TALE OF THE

BROKEN SPOKE

A SEDONA CHI MYSTERY

TALE OF THE
BROKEN SPOKE

A SEDONA CHI MYSTERY

MANY**SEASONS**PRESS

Mesa, Arizona • 2023

FIRST EDITION

Tale of the Broken Spoke
A Sedona Chi Mystery

Copyright © 2023 Paul Johnson

Published by Many Seasons Press
an Imprint of Multimedia Publishing Project
PO Box 50553
Mesa, Arizona 85208-0028
480-939-9689 | MultimediaPublishingProject.com

Book designed by Yolie Hernandez
(AZBookDesigner@icloud.com)

Paperback ISBN: 978-1-956203-33-2

Library of Congress Control Number: 2023937987

CONTENTS

Contents

PROLOGUE

Tall Boy's Last Ride

THE MOUNTAIN BIKER RODE DOWN JACKS CANYON TRAIL looking for signs he hoped he wouldn't find. He'd slipped into the wilderness area; bikes were prohibited because nature had been declared too fragile for rubber tires, as if the ageless red rocks of Sedona, remnants from ancient sea beds, wouldn't still be there long after he was gone. Two miles back, he'd cruised past the Forest Service marker threatening a significant fine if caught. As a local, he knew the trails weren't patrolled past Labor Day when the tourists left. Tourists were the good and ugly of Sedona. They brought money on the one hand, but on the other they overwhelmed the streets and trails. He kept pedaling, alone with his thoughts and the canyon's spirits.

The biker was testing his almost new Santa Cruz Tallboy 29 Carbon R bike. It was her maiden ride, with him anyway. Once he graduated from Northern Arizona University and was getting a paycheck, he'd upgrade to a CC frame, but for now the C frame would have to do. What did another tier of carbon do for performance anyway? It would have cost him another semester's tuition. The new bike had a longer frame and more reach than the old one his great aunt had given him when he graduated high school. That made it more stable. He could already tell from the bigger boulders he'd glided over. This bike had more than enough performance and speed to get him out into remote areas for his studies of past civilizations and geology.

The side canyons in this area were full of *Sinagua* ruins. *Sinagua* was the Spanish name for the Puebloan people who had scratched out a living in this part of the arid Southwest long before the conquistadors and the missionaries arrived. They were the current focus of his thesis. He had been exploring the faults and cracks of the Verde Valley and Oak Creek Canyon since he was a kid. When he began learning about the people who had lived there, in his high school history class, his path in life was set. A scholarship to NAU turned it into a professional passion. At first he'd been torn between archeology and geology. But when it came time to choose, he had opted for people over rocks.

The day was beautiful. Most fall days in Sedona are after the monsoon rains stop in mid-September. The rusty red sandstone and gleaming white Coconino formations of Lee Mountain were backstopped by a brilliant baby blue sky. They'd stood in contrast to each other for over five-hundred-million years. The large fluffy cumulus clouds softened the hardness of the jagged peaks. Biking in this setting was like riding through a Thomas Moran landscape. What better way to spend a weekday morning? The young idealistic biker basked in his good luck and promising future.

The trail had narrowed considerably, twisting and climbing a slight grade the entire way. If he rode it long enough he'd end up on the Colorado Plateau. But he had no intention of going that far or that high. Biking had to be your career to tackle that. He was look-ing for smaller unexplored faults. That's where it got really remote and challenging, off the main trail and into areas man seldom vis-ited. Archeologists were still discovering untouched smaller ruins or ones that hadn't been seen since the 1860's cavalry patrols were hunting Apache. He always looked for animal trails; passages wide enough to get his bike down. His new Tallboy opened up rougher possibilities.

Up ahead he could see a side canyon disappearing into the mountain. By the looks of it, it was a box canyon with only one way in and one way out. Those had often been places of habitation, espe-cially if there was a spring. The biker had won more than a few bar bets with out-of-state friends over which state had the most natural springs - Arizona. He'd studied how in the late *Sinagua* period there was evidence of conflict with other migrating Peoples. Hidden, easily defensible canyons with sources of water would have been popular and fought over. The *Sinagua* didn't locate based on the proximity of a super Walmart. Sure enough, there was an over-grown deer path heading into the gap.

The path got wider a quarter-mile in. He started to see recent signs of activity. Javelinas, desert rodents that looked like boars, had been lunching on the prickly pear, their signature horseshoe shaped bite marks making a fat C of the pads. Sandy areas were lit-tered with coyote scat, their undigested juniper berries still fresh. The biker even startled a group of mule deer drinking from a pool in an eroded arroyo; water, the Southwest's oil. And he saw what he was searching for - human footprints.

The biker followed the footprints and deer trail to the head of the box canyon. Staying seated on his bike, he leaned against a pinon pine. It was shady and cool. He could hear a spring gurgling; there had been a lot of rain. It was hidden somewhere in the midst of dense acacia, better known as the Arizona 'wait-a-minute' bush because of its barbed thorns. He sipped from his water bottle, listening and assessing how the deer made it down from the ridge above. He could follow their switchback trail for a ways, then lose it, then pick it up again, then just make it out as it crested the top edge forty feet above. The footprints went that way too. He couldn't hear any voices or human noises from above. The biker took a last swig of Arizona oil. Getting up and back down would be a good stress test for the Tallboy's SRAM Eagle 12 drivetrain.

The first two switchbacks weren't bad. He only had to shoulder the bike at the turns where the path went vertical for several feet before leveling off in the next switchback. After those it got dicey; the biker joked with himself it was a mountain goat not a deer trail. His total focus was on reading the rocks, slides, and roots. The latter were the worst; they could blow a tire sending him head over heels. Not what he wanted to do on an unmapped animal trail seven miles from the trailhead. After several harrowing slips and falls and navigating sections that were little more than two-feet wide, he reached the top.

The ridge top was level enough to navigate Tallboy. The biker picked up the deer path, which shortly ended at a dense clump of barbed acacia, cholla cactus, and thorny mesquite. He'd be shredded if he tried riding through. Leaving his bike, he rolled down his sleeves and waded into the tangled mess. After a hundred yards he spied a ten-foot rock wall with a small clearing in front. He guessed an ancient granary might be hidden behind the bushes fronting the wall. Granaries were small caves sealed by the *Sinagua* to store grain. Finding one was interesting, but not uncommon, unless they hadn't been opened. What captured the biker's attention as he drew closer, however, were the two wooden crates sitting in the open.

He didn't see or hear anyone, but the footprints had reappeared. Hooked by what he'd discovered, he cautiously crept forward. What a find! One crate was loaded with beaded and bone necklaces, bracelets, and rings, some decorated with colorful minerals mined from nearby mountains. There were numerous small fetishes, made from cottonwood, yucca root, and obsidian. The second crate had even rarer objects, intact pre-Colombian era pottery. A quick survey of the pots proved there was artwork from not only the *Sinagua* people, but also the contemporaneous *Anasazi*, *Mogollon*, and *Hohokam* civilizations. A few pieces were filled with sea shells traded with people living on the Pacific coast. The biker was dizzy with excitement over the wealth of intact artifacts.

Behind the crates was a figure wrapped in bubble wrap. The biker carefully removed the tape, exposing something he'd never seen in any museum or textbook. It was a life-sized effigy of an androgynous figure. Male and female characteristics were finely painted over its body, with turquoise and copper embedded in its face. It seemed to be smiling at the biker. The dominating feature was an exaggerated engorged penis. The biker had seen these types of effigies before, just a lot smaller and far less adorned. They were used in fertility rites to ensure successful pregnancies and in agricultural ceremonies to ensure a fruitful harvest. The market value of a figure this large and decorated, not including what was in the other two crates, was inestimable.

He heard a rustling at the cliff edge, away from the clearing, past a low growing juniper tree. He would have heard their noises earlier if not mesmerized by what he'd found. Two men stood thirty feet away. He recognized both of them and knew he'd stumbled on their cache. The older of the two pointed at the biker and yelled his name. Both men started running toward him. The biker rushed back into the underbrush, ignoring the cuts and scratches. If he could just make it back to Tallboy he thought. The two were closing on him by the time he cleared the brush. He grabbed his bike on the run. Another ten seconds and a couple of hard thrusts on the pedals and he'd be on the switchbacks out of their reach. He had quickly picked up speed thanks to the new Eagle 12 drivetrain. It seemed he was going to escape, when, at the last minute, the younger and faster of the two men lunged and thrust a hiking pole into his front wheel just as he dropped into the first switchback.

That was it. The biker flew over the handlebars, the Santa Cruz Tallboy spiraling behind him. He flailed and grasped with one hand for anything he could find while instinctively holding onto the bike with the other. There was nothing he could do as he plummeted forty feet. Halfway down he was knocked unconscious when his head struck a block of granite pushed out of the sandstone eons ago by molten activity originating deep in the earth. He hit the bottom hard. Tallboy landed by his side. Still breathing, his broken body lay in the gravel at the bottom of the wash.

The two men reached the biker twenty minutes later. He was still alive and still unconscious. The older man directed the younger man. He'd come up with a plan on their scramble down the switchbacks. The biker's being alive didn't alter it much. He handed his companion a rock and nodded at the biker. The younger man wanted to object, he'd been friends with the biker. He'd worked with him. But he knew better than to butt heads with the older man. They didn't have a choice anyway; his friend should have known better. After killing the biker, they moved his body behind a flowering manzanita. They threw Tallboy behind a collection of broken boulders away from the body and covered it with brush; no sense risking a helicopter spotting a metal reflection. They doubted anyone would ever find the biker, especially after the javelina and mountain lion finished their scavenging. They were miles from an official trail and even that was remote. If his remains were found, it would be written off as another crazy mountain biker riding somewhere he shouldn't have been.

TALE OF THE BROKEN SPOKE

1

THREE YEARS LATER

Sedona Chi

THE BLOND WITH THE PINK, PLASTIC, DAISY-ADORNED, FLIP flops and lavender, strapless, spandex, tube top squealed, "These rocks are hot! They burn my booty!" She struggled stretching her leopard leotards back over her silicon injected gluts. "I'm not taking anything off out here unless it's in a tent!"

Skip Rhodes groaned in shame, running his hands through his shaggy dirt-blond hair to push back the headache his clients were giving him. Never in his forty-two years...

He looked at the blonde's companion, the man with the aviator sunglasses, white golf shorts, and soft-soled loafers and shook his head. "You can film at night," he shrugged, not really caring.

Skip regretted having taken their online reservation. But they were from L.A. and with those bookings he always added an extra twenty percent to cover the inevitable pain in *his* butt.

Aviator was a producer and Flip Flop was his starlet. On the reservation form he'd indicated he was scouting locations for a film. He hadn't indicated it was actually for a sci-fi western "mature audience" cable series called Debbie Galaxy Does Westworld. It was obvious from her lack of inhibition why Flip Flops Debbie was along for the weekend with her boss. Not Skip's kind of people, but hey, the tour business in Sedona was competitive; somebody had to take their money.

"There's no service. I can't post on Instagram!" cried Flip Flops, aiming a sequin decorated cell phone. She was on her knees, mouth open and studded tongue suggestively positioned over a stack of spirit rocks. Skip decided then and there to up the California premium another fifteen percent.

Skip Rhodes was the owner, driver and sole guide for Sedona Chi Tours. His girlfriend at the time he wrote his business plan had come up with the name. They were still friendly, but he missed seeing her red hair cascading down her back while she relaxed on his couch. She had a swimmer's body, long and flat with wide shoulders. Until she educated him, *hit him over the head as he recalled it*, Skip hadn't known what Chi meant other than some tortured memory of a cartel drug lieutenant's inamorata threatening him with a machete. *Che'll cut you bad*, the mule had jeered. Not all his memories were good.

Before they'd broken up, Lilac had tried teaching him about Sedona's magnetic dynamism and the philosophy of Chi. Both important to almost everyone living in or visiting the quirky town of Sedona, Arizona. She'd threatened to shoot him and send him to his spiritual afterlife after he'd cracked half-a-dozen jokes. A discharged Tucson detective, Yoga and guns were her real loves. All he remembered now was Chi had something to do with the life force of the universe, energies that flowed around your body, and that you could manipulate it with martial arts. That's how he explained it if clients asked.

"The lighting's fantastic. I'm just not sure about getting the cameras and a futon this far out. The union will want a fortune," Aviator said, ignoring Debbie's demand for a tent.

"This part of Boynton Canyon trail is pretty remote. But Enchantment Resort would be popular with your cast. They have a glamorous pool," Skip countered, not sure why, the producer was staying there and had surely seen it. He was proud of coming up with "glamorous" though, it sounded Hollywood.

"You think they'd let us shoot in the Jacuzzi?"

"Why not? Glen Ford did scenes for *The Rounders* there." *The Rounders* had been filmed in 1965; Enchantment Resort opened in the late 80s. But Aviator didn't strike Skip as the kind to be into cinematic history. "John Payne...not the Duke...did a few B westerns out here too, along with Tyrone Power, Burt Lancaster, and Bob Mitchum. You'd be in good company."

"John Payne...any relation to Long John Pain? He's a legend."

Skip ignored the question and kept hiking. His outgoing friend Kuul Balthazar had volunteered to join the tour and tote the lunches and wine packs. He wanted to meet the motion picture people. Kuul called them Segway tours; his segue to lucrative movie adviser contracts. He was big for an Indian, a few inches taller than Skip's 5'11, and while Skip was solid, his friend dwarfed him in bulk. The wine was an Elite Tour upgrade. Big spending Aviator had ordered Riesling, specifying no more than $8.99 a bottle.

Sedona Chi offered personalized tours and hikes in and around the artsy quirky town of Sedona, Arizona. He'd initially pictured the business as a sort of Hop-On Hop-Off trailhead tour, but didn't like the idea of driving all day. Wine tours were popular, but merlot went straight to his head and if you couldn't drink what was the point. He'd toyed with a sunset tour, but decided it'd interfere too much with tequila hour. Ambition for himself had never been Skip's Chi; he was more a *Give him an assignment and he'll get it done* kind of guy.

After a few months of trial and error, he'd settled on personally guided vortex mystery and ancient monument tours, and the always popular red rock vista hikes. Pretty generic, but generic sold. He also offered a weekly Skip's Crack Tour to the south rim of the Grand Canyon. His friend Kuul had come up with the name, ever the quick wit. Most local tour companies offered hurried *Oooh-Aaah* half-day trips to gape into the mouth of time and visit the gift shops. Skip felt at home there and he respected the Canyon, his trips stayed overnight and delved deeper into the geology and the Park's human history.

He'd picked Sedona because he valued the anonymity of a transient tourist town. No one cared who he'd been or where he'd come from. In fact, he'd yet to meet anyone who actually came from Sedona. He set his own hours and business was good, as good as he needed anyway. Good enough to attract sketchy Hollywood characters...

"It's still not working," Debbie Galaxy whined, now straddling a twelve-inch juniper stump, holding her phone low and out front for the money shot.

"Give it a break, baby," said the polarized producer.

Flip Flops pouted, playfully wagging her tongue at the Aviator. Skip was surprised the tongue fit through her puffy augmented lips. The only gear in her head seized on another idea, "Hey Navajo man, how'd you like to do a shoot?"

"Navajos don't take photographs," said Kuul. "They steal the inner spirit of all living things." Kuul crossed his arms and looked to the sky. "The Great Spirit forbids it." Kuul was wearing a knockoff Yei blanket vest made by the China tribe and knee-high buckskin moccasins despite it being in the high 80s. He knew how to play a part.

Kukulkan Bonifacio Balthazar was Skip's closest friend; his only friend since Lilac Williams had dumped him. Depending on how the wind blew, Balthazar slipped into and out of the stereotypical roles of backward noble savage or Native sage. It looked like he was going with the shaman today. Kuul wasn't even Navajo, except when it was commercially viable. One night, under a *Cuervo* haze and Skip's poking at the origin of his unusual name, he had admitted he was half Mayan with a few parts Yaqui and a German great grandfather. Kukulkan was the Mayan name of their War Serpent God.

"But for you, pretty white women, you can use my iPhone. You have to have the right setting out here to access data. We are near a sacred vortex, the Chamber of Commerce has it turned off to ensure the transcendental tranquility of our sacred mountains."

Skip thought he picked up a slight Bavarian bullshit accent. You didn't need data to take or send a picture. *His pitch was coming*.

"Well, how does yours work then? Flip Flops asked. "I've seen you taking my picture." Kuul had been keeping a pictorial record of Debbie's interactions with the desert.

"I perform a Telephonic Receiver Blessing," Kuul said straight-faced.

Get ready.

"Can you bless me?" Flip Flops asked. "This is so cool; you're like a real-life medicine man, aren't you?"

Kuul winked at Skip and raised his arms over his head. Aviator was checking his phone to see if he needed a Blessing too.

"I can tell you know a lot about our customs," Kuul said. *Here it comes*. "*Dinetah*, the mother Earth, and First Woman allow me to bless human electronic possessions under certain conditions. You must make an offering to appease the Hero Twin gods."

Take the faux Navajo shtick; add in gullible tourists, a few mystic stories about the Hero Twins and Spider Woman, and the tips rolled in. Kuul usually topped his blessings off with selling *authentic* bear and moose fetishes (*Arizona never had moose*) that he molded from coyote scat.

Kuul's real job was running a plumbing service, AAA Plumber to the Stars. He marketed to the liberal Hollywood crowd with second homes in Sedona. They ate the mystic Aboriginal stuff up. That's why Kuul had jumped at the chance to tag along. Just last week he'd roto-rooted a kitchen drain for Diane Ladd. He'd pulled out a serving of yellow asparagus still wrapped in a plastic baggie.

"What kind of offering?" Flip Flops guardedly asked. *Smooth talkers, always angling for a freebie, always wanting the same thing.* Sure, the Navajo had mysterious black eyes and a great tan, and she had to admit the grizzly sad-eyed guide was attractive in a younger Jeff Bridges kind of way. But Debbie Galaxy wasn't stupid, she'd been around the universe a time or two. She wasn't about to give it for free, at least not with this hot sun beating down. Young looking skin was her trade.

Kuul bowed, spreading both arms wide, forefingers pointing to the ground, "Mother Earth asks for ten dollars per photo and post," he said cheekily. "No checks or plastic."

Boom, payday! Skip hid his grin as best he could.

"That's all?" Aviator said, opening up his wallet.

Skip knew he and Balthazar made an odd couple. They couldn't have been more different. But if the chips were down, Kuul was there to turn them over. Despite the fake façade, he was level-headed and a good thinker when he wasn't hustling. The big Mayan might take a more cautious roundabout path to solving a problem, but they always seemed to end up at the same solution. Skip had learned to trust him. That was big in Skip's book. And it wasn't a bad thing to know a good plumber.

After Kuul pocketed a Benjamin for the pictures and an owl fetish, Debbie and Aviator were done. Skip would get his cut later. It was mid-morning, and the temperature was already ninety. With the photo shoot finished, they hiked another quarter mile to a grove of desert willows where they ate lunch, and Debbie auditioned for her role with the Riesling bottle. Getting even that far on the trail hadn't been easy. The producer had dried his bare feet twice complaining about blisters, he hadn't worn socks, and Debbie tore a thong on a flip flop that Kuul repaired with a yucca stem. But Skip had quoted three hours and he didn't want any L.A. negotiating when they got back.

"You ever sell anything more than these owl figures, like arrowheads or necklaces or other old Indian stuff?" Aviator asked Kuul. "I know some people in L.A. that pay big for authentic items, painted pots, shields, pre-Colombian goods, you know."

Kuul's tone changed from his Navajo foolishness, "It's illegal," he said seriously. "You should tell your friends they're subsidizing the desecration of our ancestors. We wouldn't steal a gold cross from your church; you shouldn't steal from our holy sites." Kuul walked away before Aviator could respond.

"It was just a question," he said to Skip.

Aviator was his client, but he'd had about all of the couple he could take. "It's a sensitive issue that carries more baggage than you could imagine. Best leave it alone."

After they ate the leftover chicken tenders that Skip had made into *gourmet* chicken salad he looped back to Enchantment Resort, dropping DeMille and Bankhead at *Mii'amo* Spa for expensive margaritas and Teddy Bear Cholla flour foot massages. Cecil B. didn't tip, but Debbie had winked and slipped him her phone number.

"How about a cold Snake Charmer at the patio?" Kuul asked as they were riding back into town. He was thumbing his gratuities and whistled, "We did good Kemo." Aviator had tipped him another fifty. "I'm buying." The patio meant Oak Creek Brewery, the locals spot off Coffee Pot Road where the vats were located, not their tourist packed grill in Sedona's outdoor Tlaquepaque Mall. Snake Charmer was a dark I.P.A. with a tangy hint of grapefruit, no relationship to the amiable Mayan war god.
"Deal. I could sure use a couple." Skip said.

2

DOGIE STYLE

BIG BOB BAKER WAS SWEATING LIKE A THREE-LEGGED JACK rabbit chased by a mountain lion. Keeping up with the feisty Maggie Kempdinger, Vice President of the Sedona Westerners, wasn't what he'd signed up for. The Westerners were a local hiking club. Big Bob had just graduated into the Dogie group from the less active Amblers. Even their easier, less stressful hikes went deep into Sedona's surrounding wilderness. The Dogies were headed out Jacks Canyon Trail. On a weekday it was safer, there were far fewer mountain bikers zooming around blind curves.

As lead Dogie it was his responsibility to keep everyone together, make sure they had enough water, write a short article for the Red Rock News, and lead the hike. Thanks to Steel-Calves Kempdinger he'd already lost the latter honor. The woman was a maniac. Big Bob knew he couldn't trust her the minute he saw her two L.L. Bean diamond tipped trekking poles. No Dogie needed two poles. And her military issued Camel Back hydration pack was way beyond the pale for the easier Dogie hikes. She belonged in the more advanced Rough Rider group if she wanted to punish herself. The whole group was struggling to keep up her pace. He sure as hell wasn't carrying her ass back if she pulled a quad.

Steel-Calves had picked the hike too. She knew Big Bob would sweat a couple of five-gallon buckets on Jacks Canyon trail. All the Westerners knew Kempdinger was a sadist; that's probably why the Rough Riders hadn't promoted her. The sign at the trailhead warned them to beware of the heat because there was no shade.

"Kempdinger, slow the heck down, it's a pleasure hike not a race," Big Bob gasped. "Mustang Timmy's about to pass out."

Mustang Timmy was Big Bob's drinking buddy, and they were hungover from the VFW award dinner last night. Mustang had landed at Inchon, which put him well into his eighties. Big Bob knew for a fact that if Timmy upchucked out here, they'd clinked their last Coronas.

The group had hiked a couple miles and hadn't yet found their groove. Jacks Canyon trail was wide open in this part. It ran below Lee Mountain, but not close enough to be in the shade. Sedona wasn't scorching like Phoenix, but still plenty hot for Bob's 275 pound package and Mustang's high blood pressure. Not a whole lot of recreational hikers used Jacks Canyon. The views were Okay, but not as good as those around Courthouse and Bell Rock. The Dogie's had only seen one backpacker and he'd been out for two days. Steel-Calves wasn't even breaking to take pictures, which was pissing him off because he needed them for the newspaper.

Mercifully, Kempdinger finally stopped. She turned to face the other panting Dogies with a look that said, *you weak kneed, cry baby motherless calves, time to grow a pair and lace up your Magellans.* "We've haven't even gone three miles," she said instead.

Big Bob tried standing in the spindly shade of an ocotillo to catch his breath. Mustang Timmy sat on a red boulder and promptly fell over backwards. His blood pressure was probably impacting his equilibrium. "You killed him!" Big Bob yelled.

"I'm Okay," Mustang whinnied, rolling over on all fours trying to get up. "Two liters of Makers Mark is too much weight for my backpack. I think it broke."

The other Dogies, Crazy Eddie, Mel the Butcher, Gladys 'without a Pip' Knight, and Puddles Waylon, all panicked at the loss of refreshment and started trying to help Mustang upright. Big Bob, exercising excellent leadership skills, instructed them to not move him in case he'd hit his head. "Hold on, we need to check his pupils."

"For the love of Kit Carson!" Kempdinger said disgustedly. "Get him up and dust him off. We've got another four miles to go. You're all going back to the Amblers if I have anything to say about it." Kempdinger had a reputation in the Westerners as being a hard ass wagon master. She'd been a P.E. teacher and girls' basketball coach in Nebraska.

"Good lord, we smell like the basement of a frat house on a Sunday morning!" sang Gladys 'without a Pip' Knight, lifting Mustang's elbow while Crazy Eddie was pulling a leg the other way. Gladys got her nickname from singing once a week at Eddie's Yavapai Bar and Grille. In her seventies, her range wasn't what it was when she had performed at the Hilton. Puddles Waylon had salvaged the Makers Mark and was wringing his bandana over his water bottle.

"Leave me alone! I'm a veteran," screamed Mustang Timmy.

"Everybody settle down. Let's just rest here awhile and we'll see how Mustang feels. Then *I'll* decide if we're going on, not *Kempdinger,*" Big Bob said in exasperation, reasserting his charge as lead Dogie.

A little later Big Bob gathered his troops, except for Kempdinger who'd marched ahead. Mustang was feeling better after a few hits of the Makers Mark. "I never quit on MacArthur," he said to no one in particular. Puddles and Butcher were raring to go. Gladys and Crazy Eddie decided to head back, "We'll be at Red Rock Café enjoying some blue corn *huevos* if you all change your mind." Big Bob, Mustang, Puddles, and Butcher waved goodbye and sauntered on to find Kempdinger. They'd all agreed when they started the goal was four miles out and four miles back. Clouds had moved in cooling things off a bit, which made the hiking easier. Big Bob thought they could make it, maybe even another mile or two to keep Kempdinger from filing a complaint.

A mile farther they found Steel-Calves finishing an all-natural Quest Bar. The damn things had twenty grams of protein, Big Bob thought; she'll run the rest of the way. "So, Big Bob, we going on or turning tail?"

"You stay behind, I'm taking scout. Unless you want to go back alone and then we'll see you at next month's meeting," Big Bob ordered.

With Big Bob scouting they leisurely hiked another mile. When the others came up, Big Bob was taking panoramic pictures of the red walls. The clouds were making a dramatic shadowy effect against Lee Mountain. Hopefully the Red Rock News would print his shots in color.

"The trail looks like it splits," Bob said. One path went straight ahead and another turned off to the left toward a box canyon.

"Ain't either one of them look too good," Mustang noted. "Don't see no cairn," Butcher added, the double negative going unchallenged.

"Make a choice *Big Man*. You're the leader," Kempdinger chided. Big Bob had his foot on a boulder double-knotting a shoe-string that had come loose. He was looking in both directions and thinking. "Make sure you don't tie them together," Steel-Calves said. Finishing with the lace, he headed left down what looked like little more than a deer path. Kempdinger shook her head in mock disgust at Bob's directional acuity but followed.

A quarter mile in the path got better, more sand than rocks, easier on Mustang's knobby knees. It roughly followed an arroyo into a canyon. The farther they walked the narrower the canyon became. Red rock walls on both sides tightened around the Dogies.

Back in the day it would have been a good place for an ambush. Today the scenery was gorgeous, not threatening. Big Bob welcomed the heavy shade from the side walls.

"Pretty clear nobody's been in here for a while," Mustang said. "Looks like we'll run out of trail not too much farther."

Mustang had got his second wind. The flask he'd transferred the Makers Mark into was dry, so Big Bob knew he'd be gassed going back. Mustang didn't care much for water, or, *Chinese weak tea,* as he called it.

They arrived at the end of the trail, not counting the mountain goat switchbacks heading up through a rock slide to a ridgeline above. Big Bob put his boot on a low pinon branch to retie the annoying lace; time to turn around he thought.

"Went the wrong way, didn't you Big Bob," Kempdinger sneered.

"I don't think Mustang can make it up there," Big Bob said, studying the terrain for show. "We'll turn around here."

Mustang whacked his pole on the ground, "Hell I can't." He was about to charge the hill when...

"Hey! Over here! Jesus H. Christ!" Puddles yelled and was motioning them over to a clump of acacias away from the trail. "I found something."

Big Bob, Kempdinger, and Butcher headed that way. Mustang had found a nicely grooved seat in a boulder and stayed put. "Jesus H. Christ," Puddles repeated. They hadn't seen him this excited since New Year's Eve at the Lions Club when Lucy Chiselbottom got drunk and grabbed his *hinky*.

He was staring at a pile of bleached bones half covered with blown red dirt and years of debris. A few bones had been pulled away and spread around by scavengers. The rest of the Dogies were trying to make sense of what they'd found.

"It's *human*," Butcher pronounced with some certainty. He'd been a butcher back in Chicago before retiring. There was half an elk in his garage freezer. Big Bob had been with him when he bagged it over by Show Low.

"How can you tell, they're only a few and they're scattered all over?" Big Bob questioned.

"I carved a lot of beef and pork ribs. This is nothing like those, they've gotta be human," Butcher said, turning over a curved broken piece of deteriorated bone.

"Let me see it," Big Bob said, grabbing the bone and inspecting it closer. The idea of it being human made him nervous. The Forest Service would be all over him and the Westerners for disturbing a burial site; he'd probably get kicked out of the club. "I think it's black bear. I read in National Geographic they're genetically ninety-eight percent our match."

Puddles had wandered farther along the rockslide to take another pee. His prostate had been pressing his bladder like General Crook had pushed the Chiricahua after they jumped the reservation. With *hinky* in hand, he spied a rusty wheel as his *drip drip drip* made an unnatural sounding *ping ping ping*. "I found a bike!" Hauling it out of a clump of manzanita and fumbling with his zipper he held it up for show – the bike. "It's beat to hell."

"Maybe the bear got it," Mustang yelled, having followed what his fellow Dogies were finding from his rocky perch.

"Makes sense," Big Bob said.

Kempdinger had been quiet through the whole exchange. She'd been scratching around and found a few more bones. Looking up forty feet she got an idea of what probably happened. "Big Bob, you're a moron. Butcher's right, those are human remains. Obviously, a crazy biker tried riding up those switchbacks and fell. Whoever it is has been out here a while."

"I agree with Bob, it's a bear," Mustang yelled from his seat twenty yards away. He'd follow his Captain through hell and back.

Kempdinger yelled back at Mustang. "Daniel Boone here couldn't even follow the main trail. We've got bones and we've got a bike. It doesn't take a rocket scientist to figure it out."

"Maybe it was a circus," Puddles suggested, having shook and tucked everything away. He hated to disagree with Big Bob and Mustang. They were always good for a couple of free beers at the VFW.

Kempdinger threw up her hands, "I'm never doing Dogies again!"

3

LAZY SOB

SANDS DESERT RETREAT WAS OUTSIDE THE CITY LIMITS ON RED Rock Loop Road. The sweeping vistas of Cathedral Rock and older homesteads stood in contrast to the concrete and smaller lots in town. The retreat was owned by Zula Ballsy who had been married to a Vegas mob boss. According to local legend, Tony "Two Balls" Ballsy had been axed by his New Jersey family for skimming off the top. Whether or not Zula had anything to do with the axing and got the money to buy the retreat as a reward was another part of the rumor.

The Sands had originally been a ranch. In honorarium Zula Ballsy named the bar/gathering hole the Lazy *S*OB after Sonny O'Bryan, a famous old-time foreman who had long ago gone to the big roundup in the sky. The lazy *S* was tilted like in a cattle brand. Most nights Zula held court behind the bar, regaling guests with stories of the Rat Pack during her early Vegas years. She claimed to have been Dean's stylist and palled around with Angie Dickinson.

The whole compound was twenty acres, give or take, not including a secluded slice along Oak Creek that extended to the original two-room O'Bryan cabin. Under the terms of a month to month lease, the rustic cabin had been Skip Rhodes home for the past three years. The rest of the retreat had four two-bedroom cabins and a two-story lodge with four guest rooms and the Lazy *S*OB on the first floor. Zula bunked in the upstairs quarters.

The grounds were a private nature park. Two sides were bordered by red bluffs with prickly pear and sage packed slopes. The third side was a thick green ribbon, Sycamore trees and bear grass meandering along Oak Creek, its bubbling sounds louder or softer depending on the season and flow of water. The cabins were tucked amongst taller cottonwoods and pine in a rough semi-circle several hundred yards from the creek. The main lodge rested in the center of five acres of grass, gravel, and wildflowers. The fourth side adjoined Red Rock Loop Road; a rock driveway led to a parking lot by the lodge. Next door was the Red Rock State Park, which had been trying to buy Zula out. According to Zula, *"The government bastards would tear the Sands down, just like what had happened to its namesake on the strip."*

Most nights Skip walked the half-mile path along Oak Creek from his isolated cabin then turned left for several hundred yards past the guest cabins to the main lodge for a drink with Zula. She played the feisty frat mom role with an unending wealth of advice. Mostly it was good. The more bombed the old showgirl got, the more colorful the counsel.

Zula claimed to be seventy and anyone valuing their *cajones* wouldn't contest it. As she liked to say, she was still *spry, sly, and ready to fly*. Her birthday celebration had ended with the newly minted septuagenarian tucking Skip and Lilac Williams on the worn leather sofas in the lobby and her polishing off a second Hornitos bottle with her maid Consuelo. At two in the morning, the employer and employee had lobbed cherry bombs across the fence at the

Red Rock Park rangers' cabins. Green and white Crown Victorias crashed the retreat's gate with lights flashing. Zula had blamed it on meteors. The next week the State installed a driving range net and had been after her big-time ever since.

Seventy, as the old showgirl adamantly said she was, didn't jive with the Rat Pack memoirs. Her stories were genuine, she was just older. It was the mysterious magnetic energies released from the town's vortexes. People came to Sedona and rewrote their personal histories. The shabby cowboy drinking Budweiser at a local wine bar could be a past CEO of General Electric and worth a couple billion. And a high-kicking Vegas showgirl friendly with Sinatra and married to the mob could become a local hotelier. Skip had heard enough wiry annotations from Zula watching old Dean Martin Celebrity Roasts from her VHS collection to know her stories about sharing bourbon shots with Dean as she trimmed his eyebrows were true.

"The usual, hon?" Zula asked on seeing Skip at the bar. Not waiting for an answer, she started mixing. Pretty pink prickly pear margaritas didn't match the rough persona Skip had built, but everyone has their quirks. Zula made her own syrup, a special recipe she'd gotten from Shirley MacLaine, and he liked the sweet aftertaste.

Zula, the Vegas performer, was at home behind the oak bar with its well-worn copper rail. It came from the infamous Kitty Kat Club, an old saloon and gentleman's club in Jerome Arizona. The last drink poured behind it for a thirsty miner had been in the early 1950s, the first in the 1890s. Zula was chattering about her Vegas days with four guests bellied up to the counter, craftily refilling their drinks when they were only half empty.

"I was sixteen, but I could kick with the best of them," Skip heard her say to her attentive customers as she was shaking his drink.

"Sammy would come in after the show with Quincy Jones. They'd take Angie, Shirley, and I out on the town. Just for kicks you know. The Jersey gang didn't like us white girls being with Negroes, but it was Sammy, so they let it pass. This was before I met Two Balls."

"I thought you had to be eighteen to work in a show lounge," asked a girl with long straight brown hair and a fringed leather jacket. She was sitting next to a boy with aluminum foil wrapped around his shirt cuffs and the bottom of his jeans. They both looked like college dropouts.

"Not back then, sweetie. As long as you were 5'8" and had big boomers and long legs they didn't care. You'd have had your pick of jobs."

The girl laughed, "Thanks for the compliment."

"Boomers?" Aluminum Foil asked.

"These, baby doll," Zula said, brushing her frizzy shoulder length gray hair back and thrusting her still ample breasts up and forward. "Breasts, titties, baby bottles." Zula didn't have an off switch or a mute button.

The kid turned red and took a sip of his Cosmo. "Oh."

Zula finished showing off her girls and straining Skip's margarita. The tequila was from a private stash of Don Julio Anejo 1942 Black that she kept just for him. She placed the blushing pink drink on the bar and Skip headed outside to the porch for sunset.

As he pushed open the old-fashioned, wooden, screen door he heard the mob doll from behind, "Tony Two Balls and I had a fancy red velvet davenport we banged on every Saturday night..." *More information than Aluminum Foil could probably process.* The porch was a wraparound with kiva poles as posts and a railing made of juniper limbs. He sat down in his favorite Kennedy rocker with Don Julio.

Skip anticipated a vibrant sunset. The clouds were thin wavy ripples with royal blue bands in between. In another thirty minutes they would be blended streaks of red, orange, and pink, with a purple backdrop. The rust hued rocks were already glowing like the

Sedona Theater Club had aimed yellow spotlights on the protruding points. Before they threw the switch, Skip planned on watching the light walk its way up the cliffs. No matter how many times he sat here the shadows always revealed a different pattern of cracks and holes.

The lodge was peaceful at sunset. The buildings reminded Skip of the cabins he'd built when he was a kid with his Davy Crockett Lincoln Log set. That embedded memory was probably what sold him on living there. That and Zula knocking a hundred off the rent if he lent a hand when needed and ran errands from time to time. He would have helped her for free; it gave him something to do when he didn't have a tour.

Zula wandered out with a *cerveza* pilsner in a frosted mug, a wedge of lime floating on the top. "Guests leave?" Skip asked.

She rolled her eyes. "The kid was trying to cuddle up next to the girl. It was like little Frank Jr. trying to hit on Kim Novak. Hands all over her. Though it's good to be that age and horny." Zula followed their ritual and took the rocker next to Skip's. She pulled the lime out, took a bite sucking the juice, and drank half the beer. "Not sure that young man knows what he's in for. That girl's got a head on her, not like the rest of them."

"Time slides by," Skip said, Don Julio and nature's spectacle making him philosophical. "Who are they?"

She chuckled, "They're part of a group that booked the retreat this week and next. Head man is a preacher, Dr. Reginald Landish." She enunciated the last name like she was introducing a British lord. "Quite a name, huh? Another one of those astro groups doing research on aliens and UFOs. Like we don't get those nuts all the time, right?"

"Right, what's the 'Dr.' for?" Skip asked, stirring the rosy froth of his margarita with his little finger.

Zula thought about it a few seconds, "Don't know, but he booked the meeting room for lectures every third night. He's a big man, bigger stomach. His groupies keep bringing him Double Whoppers from Burger King. It'd be comical except he's not buying my pickled-jalapeno, hatch-chile, super-green salsa, hot dogs on pepper jack buns."

"Imagine that," Skip said with the utmost respect.

Right on schedule there was rustling in the yuccas below the porch and Spike trotted up. Skip had watched him rooting in the desert poppies before his mother came out. Spike was smart; he'd blame the mess on deer. The hairy *javelina* was Zula's pet. She'd found him when he was barely weaned, and he had adopted her as a surrogate mom. Zula hid a piece of bacon for him in her apron.

"You know a javelina isn't a pig. They just look like one. Call them a pig and they get mad. No telling what a mad javelina will do. They're actually peccaries, more like a big rat," Zula said, throwing him the piece of fried pig.

She always made sure Skip understood Spike wasn't a cannibal. Most people in Sedona had dogs, bull snakes, or pet tarantulas. Normal people anyway. Zula and the javelina were close the same way. Zula heading off into the woods with Spike was a common site, a homemade backpack strapped on his back to carry their lunches with a side holster holding her Smith and Wesson Model 60 - she was known to shoot anything that rattled in the bushes and didn't answer.

"Damned deer have been eating my poppies again," Zula observed. "We'll have venison steaks on the menu this week if I catch them." Skip swore Spike grinned as he lay beside Zula's rocker.

They sat quietly and enjoyed the remnants of the sunset. The fiery globe had disappeared while Spike was eating his bacon. The mountains across the creek were now a black silhouette positioned in front of a ginger and eggplant sky. The skiffs of cloud were dark shapes floating above the jagged profile. Before long coyotes would be yelping, and the desert sky twinkling with stars.

"You want another one?" Zula asked.

"I'm good."

"Good. We're about out of Don Julio. You need to pick some up or it's *Sauza* tomorrow."

Sunset was over and Spike trotted off to inspect the trash cans by the guest cabins. It wouldn't be long before they'd hear screams. "That pig will eat anything," Zula said.

"It'll hurt his feeling he hears you call him that," Skip joked. "Any mail for me today? I'm expecting a check."

Skip's mail was delivered to the lodge. He had a slot behind the front desk but forgot to check it. The installment check from the Arizona Lottery Commission should have come. He'd only played once and that was when Kuul Balthazar dared him. Skip had always figured he'd wait to play until he really needed the money. He'd heard too many bad stories about lottery winners; new friends that weren't friends, girls that all of a sudden swore you were a doppelganger to Brad Pitt, and sleazers trying to sell you a condo in Venezuela. Not for him.

He could have held off, but Kuul had badgered him while they were gassing up at the Circle K. Sedona City Council had been debating a wheel tax on day trippers from Phoenix to deal with traffic congestion, and he'd lost five bookings that week. The machine picked the numbers and a week later he won two million. Not enough to retire and live like a king, but enough he didn't have to worry about cancelled bookings any longer. He'd managed the publicity by threatening to smash the teenage Red Rock reporter's tablet.

"It's in your box." Zula Ballsy flashed her Viva Vegas smile, "And by the way, rent's due tomorrow."

4

ESCOBAR AND THE MACHETE

SKIP STUCK AROUND AND WATCHED THE 10PM NEWS ON THE Lazy *SOB*'s flat screen before walking home. Zula had installed the wall mount herself without a level. The result was an imbalanced view of local events. To see things straight risked permanent spinal damage. Lilac had said it improved his perspective – *but not enough*. The Diamondbacks finished a sweep of the Cubs and a dental hygienist from Apache Wells was arrested for selling Novocain to seniors at the Last Wagon Train Day Center. The Center Director noticed something was wrong when they kept running out of bibs and he couldn't understand a word of the Hello Dolly production. The weather woman warned of a late season haboob that could blanket Tempe with up to two inches of sand.

The path to O'Bryan's cabin was long and overgrown, keeping any unwelcome guests from the retreat from wandering into his yard. The only time the small wooden structure was noticeable from the lodge was when Zula closed the retreat in January. Even then it was only the smoke from the chimney that was visible. That's the way he liked it - alone, on his own. He could tune out the world and forget about all he'd done. When he'd first seen the location, he offered Zula three months' rent before even entering the cabin. Zula said she liked the cut of his jeans and took the money; she'd been to enough rodeos to be a good judge of character and not ask questions.

The stars were visible through gaps between tree branches. As a child, he remembered the awe upon discovering some stars were in galaxies millions of light years away. That was a long time ago; he'd walked below a lot of skies in a lot of different places since then. He loved the night smells. The creosote bushes and desert willow lining the bank mingled to create a sweet cinnamon fragrance. The full moon guided Skip along the worn path in the soft earth. Usually, it was so dark the creek and the path were lost in the night. The Sand's dim yellow porch lights and solar powered sticks along its walkways had long since disappeared.

He followed the creek a quarter of a mile and turned right at a large billowy tamarisk. His home was a black shadow fifty yards ahead. Aged sandstone steps carved into the bank led from beside the creek to the front yard that he had cleared to allow a little sun and improve the view. The cabin wasn't technically off-grid; he had power and O'Bryan had put in a well pump with piping that fed the cabin. It was rustic, but functional.

Skip stepped onto the porch via three sturdy concrete blocks. The porch was outfitted with an old metal glider left by an earlier tenant that squeaked when sliding forward, an ancient wooden table with camp chairs, and a colorfully striped Mexican hammock slung between posts. He had picked up the latter at an estate sale along with the three hummingbird feeders hanging from rusty nails in the rafter beams. Skip wasn't an ornithologist but he was captivated by the warring dive bombers that buzzed his yard defending their territory. The least he could do was feed the buggers.

His favorite time at the "ranch" was cocktail hour, on occasion spent with Kuul or Zula, anytime between five and midnight. Or Lilac when they were together, sitting in the glider or around a campfire wrapped in a Pendleton blanket. That's the hour the light turned magical and the wildlife came out for a drink and dinner along the creek.

The bell hanging inside jingled as he opened the split farmhouse door - his homemade alarm. He'd thought about installing a state of the art security system, but if any past associates got this far it wouldn't make a difference. They could disable it. The low-tech bell would work just as good, giving him a few seconds to react. The cabin had three rooms, the main room with a fireplace O'Bryan had built from river rock. On lonely nights like this, he could still picture Lilac lying on the worn leather with the glow from the fireplace firing her copper hair. There was a small bedroom, and a bathroom with john and sink added after the foreman had passed. Skip had installed a deadbolt on the bedroom door; it would give him a few more seconds. There was a two-burner stove and three-quarter fridge along the back wall of the main room. O'Bryan had been a simple man.

Skip seldom went to sleep before the end of Happy Hour. He chiseled an ice cube tray from the frost-capped arctic inside his freezer. Four parts Don Julio, one part sweet and sour, two parts lime juice, and a splash of Zula's syrup, shaken not stirred. He went out to the porch and swung into the hammock, careful not to spill his drink. He peered into the moonlight reflecting more on the secrets it hid than those it revealed. He finished his quiet time with Don and closed his eyes.

He was running through a market. Escobar was chasing him with a bloody machete. He thought of turning and using his Sig Sauer to stop the kingpin in his tracks, but for some reason he couldn't stop. He kept running. Every time he looked back Escobar was close, swinging his blade. Somehow, he kept running without slowing down and Escobar's machete never broke his skin.

He kept running.

The next thing he knew a man in a serape stepped out from a cart selling sharks and handed him two baby hammerheads. He threw one over his shoulder at Escobar and dropped the other. He looked back. Escobar was gone. The other shark had grown legs and was chasing him now. The shark had dark sunglasses and was carrying a briefcase. He kept running. The shark pulled something from the case and threw it at him. He couldn't make out what it was. His head started pounding and he stumbled, the shark almost on him. He fell and landed on top of Escobar's severed head. His own head was splitting, his vision limited to pinholes. He tried to lift his arms but couldn't.

Skip wrestled with his brain to wake up. He'd thrashed around and was twisted in the hammock. Sleep won the match, his body quieted, and he fell back into the dream.

Now he was strapped in a chair. Escobar's disembodied head was threatening him. Escobar wanted him to tell him something. He couldn't piece the words together. There were vowels floating in front of his face. A machete cut through an e. The straps kept tightening. The one around his neck was choking him. He tried screaming but nothing. He saw himself slumping in the chair, not moving. The lights went out. He was running again, this time in darkness, knocking into objects he didn't see. There was light up ahead. He kept running. Footsteps. Someone was following him. The light was getting bigger. He couldn't see past it. Thump, thump, behind him they were closing in. He felt air blowing in his face. He hit the light on the run and pushed it. He jumped forward. The wind was so strong he was flying. He could see down. There was nothing.

Skip could hear noises. A moaning that seemed familiar. He wanted to find whoever it was, but he kept falling back asleep. His eyes wouldn't open and the fog in his mind thickened.

He was in a bunker. There were too many men to count circling around him. He was surrounded by phantoms. They forced him on his knees in a barred room. He felt chains on his ankles. There was a sharp burning sensation in his arm. Spanish voices with English murmuring in the background. He heard a woman calling him Gringo. She disappeared in a red mist. The mist became solid and melted over him. The men were still circling. Their faces all looked the same. He was up and swinging the chain. Black smoke came through a window. Running water in his ears. COLD, wet sensations washed over him. He had a jarring feeling and then was trying to climb out. A tree pulled him up. Hearing a noise, he turned. It was Escobar coming out of the smoke. He watched the machete disappear into his chest. Pain.

Skip pushed harder to open his eyes. His brain synapses started clicking and he began to understand the moans were his. He fought for consciousness. There was a flash of metal behind his eyelids, and he woke up, blinking and scared, shaking, soaked with sweat, and sitting on the swinging hammock. The same nightmare again and again, his suppressed memories forced their way in when he slept. He couldn't control them. The details were already disappearing. They were fewer now, but those he remembered were vivid. He was running, chased by men, and trapped. He knew the story would catch up with him some day.

Fully awake and oriented to his surroundings, Skip felt safer. The lack of neighbors, the woods, the creek, the elevated porch covering the clearing; he had picked the cabin and its location for reasons other than cost. It was defensible. It would make a good kill zone if he stopped running.

5

BUNION CHAKRAS

"MY FRIENDS!" DR. REGINALD LANDISH SHOUTED. "THE CHURCH of Astro Departure needs your help."

The Doctor was speaking in the Sands meeting room, a screened outdoor porch off the *SOB*. The furnishings Zula had picked up at auction when the Days Inn closed. Landish was lecturing to his followers and a roomful of locals who had seen his posters around town: tonight's topic - Esoteric Correspondence between Subtle Energies and Psychophysiology. It was free to the public. The first hour was spent on breathing exercises, creative visualization, and sacred mantras.

The crowd all closed their eyes and repeated over and over, *"Support Star Travel, God, our Troops, and the USA."*

The mantra primed the pump of support and donations for when the speaker challenged their patriotism. Most of the attendees hummed right along proud to be an American.

"What's he shouting about?" Minnie Two Feathers asked her husband Clyde. "There are only twenty of us, we're in the back and we can hear just fine." Minnie was hoping to learn more about chakras, various focal points in the subtle body used in ancient Tibetan Meditation practices. Her girlfriends at the parlor said they could help her bunions.

Clyde spit in his empty peach can. "White *di-yan* likes to hear himself." Why he let Minnie drag him to every crazy sermon he didn't know. He'd rather be having a corn beer out behind their doublewide.

"Doesn't that look like ketchup with a piece of pickle on his cheek?" Minnie whispered.

"The Church doesn't work in a vacuum," Landish continued. "It takes a village to hunt buffalo." The Doctor was aware of the Natives in the crowd. He liked throwing in a little local lingo to help them relate. "If our world, led by our great nation, is ever going to communicate with the great spirits about an intergalactic cultural exchange program, *We Need Your Support*."

"Lock your purse, Minnie," Clyde said loudly enough to get a few glares.

Doctor Reginald Landish wasn't a legitimate doctor, or a real minister, or even an honest salesman. He didn't believe in little green men, psychic energies, space travel, or even universal suffrage given what he saw in the crowd before him. Doctor Reginald Landish was what and is known in Arizona as a sidewinder - a no-good, low-down green belly scum-sucking shyster. He'd sold mobile home lots in the Everglades, hand-signed bibles by Luke in Iowa, melanoma insurance in North Dakota, and too many other money making schemes to count. He'd done time in Louisiana after being arrested for spiking swimming pools with gators in order to sell alligator insurance.

His latest venture was born when he discovered that for $5.99 anyone could be ordained after a short, online tutorial.

Adding the title of Doctor of Philosophical Journeys seemed innocent enough. He'd registered the Church of Astro Departure in the Caymans while researching the viability of selling seawater mixed with Red Stripe as a boutique sun tanning oil. The good Doctor always liked to have a fall back plan. Establishing the Church as a legal entity allowed him to solicit investors and donations as long as he wasn't committing fraud. The latter part seemed like quibbling to the Doctor.

"My friends, preparing for ecclesiastical exploration of the stars is expensive." He gestured toward the sky as if the plywood painted ceiling wasn't there. "The psycho-spiritual vortices at the top of Bell Rock, the positive and negative magnetic forces spiraling from the earth being center, all point to a powerful impact on our subtle bodies. The *dhamachakra* frees our subtle body from temporal decomposition...uhh, I mean *dispensation*."

Clyde shifted in his folding chair. Zula Ballsy should have chairs with cushions if she wanted to attract more business, like the Cliff Castle Casino had for the Hopi Origami Convention Minnie had insisted on attending. He was uncomfortable with all the junk crammed in his jeans. "What a load of crap, Minnie. No way in hell this Doctor is helping your bunions."

"Shut up Clyde, he's just getting to the good part."

"What's the chakra for my hemorrhoids? My ass feels like a packrat in a forest fire," Clyde whispered, scooting down in the chair to change position. "We're stopping by Safeway on the way home for some butt cream."

"My subtle body and mind will be free from the karmic, emotional, and cognitive cycles that tie it to time and space. Bell Rock is an energy center, like a medicine wheel with spiritual and cerebral subconsciouses emanating from its central point. These subconsciouses travel through galactic continuums signaling to beings in galaxies far, far away where no man has gone before," Landish rambled on.

"That's what I want Clyde. I want to be free of these bumps." Minnie elbowed him in the ribs; she'd seen his head bobbing.

Landish was on a roll. He might have gotten carried away with the Star Trek and Star Wars references, but judging from the crowd's intensity, they didn't notice. What he was preaching was psychobabble nonsense any beginning yoga student would have picked apart in a minute. But yogis weren't his market, and the Sedona mystics were too pretentious to come to an open meeting. He knew small towns. And when you scraped off the tourist crust that's all Sedona was. His targets were the gullible nail specialists, wealthy retirees who watched the Home Shopping Network, and bored pickleball players searching for an easy edge to a better life. The Doctor preyed on the innocent, and the tonic he sold was always the same – Hope.

"That message will be received, my good friends. It already has. Aliens have been travelling light years to get here." The Doctor paused and the people in the front rows leaned forward in anticipation of his coming announcement. "And I plan on being here to meet them. Pracman from Atari 26 in the *Obienobbykneedo* Galaxy, fiftieth rock from the sun, spoke to me in my dreams." The Doctor paused and lowered his voice to build suspense. "Their cloaked mothership will beam my subtle body and consciousness aboard for a five-year journey to their home planet. During that time, they'll teach me the sacred mantra to spiritual power and enlightenment."

A voice from the back of the room, no one saw who, asked, "When is this beaming going to happen Doctor?"

The Doctor of Philosophical Journeys shaded his eyes acting like he was trying to pick out the questioner. Giving up, he scanned over the crowd, building the excitement, "On the eve of the winter solstice or when the Church of Astro Departure raises $300,000, whichever comes first. Pracman from Atari wishes in exchange for mankind's enlightenment that he be allowed to study our currency. He wants to understand our ways, and I advised him that our people always follow the money."

"Seems reasonable," the same anonymous voice said.

"That concludes tonight's lecture," Landish said. "Are there any questions?"

Doosey Cucumberson, sitting in the front row, raised her hand. Doosey was an 80-year-old three-time divorcee and docent at the Mary Fischer Arthouse Theater. Their films were a little too artsy for her taste, but the Cabernet was free to staff, and wealthy, lonely widowers were members. Her eye was on a potential number four, a retired plastic surgeon from San Antonio. Her last husband had been the owner of the Albuquerque Isotope minor league baseball team - before their extra inning divorce. She'd taken him to the cleaners just like her first two. The New Age Retirement Center had suspended her volunteering when they found her in a broom closet with poor Delbert Dunghauser who'd recently lost his wife to food poisoning from bad bananas.

"Is there a sexual energy chakra?" Doosey asked. Her temporary boyfriend sitting next to her, a barista at Starbuck's with a lava bead nose ring and blue tipped ponytail did a fist pump in the air and yelled, "Can't get too much of a good thing, Doc."

Doosey patted him in the crotch, "Later muffin."

"Yes, there is," Landish answered. "The strongest chakras spiral in the inner core around the spine. Those are easily manipulated through visualizations of the Kama Sutra, which you can order on Amazon. But we'll delve more into sexual potency and erotic expression in our next lecture."

The barista put his arm around Doosey and said, "I'm up for that, Doc."

"Any more questions?"

Clyde caught Minnie Two Feather's hand on the way up, pulling it down as gently as he could. Minnie outweighed him by a buck twenty and he didn't want her to throw him against the wall. He'd never live it down. Minnie grabbed his fingers and peeled them off like she would with the hide of an elk.

Minnie's hand shot back up and the Doctor nodded at her. Clyde prayed she hadn't been sidetracked by Doosey and asked about his little problem instead of her feet.

"How about bunions?" she shouted seriously. The crowd laughed loudly, except for Doosey and the barista who were otherwise engaged. A few heckled Minnie about toe separators and fungal deformities. It was like she'd told a poop joke to a bunch of fifth graders.

Clyde had had enough. He didn't want Minnie to ask her question, but he wasn't about to see his woman embarrassed. His honor was at stake.

"You need to call a podiatrist," Landish jested.

The crowd laughed harder, and one joker shouted, *"Do you have warts too?"*

Clyde jumped up reaching into his pants, fumbling around to find what he wanted. Doosey was close to ecstasy when he unzipped and pulled out his Desert Eagle L5 357 Magnum; she'd never seen that big of a barrel. He'd bought it in the parking lot at Big 5 Sports during their annual tent sale. Concealed was prepared in Arizona. Raising his gun he shouted, "You all show some respect. She's suffered with those toes for years."

"There not that bad, Honey," Minnie shrieked.

Clyde had no intention of firing, but the man in front of him dove to the floor sliding his chair into his knees. BOOM! The four bulb fluorescent overhead light exploded, showering glass all over Clyde and Minnie.

Great Spirit, please don't let her step on the glass with her gangly toes, Clyde thought.

She had worn her good calfskin moccasins; she wouldn't listen when he told her to wear the orthopedics.

Pandemonium ensued as the shot reverberated. Doctor Reginald Landish was the first one out the door, beating the barista who'd left Doosey on her own. People were stumbling over each other and pushing their way out. It was like a Phoenix nightclub at last call. A few Baptists were on their knees praying and Steel-Calves Kempdinger was vaulting out a window with the help of the hiking pole she always carried. Clyde was still standing with the Desert Eagle over his head. "I didn't mean to shoot, I didn't mean to shoot," he kept repeating.

Zula Ballsy was tending the Lazy *SOB* waiting for the meeting to end. She'd stocked up on Oak Creek Ambers, *Sauza* tequila, and Great Value margarita mix. It was going to be a big night. When she heard the unmistakable roar of a 357 Magnum, that's what Angie had used in Police Woman, she reached below the bar and grabbed her 12 gauge Beretta Silver Pigeon and ran to the sound of gunfire. *Not in her bar, not today.* Tony Two Balls had taught her to protect herself and she'd done some skeet shooting with Peter Lawford and the Kennedy boys.

By the time Zula got past the crowd which magically parted upon seeing the shotgun, Clyde had stuffed the Eagle back between its denim resting place and his BVDs. Minnie was hugging him. "I didn't mean to shoot," he told Zula. "They insulted Minnie's feet."

"Keep it in your pants next time," Zula ordered. "How about a cold amber?"

6

GRAB THE BIRD'S TAIL

THE SAND'S PREVIOUS OWNERS PUT A SMALL BATHROOM ON the back porch of the O'Bryan cabin. They'd lived there while the lodge was being built. Knowing it was a temporary stay they ran a pipe from the kitchen sink and stuck it through the wall to make an outdoor shower. Skip added privacy by screwing a few pallets end to end and laid pavers to keep from standing in mud. It suited him fine, more than O'Bryan had.

He was showering early, gazing at open sky as he lathered his shaggy graying hair. The salt and pepper stubble gave him a weathered rustic look that matched the cabin. Quite the change from the buzz cut and razor scraped chin he'd had for so many years. He rinsed and slipped on a pair of cutoff jeans and a sombrero-wearing hot dog t-shirt hanging on a rusty hook attached to the cabin's siding. The sporty attire was for his morning creek-side workout and a long run in the woods. He'd decided against coffee before exercise, he'd go to the lodge afterwards and have a cup with Zula.

Logic dictated he take up Tai Chi, Skip's logic at least. To him it seemed a requirement since he'd named his business Sedona Chi. He did a little Judo as a kid, but the smooth choreographed motions of Tai Chi were a better match to his forty-two-year-old joints. Qigong Tai Chi focused on breathing, movement, awareness, and meditation. The meditation he normally saved for the evening on his front porch with Don Julio; his favorite mantra being *Lay Down Sally* by Eric Clapton. Lilac turned him on to it, Tai Chi not Clapton. She claimed the rhythmic gestures would balance his ying and yang polarities. He'd been pretty keyed up when he first arrived in Sedona. He wasn't sure about his polarities, but the breathing and meditation she taught him helped him relax. Sex after stretching had its benefits as well.

For two weeks he'd been repetitively practicing and mastering a new movement. It was based on the *Grab the Bird's Tail* motion. Pivoting on his right heel he stepped away from his left foot. Extending his bottom hand, he led with his palms facing his chest, then flipped and rotated that hand, aligned his back hand, and ended with the back of his hands facing each other. Punching was permitted only if acting in self-defense. It took Skip two weeks before he was doing the Bird in his sleep. *Rip the Tail off the Donkey* was his own creation. The Donkey started from where the Bird ended, yanking the tail back violently with both hands. It would come in handy if he was ever in a bar fight holding some redneck from Cottonwood by his ear or nose; a situation not all that uncommon.

The run was challenging. It wasn't the distance but the terrain of rocks, water, steep grades, and loose soil. Skip had done it so many times he could just as easily do it in the dark. He ran three miles toward Cathedral Rock, including two crossings of Oak Creek, hopping from rock to rock. Most of his course followed Baldwin Trail, the back of which had the severest grade. Running came easy for him, he had been doing it most of his life. He ran Cross Country in school and, later, dashed through more than a few back alleys.

Back at his cabin, he sat on the concrete steps sweating, breathing too hard, and drinking a liter of cranberry juice. Breakfast was two hard boiled eggs. The last brown sugar cinnamon pop tart was tempting, but he decided to save it - *Time for coffee.*

"Joey liked a raw egg floating on top," Zula said at the *SOB*, handing Skip a cup of steaming Kona blend in a souvenir cup that said *It's Better in the Rocks.*

"Bishop?"

"Who else?" Zula responded. "He was a funny guy. Didn't always get along with Frank though. Politics," she tsked without explaining. "How's the donkey thing coming?"

"It's getting there." Skip liked the coffee but could do without all the conversation this early. He was sitting at the bar, the only one up and moving other than his landlady. He'd always been an early worm and Zula was always prepping for breakfast by five o'clock. She seemed extra wired this morning, standing behind the bar fussing with the Bunn.

"Could have used that burro busting move last night with Clyde Two Feathers. I expected to see you running up here after the shot."

Skip had slept through the ruckus and had no idea what Zula was talking about. *What shot?* He should have made a pot of Folgers at the cabin, sat on the porch, and watched the Gambel quail doing crazy 8s in his clearing. They always made him feel like he knew where he was heading.

"That crazy Apache shot off his 357 because of Minnie's bunions."

Skip rolled his eyes and took another sip of coffee. *Only in Sedona* – he didn't care to know more. If he didn't ask maybe that would be the end of it and he could get another cup to enjoy the morning silence. Zula was mixing homemade biscuits with her back to him. He leaned over the counter to reach the pot. Overhead on the flat screen, *The Morning Show* with Butch Snowboard and

Cassidy Sinclair was on. Butch was reporting everything his viewers needed to know that happened overnight in Phoenix. Cassidy kept nodding, apparently agreeing with Butch's news. Skip kept watching to catch the weather; he had a tour in the afternoon.

The reporter blurted out a report:

"And up in Sedona, where the Arizona sun always shines, a group of hikers informed authorities of a body found along a local trail. There were initially questions as to whether the victim was killed by a grizzly bear. The head of the hiking group had reported it as such. Captain Hoot Hooton informed News Channel 5 there hadn't been a grizzly sighting in Sedona since the 1930s. They only have an occasional black bear. Upon inspection, the bear was determined to be a set of human remains. A mountain bike was also found nearby."

"Captain Hooton said it is the 825th biking accident reported this year. He recommends all mountain bikers take a safety course from Bootsy Hooton at Hooton's Bike Shop in Uptown or their convenient location in the Village of Oak Creek before riding Sedona's trails. On a lighter note, Wickenburg's annual golf tournament, raising funds for the Society of Irritable Bowel Syndrome survivors, is this Saturday at Flushing Green Golf Club. Sounds like a mess Cassidy. In Tucson..."

The news about the mountain biking accident caused Zula to burn the biscuits. "Oh My God!" she cried, anguish in her voice.

"What?" Skip said, alarmed. "I've never seen any bears out by the cabin. If you're worried about them at the Retreat, you don't need to be." It wasn't often he saw Zula startled and upset, especially in a sad way. But if anything could do it, it would be a grizzly.

"The biker..." Zula hesitated. "He has to be my great nephew Zebulon. I feel it."

Skip noted the family's unusual use of names beginning with Z. "I didn't know you had family here."

"Not now!" she snapped. She looked at Skip and took a deep breath, easing it back out. "Sorry, I didn't mean to bark."

Skip never knew her to apologize. She was more the double down, take the hill and damn the torpedoes, ask for forgiveness later type. "What makes you think it's Zebulon?"

"It fits. Zebulon disappeared three years ago last October. His car was found in the parking lot at Bell Rock Plaza. The bike rack was empty. God, that child loved riding the back trails. I reported him missing after his roommate at NAU called. Everybody looked for him, but there were just too many remote areas to cover. The Search and Rescue helicopters flew for two days."

Zula's eyes were tearing. "It's just so hard, I always hoped he would..." she stopped, her voice breaking with emotion. "He lived with me during summer vacations. You just missed him. You showed up six months after all this happened. I couldn't talk about it back then."

Zula added a strong dose of whiskey to her coffee and looked at Skip who shook his head, *None for me*. "The kid's parents were a pair -- Angelo and Katey Sue," Zula said, looking at the ceiling like she was remembering two people she hadn't thought about in a long time. "Angelo and Tony could have been twins, except Angelo didn't have my Tony's heart or brains. Not that Tony was an ace in a deck himself."

"So, what happened to them? They still around?" Skip asked. He held his cup out, changing his mind, and Zula poured a shot. This sounded like it was going to be a long story.

"Divorced. Nasty one too, which was hard on Zeb. Katey was as flaky as a French croissant and Angelo always assumed other people's money was his own..." Zula hesitated, staring at nothing again. Skip guessed she was reflecting on her late husband's financial faults.

"Same as Tony, I guess. I never understood where they got it from," she said wistfully before returning to Zebulon's story. "The poor kid was caught in the middle. It was amazing he turned out as well as he did with the genes he inherited. The last I heard, Katey

Sue moved to Penang with the New Delhi acupuncturist she'd had an affair with and Angelo was surfing in Maui, living off a sugar momma."

"I'm sorry Zula," Skip said. "Maybe the body's not him." Zula winced and Skip immediately regretted saying *body*.

"It doesn't make any sense he'd fall off a mountain," Zula said. She'd already made up her mind it was her nephew. "That boy was careful, the serious kind. Not like his parents, or Tony. He was a good student and applying to graduate schools. He knew what he was doing on a mountain bike; he'd even won a few junior championships. It just doesn't fit."

Skip was about to suggest even the best make mistakes when a slickly groomed man in a Seersucker pinstripe suit walked into the Lazy *SOB*. He was big, over six feet, with a gut that looked like he'd swallowed a hot air balloon. His face was splotchy red, and poorly dyed black hair wisped from left to right across a balding top. There was a small posse following him, including the long-haired girl Skip had seen at the bar and the kid with the aluminum cuffs. Junior's belt was wrapped in aluminum foil this morning. Long-hair looked Skip over from beneath her purple eyelashes and grinned like people do when they make a smart joke to themselves. Or see something they like. The fat man had two other attending acolytes; a girl with a fire engine red buzz cut, and another young man, short and skinny with a tattoo of ET in a bike basket. They all sat at a table across the room, and ET handed a bag of Skittles to Seersucker. The big man started picking out the green pieces and setting them aside.

"That's Landish," Zula said, temporarily distracted from thoughts of her great nephew. "The Doctor, I told you about, with his group of looney tunes. The girl with the long hair is nice, a bit of an oddball, but nice. It's a shame she's hooked up with that blow hard. Wouldn't give a spit for the rest of them."

Skip watched Landish sort the rest of the Skittles by color and start eating them two at a time. Landish looked up at the bar and motioned for Zula. Skip doubted colored bits of sugar were going to cure his appetite for long. Zula grabbed her hand written menu card for the day and headed for their table. "Their money's green though," she winked. "Don't go anywhere." Skip reached over the bar, found the pot, and poured another cup of coffee.

Zula came back after taking their orders, which hadn't taken long because the only item on her breakfast menu was blueberry pancakes with prickly pear syrup. It sounded like an odd fruit pairing, but Skip knew the blend didn't matter when Zula added a little blackberry brandy to her homemade mix. He watched her pour store-bought batter onto the griddle from the cutoff milk carton. Apparently, the doctor didn't rate the brandy.

Gesturing with a spatula, Zula turned back to Skip. "I didn't buy Hoot Hooton's saying Zebulon had an accident." She was definitely convinced the skeleton found with the bike was her great nephew. "And if it wasn't an accident..." she said, pointing the spatula at him, splatters of leftover batter landing in his coffee. Tasting it, he made a mental note to offer the formula to Coffee Mate.

"Then it had to be foul play," Skip heard himself finish her sentence. He didn't usually let his mouth get in front of his brain. He'd learned the hard way to think and analyze before speaking, if talking was even necessary. Otherwise, you boxed yourself into a direction you might not want to go.

"That's right! How about you go with me to see Hoot this afternoon?" Zula said, the spatula targeting him again. "I might need you to hold me back. Hoot and I aren't on the best of terms you know. I need to remind him about Zebulon. The cops always know more than they tell the press. You wouldn't believe the stuff they held back about Tony."

Skip didn't know they weren't on the best of terms or why. He started to say *ok* before remembering he had a tour later. "How about tomorrow morning? That producer Kuul and I had the other day wants to check out Made in the Shade. He said the trail name fits and the shade would solve their concerns with the hot rock nude scenes."

"Porn stars have a love-hate relationship with UV rays. Wrinkles cut a career short and tan lines look slutty in adult films, but an exotic Mediterranean look sells. Tomorrow works for me," Zula said. It crossed Skip's mind that she knew a lot about tan lines.

"Now *those* boobs," she said, pointing at Landish and his entourage, "are keeping me hopping. Fat boy already asked what's for dinner and I haven't even served the pancakes. I told him whatever the special is at Pisa Lisa Pizzeria. I sure don't envy those aliens he's going to hook up with. They better have burgers and candy on their planet."

"Better flip the cakes, Zula."

"You want any? I can use the good mix. I've got some brandy. The blackberries reduce free radicals," Zula grinned.

Skip licked his lips, "Zula Ballsy, where have you been all my life."

7

PETRIFIED STRIPPER

RIDING WITH ZULA WAS NOT FOR THE FAINT OF HEART. SHE DROVE a bulletproof white classic 1982 Cadillac Fleetwood Brougham De' Elegance. Tony Two had willed it to her. It looked like the Good Fella car it'd been. The car was a crowd pleaser at Sedona's raucous St. Paddy's Day parade with its emerald-green landau top and monthly wax jobs from Cowboy Way Detailing. Zula had raced around Red Rock Loop Road, fishtailing in the wrong lane on most curves, blasting her horn as a signal to get out of the way. Once she hit State Route 89a at Lower Loop Road, she pushed the speedometer up to eighty in the fifty-five zone. The big V8 didn't break a sweat as it passed the Yavapai County Sheriff's SUV. The Deputy and Zula exchanged waves. Skip was glad she wasn't in a hurry.

"Looks like they're putting in new flood lights for the Scorpions," she said with one hand slung loosely over the wheel, the other pointing at Sedona High. "Best view in town." She slammed on the brakes with her left foot as the light ahead turned red and two Hummers with open seating pulled out from the Marriot for their morning tours.

"You think they'll win a game this year?" The Sands had an ad on the scoreboard, which in Zula's mind made her part-owner of a pro team. The Scorpions weren't known for their football prowess. Despite the millions of annual tourists, there were only twelve thousand fulltime residents and most of those were old enough to have watched Lee Harvey shoot Jack Ruby on their black and white Motorolas. There weren't a lot of teenage athletes to choose from. "The Carter twins are starting at tight end and wide receiver. Neither one of them could catch a cold in a Minnesota emergency room with nothing on but their skivvies," Zula scoffed.

Skip was relieved they'd stopped and that his own skivvies were still clean. Idling gave him a chance to steel his nerves for takeoff. Zula's right foot was hovering over the gas pedal and there was a funeral procession up ahead.

"That Hoot Hooton better shoot straight," she warned. Skip hoped she hadn't brought her Smith and Wesson. "He better not try to tell me it wasn't Zebulon." Skip cinched his seatbelt as she revved the Fleetwood's 7.0 liter engine, with her other foot still on the brake. *He should have driven.*

The Sedona Police Department was located inside City Hall, a half block from the Fire District, which would come in handy if the Cadillac overheated and burst into flames. Zula backed into a parking spot doing twenty, the long trunk of the Fleetwood pinning a beautifully flowering cholla against a stucco wall.

"Hell of a place to put a cactus!" She was in a prickly mood.

The counter at the police department was staffed by a short pimply noodle of an officer whose badge was the only part of his uniform that stuck out. The Fire District got the good-looking muscle hounds; they lived in frat houses, pumping iron and heroically fighting wildfires while the police dodged vomit from drunken tourists. Every red-blooded Arizona kid wanted to be a firefighter. It was the firefighters who executed the search and rescue mission that collected the biker's remains before turning the case over to the police. Officer Noodle saw Zula Ballsy heading into the station, but not in time to run.

"Mrs. Ballsy," he stammered while standing. The Police Department picnic had been at the Sands last year when he was a rookie. He was still living down the lawn dart incident. Hard-ass Sergeant Buckleroy had told him if he didn't get the next dart to the ring he'd be directing traffic in Uptown until he retired. He had been determined not to leave it short and let it fly. The dart bounced off a bat house nailed to a tree and dropped harmlessly into Bootsy Hooton's new breasts; Captain Hooton had just made the third and final installment payment. To make matters worse a startled bat caught a wing in her hair in its confused attempt to escape. Sergeant Harry *friggin'* Callahan had pulled his standard issue and shot it like William Tell plucking the apple off his son's head. Officer Noodle had been behind the front desk ever since.

"I'm here to see Hoot, let him know I'm here," Zula commanded. Skip was amazed how authoritative the ex-showgirl-turned-Sedona-den-mother could be when she wanted attention. He pitied the poor officer behind the counter if Hooton wasn't in. She was looking in disgust at the open box of Twinkies on his counter.

Officer Noodle nervously punched buttons on the new phone system with Zula hovering over the counter. They all heard Hooton's voice boom over the wall speaker. "I saw her in the parking lot, tell the petrified old stripper I'm not in." After an awkward pause, the Captain came on air again, "Officer Dickie, you hit the intercom button again didn't you?"

Here we go, Skip thought. Poor Dickie was headed even lower down the ladder if that was possible.

Zula was already charging into the captain's office. Skip followed. He'd grab her if she went for anything in her pockets. Same thing went for Hoot if he opened the gun cabinet.

"How they hanging Hoot?" Zula asked with a gleam in her eye. "How's Bootsy? I hear she's still deflated because you were too cheap to buy the warranty." She had a wicked streak if pissed.

Captain Hooton jumped to his feet; he was a striking character in a town full of them. His good eye was glaring at Zula while the other lazy one was searching up, down, and sideways. Skip couldn't help but follow it until it settled on the ceiling fan. Both eyes bulged from their sockets and quivered due to an undisclosed medical condition, making the wandering orb even more disturbing. He stood 6'10", had a busted knee from a botched traffic stop that left him with a limp, and one ear sat noticeably lower than the other one. His shiny dome was bald as an onion except for one eyebrow that was black and one that was red with a gray stripe. He looked like the offspring off Tennessee twins who'd committed incest.

"Zula, you know it takes a long time to get a squad car out to your place," Hooton warned. He'd guessed the purpose of her visit. His distracted eyeball was on the move again. Skip watched it bounce around the room until it landed on the coffee he'd just spilled on the floor. His good eye had stayed fixed on Zula.

They were both getting ready for round two when Skip jumped in. "Zula thinks the skeleton found out Jacks Canyon was her great nephew." Both of the Captain's eyes settled on him, which was unnerving. Hooton shook his head affirmatively and the eye took off again.

"I tried to tell Lurch something happened to him three years ago," Zula spit out.

Hooton sat back down and made a show of moving papers around before looking back up with his good eye. "I had the same thought Zula, but we can't be sure until some tests come back. I was waiting until then. It wasn't unreasonable for us to think the kid had just taken off. Like his parents. It happens all the time with young people that age."

"Humph," Zula muttered. She started to say something, but Hooton cut her off.

"Zula, it's under investigation. Look, it's our working assumption it's Zebulon. When we know for sure I'll come out to let you know. I'm sorry we didn't find him three years ago, but it wouldn't have made any difference. It was an accident. There was the body and his bike. It was pretty clear from the bones that he'd fallen. He probably died when he hit his head. We dug up a broken skull."

"Who found him?" Zula barked. She was still simmering.

"Big Bob was out there with the Dogies. He called Search and Rescue, and Chief Drummmaker sent the Fire Department's recovery team out."

Skip had been closely listening and watching Zula to make sure she didn't go for a pocket. "Captain, I don't want to tell you your job, but it seems premature to call it an accident. Did you set up a search grid? If it was a fall, there must have been some sign of how it happened; debris, broken branches, scraped rocks, that kind of thing. Were there any fingerprints on the bike? Could you tell how the body was laying? The area's still taped and closed off I assume?"

With one eye, Hooton stared at Skip as if he was ready to throw him out the door. The other eye had a *WHO is this guy* glare. "We didn't actually go out," Hooton finally said. His lazy eye started fidgeting and darting between Zula and his holster hanging from a hook on the wall.

"Why the HELL NOT?" Zula howled.

Hooton was back on his feet. "Big Bob said it was a *bear*! WE DON'T DO bears! Call the damn rangers, Zula!"

Skip held Zula back. She'd braced herself on Hooton's desk, preparing to launch over it into the captain. She was like a bull charging a red cape with two good-looking cows behind it. Skip was fighting to hold her back. Hooton's bulging eyes were fixed on her and shaking like jello.

"Where's Zebulon now?" Skip asked, blocking a high kick from the old dancer.

Skip felt Zula's muscles deflate. Thinking about her nephew's remains sobered her. In her anger, he doubted she would have thought to ask about Zebulon's body.

"The *remains* are at the coroner's office in Prescott. Jacks Canyon is in Yavapai County. An autopsy is being performed to confirm the cause of death...if there's enough left; it's been out there a long time. The coyotes and big cats have been at it. If it's him, where do you want the bones sent, Zula?"

"I'll let you know. You're worthless Hoot," Zula said and stormed out.

• • •

The dash from the Police Station was as reeling as an angler with peanut butter at an overstocked trout farm. The homeless hiker at the corner by McDonald's barely leapt out of the way in time. Zula picked off the collection basket he was shaking with her driver's side mirror. By the time she whipped into the Safeway Plaza and skidded to a stop in front of Café Jose, Skip had exhausted his short list of prayers. Scarlet flowers from the cholla she'd backed into at City Hall were still adorning the Cadillac's back bumper. A girl sitting in a parked Sahara Jeep in the next spot wearing a Grateful Dead bandana gave thumbs up and said, *"Cool begonias."*

Safely seated in a vinyl booth, Skip chose Café Jose's scrambled egg, hash brown and avocado burrito with a side of grits. It came with tater tots or jalapeno poppers. Zula had cooled off and ordered the BLT with a side of fruit. Café Jose was owned by Ted 'Lucky' Cackling who also had the Golden Goose Steakhouse across the street. Every year Jose won the Best of Sedona Enchilada Meat Loaf Combo – probably the best enchilada meat loaf in the world.

The glass sculptures hanging on the walls came from Lucky's black-jack winnings at Circus Circus. He and Zula went way back.

"Coffee or water?" the waitress asked.

"*Dos Pacificos*," Skip answered, both beers for his nerves.

"Hoot Hooton's full of elk spit," Zula said. "He's all set to close the case as an accidental death and he didn't even bother to go to the scene." Skip glanced at the kitchen hoping her BLT was on its way before she got riled up again.

"That's a long hike with that eye and a limp," Skip said. Zula shot him a hard look as the waitress placed a bowl of fruit on the table. "Maybe the coroner's report will shed some more light," he added.

Zula poked at her fruit. "I need to talk with Lucky, this is all bananas and pineapple. Oh, wait a minute, there's a strawberry." She didn't care about the fruit. She was working out in her head what to do next.

Skip shoveled fresh mango salsa on his burrito and grits. A taste of the Caribbean, Mexico, and Alabama all rolled together. They both ate in silence. Zula stole more than a few of his jalapeño poppers. The avocado was a tad mushy, but Skip wasn't complaining. Burritos at Jose were famous; the size of a sycamore log. Leftovers would be dinner if he survived the ride home.

Zula was absentmindedly spearing bananas with her fork. "I had a vision last night, it wasn't the first time," she said, spinning her silver Kokopelli bracelet. Skip was adding ketchup to the last popper and dabbed it in the last of the salsa.

"You've got an iron stomach. Tomato and mango?" she chuckled. "No wonder you like my cooking."

"What, they're both fruits. What'd you see in your vision?"

"Ever since I bought that cannabis oil infused pillow they're more vivid. Accurate too, not counting the one about Foster Brooks and Dom DeLuise making out in the backseat of my Brougham. I swear I'm never drinking buh-buh-bourbon while snacking on éclairs again."

Skip was aware of Zula's visions. She claimed to have had one the night before he showed up at the Sands the first time. She'd seen a Mexican flag and a big knife cutting a stranger chained to a chair in a cargo container. It explained why she had carried her Beretta to show him the cabin. She later confessed she rented it to him because her vision also revealed Skip had a true heart and deserved a break.

"Zebulon was murdered. I saw him running and then falling after being pushed." Skip wondered if their wires weren't cosmically spliced together: Her visions sounded a lot like his dreams. "I woke up when a shadow was standing over him."

Empathy had never been high on the list of Skip's virtues. In his defense, it was a short list, so there wasn't a lot of room. But he was loyal. Zula was hurting and it was clear Hooton was only looking to check the boxes and be rid of the case as soon as possible. Zula deserved answers.

Well, what the heck, he thought. *You don't have any tours on the books for a few days...*

8

TURQUOISE PENIS

HIDDEN SEVEN THOUSAND MILES AWAY SAT A COLORFULLY DEC-orated life-sized androgynous figure. It rested in a subterranean vault below a Chinese art gallery several blocks off Nanjing Road in Shanghai. Its owner had put the statue in a separate room inside a glass case with its carved penis sticking through a hole. The lights in the case highlighted the turquoise and copper encrusted face. The room had no other furnishings or art with the exception of a double bed placed perfectly in line with the figure's impassive gaze.

The collector was one of the expanding breed of super wealthy Chinese industrialists searching for ways to invest their profits. He was in his late seventies, but looked twenty years younger because of the cosmetic work he'd had done. The son of a Japanese soldier and a Chinese woman impressed into a local brothel during Shanghai's occupation, he'd survived the Cultural Revolution and succeeded beyond his imagination after Mao's death and the country's economic liberalization.

The gallery off Nanjing road was really a front for his import-export business. He acquired and distributed pre-Colombian artifacts. There was an unquenchable thirst for Native art in the world market, even pieces that couldn't be displayed publicly. The collector specialized in Southwest American objects from 500 to 1200 A.D. They sold fast and were easily attainable. There were still undiscovered ruins throughout the area and no shortage of looters and entrepreneurs with shovels. From Arizona and New Mexico, it was a short drive across the border to Mexico where a few well-placed pesos could buy anything, including the packaging and shipping of illegally obtained artifacts. The Mexican and U.S. border authorities were only interested in keeping people and goods out of the U.S.; the reverse trip required little more than a wave. Even something as large as the androgynous figure sailed right through.

Most of the items the collector attained were sold within three months to buyers throughout Asia, Australia, and Europe. He'd recently made some inroads with the Russian oligarchy, but he needed to grow that line slowly. The two private rooms he kept sealed from the larger vault were for his own pleasure. The collector called them the Smithsonian, a jab at the venerable American Institution whose own collections had been stolen by American archeologists they'd financed with grants to American universities. He was only doing the same.

In one of the rooms the collector displayed his most valuable finds. He liked to impress his friends with Montezuma's headdress and a rare Mayan calendar. Occasionally he would tire of a piece and sell it, making room for a new purchase he'd decided to keep. The other room was for the androgynous figure with the jeweled face and polished penis. It was a rare fertility goddess, and its powers were said to ensure successful pregnancies. For five million a night, he offered the bed to Asia's most powerful business leaders. He charged the Japanese auto kings more because of his mother. They had built the planes, bombs, and military hardware that had raped his country. The camera he'd installed in the turquoise bead on the head served as insurance against their reprisals.

The collector was waiting on another order he'd placed for bid with American middlemen. The call had been for Ancestral Puebloan jewelry and Apache collectibles. A Russian buyer had asked for specific designs and colors originating in the Four Corners region of Colorado, Utah, New Mexico, and Arizona.

9

GUNS AND POSES

THE SEDONA LIBRARY WAS A HIDDEN GEM IN A SCENIC SETTING out Dry Creek Road. It was privately run with donations from wealthy blue-haired patrons who reappeared every winter. The library had a large Arizona History section that Skip liked to spend time in researching stories to tell his guests.

He had been doing an in depth dive into the Navajo Long Walk from Fort Defiance to Bosque Redondo and the People's five year internment in that poisonous hellhole. The Navajo had endured alkaline tainted land, no firewood for the harsh mountain winters, and endless Comanche raids from Texas. To compare and contrast, he was also studying the Yavapai Wars conducted by General Crook. The Yavapai had been marched nearly two hundred miles over mountains and across icy rivers in February 1864 to be imprisoned with the Mescalero Apache in San Carlos. Both tribes had been screwed. The Navajo came home after five years; the Yavapai after twenty-five.

In the outside courtyard he tipped his baby Stetson to the life-sized sculpture of the pretty young woman holding a basket of apples in the courtyard; Sedona Schnebly. Her pioneer husband, T. Carl, had originally sent Red Rock Crossing to the postmaster general as a name for the new town, but that took too much ink for a stamp. T. Carl's brother had suggested *Sedona*, which made Skip wonder what was cooking between him and the smiling bronze woman depicted in the statue. White and European, none of the invading settlers or their heirs were ever force marched and held captive away from home.

Skip walked through the double doors and past the racks with worn paperbacks for sale. An adventure book about two buddies looking for a confederate warship in the Sahara Desert caught his eye. He put it back because the plot seemed a little too far-fetched and complicated. He preferred easy reading when he wasn't researching dry historical records. There were two volunteer librarians working the information desk. In sing-song they both asked if they could help him find something. He chose the older of the two, he liked the sparkles she'd sprayed in her obviously dyed black hair.

"Hi, I'm looking for old copies of the Red Rock News."

"How far back?"

"Three to four years," he answered.

"Not a problem. We have those electronically." She eyeballed his battered felt Stetson, his T-shirt honoring a 2005 Beach Boys concert in LaJolla, and his hiking boots with the mismatched laces. "Follow me, I'll show you how to find what you're looking for." She left the info booth and headed toward a side room with a sign above it that said RESEARCH. Skip wasn't sure he could have found it on his own, what with the room being so well hidden.

"Skip Rhodes. What's your name?" he said, wanting to be friendly. He hadn't run across this woman before despite spending quite a bit of time studying there the last few months. That wasn't unusual; the library attracted a lot of retirees looking for an air conditioned place to volunteer and a chance to make new friends. Faces came and went often.

"Agnes Speer, I just started this week. I moved here from Goober, North Carolina after Mr. Speer passed from a strangulated hernia that ruptured. If you ask me, that's what caused his last heart attack. He'd had three. Although the doctors say it was the diabetes that got him. My sister lives on Lost Wagon Road and I moved in with her a month ago. Do you like the sparkles? I saw you noticed them. Gladys said they'd help me fit in. I'm not so sure they don't just make me stand out," she half giggled.

"I like the pink ones when the light from the overheads hit them," Skip said. Agnes had stopped in the central hall to introduce herself and tell her life story. She glanced at the overhead lights and blinked. Then she blinked again...and again. Skip thought she forgot where they were heading, another thing that wasn't unusual with retirees in Sedona.

"Gladys talked me into trying contacts. She said the trick in Sedona is to look as young as you can without looking like a painted floozy from a saloon. I've seen some of those...no thank you. Mr. Speer and our pastor at Goober First Congregational frowned on women wearing makeup. Gladys and Mr. Speer didn't get along."

Skip wondered what Mr. Speer would think of the sparkles and dyed hair.

"Right, the Research Room, Red Rock News," she said, remembering where they were heading. "Gladys said the first thing to do when you retire is buy new underwear. So that's what I did, pink and purple with a band of lace...makes me feel like a new woman. Gladys hooked me up on a date tonight with a local named Mustang Timothy. Isn't that the cutest name? He's younger than me, but that's Okay," she said, winking at Skip. "I'm picking him up at Sedona Winds Retirement Center. It'll be my first date since I met Mr. Speer at Duke. Not sure I'm ready, but I'm not getting any younger."

Skip was doing his best to block the mental image of Agnes in her new panties riding a Mustang. All he'd done was ask her name. If things got any more intimate, she'd be inviting him over for tea and cookies with Gladys.

Agnes walked him over to an empty computer terminal and pointed at the seat. Skip followed her instructions and clicked on the blue curly icon. She leaned over and typed in *Red Rock News*. "When it comes up, click on the tab for past issues. That should lead you where you want to go. If you need to print anything let me know. It's ten cents a page."

"Thanks, Agnes. You seem to be catching on. What did you do in North Carolina?" Skip regretted asking as soon as the words left his mouth. He'd opened another door that wouldn't close any time soon.

"Well," Agnes looked at him conspiratorially. "I was an investigative journalist for the Goober Times. In Goober that meant following the School Board's book purchases and the Rotary Club's decision to pay for a new stop sign outside their president's Fish and Chip diner. I could have made it big in Durham if Mr. Speer hadn't accepted a job in Goober with the County Ag Office. He inspected tobacco and tracked the yield per acre based on what type of manure the farmers used. That man loved crap. Then we had Sissie and Leroy and our life was set. Leroy's a gynecologist in Winston-Salem. Sissie divorced last year. The years go so fast. The only professional mark I left was uncovering a fixed pie-eating contest at the county fair. That was nominated for a Cronkite Award; placed second to an expose on recruiting violations for Croatian athletes at Appalachian State. Basketball's big in Carolina."

"You sure shook things up in Goober. Sorry about Sissie," Skip said.

"What exactly are you trying to find in the Red Rock News. It was three years ago?"

"Three years ago, last October."

The home page for Red Rock News had come up on the screen while Agnes was sharing her professional accomplishments. She leaned over Skip again and clicked a tab, waited, clicked another tab, scrolled to 2016 and clicked October. "There you go. It only comes out once a week. It shouldn't take you too long to look them over."

"That's great," Skip said. "I would have just typed a word into the search box and hoped for the best. Looks like your fellow librarian needs help." There was a line three deep at the main counter.

Agnes gave him her Dan Rather stare, not quite sure if she'd just been hoodwinked. "Providence gets overwhelmed by herself. Weird name, huh. Let me know if you need any more help," she said and scurried back to save Providence.

It didn't take Skip long to confirm most of what Zula and Hooton had said about Zebulon Ballsy and his disappearance. There was one story on the disappearance and two follow-up stories on the search. The police in Flagstaff had been contacted by Zebulon's roommate when he didn't return from Fall Break. He'd also called Zula who contacted local authorities the same day. The Sedona police found his car at Red Rock Plaza in the Village of Oak Creek. The bike rack was empty, and the assumption was something had happened on a trail. According to his aunt, he was known to ride alone. A ground and air search yielded nothing. The helicopter pilot had been disappointed, telling the reporter, "We had an emergency packet of water, blankets, aspirin, and trail mix ready to drop if we'd found him somewhere we couldn't land."

An unrelated article below the last story caught Skip's eye. Not only was he a southwest history junkie, but Sedona Chi had turned him onto archeology as well. The news article was about a home in Prescott belonging to a respected doctor being raided in the middle of the night by federal agents. The doctor had been involved in a smuggling ring. Crates of sensitive archeological and cultural Native American artifacts were found in his basement and seized. Skip read on, shaking his head. *This stuff happened all too often. He hoped they caught all the bastards and shipped them to Yuma.* The scope of the operation had been discovered through an informant fitted with a miniature camera in a button. The informant had recorded hours of digital conversations between sellers and collectors, including the doctor, negotiating prices and sourcing of objects. The federal attorneys believed it was just the tip of the iceberg.

One crooked doctor got Skip thinking about another: Doctor Reginald Landish. He googled the name and just as he expected, there was nothing. He tried variations of the name, and no one fit the Landish staying at the Sands. The closest he'd found was a Reggie 'Batman' Landish in Mobile who had been arrested for attempting to fly off the U.S.S. Alabama in his boxers and a ski mask. The Church of Astro Departure did result in a few hits. None of them was very enlightening. They were all recent notices of meetings and lectures in Utah and Arizona. Apparently, the big man who liked Whoppers was an expert in dark skies, the mystic heritage of Celtic peoples, vortex synergy, and alien birth rituals. Each notice disclosed that offerings in support of the Church would be solicited.

When he finished, Skip backed out to the computer desktop like Agnes had asked. On his way out he picked up the novel about the confederate warship, the weird plot had hooked him, and stopped at the front desk to say goodbye. It seemed the polite thing to do and he needed to pay for the book. Agnes was checking in returns and brushing glitter off the scanner; Providence was cleaning up the children's section after a sand painting class.

"Thanks again for the help, Agnes. I've got a book here I'm buying."

"You didn't really need my handholding, did you? Patronizing an old lady's not a nice thing to do," she winked. "Once I get to know you better, Gladys and I'll have you over for barbecue. She likes to cook and I like to talk. Mr. Speer wasn't much for Mexican food. I don't care much for it either, too spicy. Brisket and pig knuckles, that's what we do in Carolina. It's all about the sauce. Most people overdo the Worcestershire. I go light on that and heavy with the Dijon and chili powder, then sprinkle on crumbled blue cheese. Gladys spikes her baked beans with good Kentucky sour mash. Mr. Speer and I brought a case back from Louisville once. He wanted to visit the bat factory. I've taken up pickleball out here."

She winked again and lowered her voice to make sure Providence was out of ear shot, "Gladys says Mustang Timothy plays close to the net." The innuendo and future invitation told Skip she was flirting; the enticement of blue cheese said she was out of practice.

"I'll see you around," Skip said and then leaned in and whispered, "Watch out for Mustang. He has quite the reputation with the ladies. Bad hip and pacemaker aside, you will need to set boundaries." Now knowing Agnes as well as he did, Skip felt a certain responsibility with Mr. Speer being gone and Leroy in Winston-Salem.

• • •

Lilac William's left foot was wrapped around the back of her head itching her right ear, avoiding her swinging red pony-tail tied with a yellow scrunchie. The pose was known in yoga as *Eka Pada Sirsasana.*

Skip turned over rocks, studying his ex-girlfriend's profile against the Sedona scenery, as she progressed through her third series of breathing exercises and low impact movements. Standing six-feet and wearing an extra-long pair of spandex leggings, there was no ignoring her tall athletic frame. The noticeable biceps on her otherwise graceful arms and her taut well-defined pectoral muscles sent a strong message that she could hold her own. Her breasts were expanding and contracting with each breath. *She had good lungs*, though smaller than her build would suggest. *Maybe it was the tight sports bra.*

Her body wasn't the most feminine he'd enjoyed, but the workouts had been extreme. Her soft brown eyes were wild and enthusiastic while making love, but afterward they'd made him feel nurtured like he was snuggling with a teddy bear. He'd once told her they were the warm color of baked clay with miniature brown and gold lightning bolts radiating through waves of soft flower petals. *He'd read it from an art description of the Greek goddess Diana the Huntress.*

"Give it a shot, just trying will stretch your back and improve your karma," she told Skip.

He sat on a stone ledge and reached his left hand around the back of his head and scratched his right ear. The move kept his rotator loose.

"Very funny." She transitioned to an easy Wide-Legged Standing Forward Bend. It kept her hips flexible and strengthened the leg muscles. Lilac had taken up yoga after losing her private investigator license, thanks to an unfortunate incident and dyslexic hotel clerk. There's no sense of humor down in the valley.

Before he met her, she had specialized in divorce investigations in Phoenix; philandering husbands only, she refused to take cases against cheating wives saying they deserved a choice. She started in law enforcement chasing criminals with the Tucson Police, but after eight years of challenging the males in charge and bouncing off the glass ceiling she decided to set up her own shop in Phoenix. She had certainly challenged Skip.

Lilac's PI business had been good until an informant with dyslexia transposed the numbers of a hotel room. She was caught photographing a tangled *ménage trois* in Room 192 at the Hampton Inn in Mesa while her mark was actually in Room 129. The District Attorney was in 192 with two young, enthusiastic, and very ambitious court reporters – neither one was Mrs. District Attorney.

She'd come to Sedona to find "inner peace and harmonic absorption" and discovered her calling as a yoga and firearms trainer. Her slogan was, *Relax in the Warrior Position and Squeeze it Softly*. Instead of working from home she met her clients outdoors in Sedona's most enchanting locations. Her go-to session was early morning yoga at the base of Doe Mesa (an optional run up top for the millennials) with an afternoon session in Camp Verde at Smoking Joe's Gun Range blasting away with a semi-automatic Glock 19. She held two sessions a week and had to limit enrollment to three unless they drove themselves. It was so popular her "girls" had started carpooling.

Lilac was in her patented *Kick the Crap out of a Jerk* pose, which was an add-on to her usual cooling down routine whenever she went out with Skip. They'd hiked from the trailhead at the end of Verde Valley School Road to a grassy field below Cathedral Rock. Skip had brought a camp chair to enjoy the view.

"How'd dinner with the Chamber of Commerce guy go? Let me guess, he took you to *Dahl and DiLuca*." D&D was a fancy Italian restaurant in West Sedona that charged an arm and leg for linguini and frozen clam sauce. A guy taking a date there meant he expected a little Dolce Vita later that night.

Skip admired her toned legs as she cycled between Up Dog and Down Dog poses, which were her favorites. They brought back warm memories. They'd met at a Sands party and been exclusive until a year ago when they mutually decided the "friends with occasional recreational benefits" route was a better option.

"Who's the investigator now?" Lilac joked. She switched to a Triangle pose with her legs split and one arm stretching to the sky. It opened up her lungs. She took a deep breath and let it out. "Jealous?"

"Just curious." *Hell yes, he was jealous. Who wouldn't be after watching her bend and twist through half the Kama Sutra?*

"One and done. He didn't appreciate my passion."

Skip suspected it hadn't been a match made in heaven. Lilac was hot tempered by nature and highly unpredictable when mad, which was her go to mood – at least around him. He doubted the Chamber guy could stand up to her, which is what she really wanted. If it had gone well she would have been rubbing it in.

She didn't elaborate, continuing her routine. Skip watched her move effortlessly, flowing from one position to another. His sore joints had been a poor match, and their personalities, likewise, just hadn't meshed for a serious long term relationship. He could never tell if Lilac wanted to punch him or jump him. He suspected she decided on the fly. They still enjoyed each other's company, just not in the same way. Today's hike was what they were now – easy company with the occasional hint of regret.

Lilac finished her workout standing on one foot with her palms pressed together in front of her undersized chest. She was in another realm, gaining focus and clarifying her place. Skip stayed quiet until she broke the trance. She flashed him a peculiarly frustrating look and grabbed her water bottle.

"It was all going perfectly until he asked the waiter if he could get Gouda on his smoked salmon enchiladas. He should have ordered the linguini if he wanted a white cheese sauce. Who has Gouda on Mexican? Fusion is one thing, but that's just wrong. What was I supposed to do?" She asked the question like the answer was obvious.

Skip decided nothing good could come from opening his mouth.

"I politely asked to see the chef," Lilac said, answering her own question.

"That's all?" Skip said.

Lilac smirked. "The chef was pretty uppity when he came out. Downright insulting actually. Apparently, he doesn't like leaving his kitchen. I asked him if he could explain to my date why you shouldn't use Gouda on enchiladas, or tacos, or burritos, or anything rolled in a damn tortilla. *Surprise!* He ignores me and apologizes to my date, saying the customer is always right. *Like who am I?*"

"Uh huh. And that's all?"

"I *might* have showed the chef my Glock and threatened to make Swiss out of his Gouda," Lilac answered shrugging her shoulders.

Skip chuckled, "You should have gone to *Tamaliza*. It's hard to screw up tamales. What did Mr. Chamber do?"

Lilac frowned, "*Dahl and DiLuca* is up there on the Chamber list, and he didn't appreciate my antagonizing one of their bigger members. The guy was a smug jerk and apologized back to the Chef for my behavior. *So...*I threatened his manhood with a butter knife. He said something about my anger management issues and we called it a night. And he said he'd eat Gouda on any damned thing he wanted to."

"And you wonder why you're out here with me."

They started walking back to the trailhead. It had been a week since they'd seen each other, so they caught up on what was new. Skip told her about the Hollywood XXX tour and Lilac talked about a couple from Albuquerque who'd each insisted on posting the other's picture over their targets at Smokin Joe's. They ended up crying and hugging after the woman plugged the man between the eyes.

Skip brought up Zebulon Ballsy. "You heard about the hiker they found out Jacks Canyon, right?" Lilac nodded. "Zula thinks it's her great nephew." Skip relayed his and Zula's visit to Hoot Hooton and what he'd confirmed with Agnes at the library.

"I knew Zebulon. Not well, but I'd run into him out at the Sands. Nice kid, Zula was broken up when he disappeared," Lilac said. She and Zula went further back than Skip and Zula. Zula was the one who introduced them at a Lazy *SOB* Tequila Party.

As usual, Skip was gassed keeping up with Lilac. She could walk faster while talking than anyone he knew, and she'd just finished a strenuous routine. Her long legs covered a step and a half to each of his. She wasn't one to slow down for anyone either, she'd be more likely to pick up the pace. He could maybe outrun her on the rocky trails because of the power in his bigger muscles, but competing on a level path was a different story. She kept her blistering pace until they were back at their cars.

"You aren't working out enough. Push the Tai Chi," she advised. "Control your breathing."

She was right, he should double down on his morning workout. Skip was sitting on the rusty dented tailgate of his Ford Bronco trying to catch his breath. He grabbed two cervezas from the Coleman cooler he kept in the back. The Bronco needed to be put out to pasture; the check engine light laughed at him, and the transmission couldn't find the third gear...but the cigarette lighter kept the beer cold. Lilac accepted the icy can and sat beside him, hoping the back of the old warhorse could hold both their weight.

From their angle, Cathedral Rock rose in a postcard view; two red and tan horizontal striped sandstone monoliths soaring in front of them like the twin bulwarks of Notre Dame, with Disney Castle turrets rising from the flat roof in between. Mother Nature's *Reach for the Heavens* pose. Most tourists climbed to the saddle from a trail on the other side leaving this side to the enjoyment of locals.

The embarrassment of fainting and the danger of cardiac arrest had been avoided. The beer was cold, and Skip was enjoying the company of a good friend. For once, they weren't arguing, they were just enjoying the moment. After a few minutes Lilac crushed her can between her hands and tossed it over her shoulder behind the Bronco's duct-taped seat. She jumped off the tailgate and a piece of rusty metal joined its iron oxide brothers on the ground. *Silence broken.*

"I was on the search and rescue team that went out for the body. There's no way you'd be out there unless you knew where you were going."

"Hooton and the Red Rock News both said it was remote and hard to get to," Skip said, uncertain where she was heading with the comment. He figured she might have been on the team; she volunteered and was popular with the firefighters.

"Not really that hard, if you're in shape," she said eyeing him. "But you certainly had to have a reason to be there. It wasn't a marked trail. Most hikers and bikers would go right past an animal trek off Jacks Canyon, and that's all it is – wouldn't even notice it. I'm not surprised it took three years before somebody found him. He was a mess, Skip."

Skip drained the last of his beer and put the can in a box he kept beside the Coleman. He needed to empty it. Maybe he'd stop by the recycling bins behind Clark's Grocery. Lilac was heading to her car and stopped.

"One thing struck me as odd," she said. "The bike was too far from the remains. If Zebulon had fallen from higher up, he would have had hold of the bike. I've seen enough bikers flying over these rocks to know the last thing they'd do is let go of the handles."

"So?"

"So... the bike should have been by the body. Or at least close by. He lost control somehow."

10

PLUMBERS TO THE STARS

SKIP GOT A CALL FROM KUUL BALTHAZAR ASKING IF HE WANTED to help with one of his celebrity clients. The client's toilet was clogged and Kuul was his "little friend" when it came to plumbing. Last names were *verboten*, Kuul had warned him. *"When they're in town they like to pretend they're normal folk."*

Balthazar had been a consultant on a crime movie partially set in Navajo Nation and one "Goodfella" actor had referred him to another to replace a water heater. After a dozen referrals famous clients, he had changed his business name to AAA Plumbers to the Stars. Kuul thought Stars was a clever double entendre for his Hollywood clientele and Sedona's dark skies. He was also AAA Plumbers *only* plumber. If he needed an extra hand, he often called Skip.

The producers had assumed the Mayan was Navajo because they'd rented his Hogan for a month to shoot a sweat lodge scene. Kuul hadn't seen any reason to correct their mistake. After a few emails back and forth they'd also hired him to advise the big name director on all things Native. The liberal Hollywood set wasn't about to insult an authentic Native American in his own home by checking references. His ancestry never came up. The consulting business had turned into a profitable sideline, and he'd just finished a Netflix series on Kit Carson starring a famous Australian gladiator.

"Al, take a look down this snake." Kuul had run a cable with a camera down the toilet into the home's main sewer line. He'd hit a spot four feet below the Venetian marble tiles where the plastic line ended in a pocket of dirt and gravel.

Al's Sedona home was on a private eight acre tract in a newer, gated subdivision plowed up against Horse Mountain. The local environmentalists had gone bat crazy during the approval process, chaining themselves to the construction gate not thinking the developer had multiple bolt cutters. Most of the houses were built just before the market crashed in 2008, when developers couldn't throw them up fast enough. More than a few corners got cut in their rush to cash in with subcontractors working seventy hours a week.

"Whoa, did I do that?" Al said. "No, wait, Martin was the last one who used this."

"It's gravel Al, no bio. The line's broken or more likely was never connected."

"That's some heavy shit, man. Martin's going to owe me. There'll come a time when I ask for a favor." Without a screenwriter in town, Al was on his own for lines.

Skip was along for the ride, helping with unloading and loading equipment. Mostly he was just keeping Balthazar company. With his celebrity customers, Kuul let him pass out Sedona Chi cards and plug his tours. L.A. was a lucrative market - despite the nut jobs. He also got a kick from watching Kuul's Navajo act. He'd asked once if it wasn't demeaning playing the Indian shtick. Kuul had said, *"Any time an Indian can get money from a white man, it's a win."*

"Wha we gotta do?" Al asked, slipping into his Little Italy brogue.

Kuul pulled out a rawhide pouch with corn starch, sprinkling it in a spoked pattern in front of the toilet. "Sacred sand," he said solemnly. "Make sure bad spirits don't come back." Al respectably nodded. Kuul wasn't done. "We should do a pipe blessing too before breaking our Great Mother and messing with the toilet water." Al crossed his arms and nodded reverently.

Skip poured leftover corn starch in his friend's cupped hands. Kuul mystically raised his arms over the tank and clapped a cloud. They had watched LeBron do the same act at a Suns game in Phoenix. Kuul stared at the dusty plaster cupid in the ceiling and mumbled a few sentences of Navajo that suspiciously sounded like an order off a Taco Bell menu with a side of Pad Thai. Al bowed his head.

Finished with the corn, Kuul said, "We're going to have to jackhammer up the floor, excavate down to the break, put in a new section of PVC, and then close everything back up and reinstall the toilet. I have a buddy that can do the tile work, but that's separate. It's a big job, Al, mucho pesos. I'll have to charge by the hour, but since you're a repeat I can knock off ten percent. I'll add the pipe blessing to the final bill.

"Yuh gotta do wha yuh gotta do," Al moaned.

"We need to smoke over it," Balthazar said.

"Now you're talking!" Al took off down an extra-wide hall lined with mirrors and a gold leaf chair rail, matching solid gold chandeliers hanging from the twenty-foot-high ceiling. "I've got a private stash hid in the tenth bedroom. I'll be right back."

Skip snickered at Kuul, "You're unreal."

"Like you don't play up that story about Sedona, T Carl, and his brother to everyone on a tour. Double standards Kemosabe… double standards."

Balthazar and Skip gathered up the protective tarp and put the tools in a snap bag. Al still wasn't back so they waited for him in the lobby; the entrance was too grand and big to be called a foyer. A five-tiered blue and green Chihully chandelier shaped like a dream catcher hung in the middle of the room; Skip trusted the eagle feathers were legally obtained. With time to kill, Al apparently had taken a wrong turn in the south wing, Skip told the Zebulon Ballsy story. A regular at the Sands, Kuul had known the kid well.

"He was going to make a good hombre. He used to quiz me about Mayan culture and the history of Indigenous People. He was serious about helping us preserve our heritage and beliefs. I hope Zula's wrong. I always figured he'd show back up some time. My ex knew him too. Zeb drove for Pink Jeeps with her for two seasons."

"Which one?" 'Skip joked. Kuul was not monogamous; wedding vows were just another European custom. Skip had lost track of his Mayan friend's ex-wives and girlfriends. They kept popping up. He kept in touch and was fast friends with all of them. They'd do anything for him, and he was always around to fix their plumbing.

"Bong Cha, you met her."

"I met a lot of them."

"Bong's the only Korean that drives for Pink Jeep. As far as I know the only Asian jeep driver in Sedona. Her new boyfriend is a manager at Ace Hardware. I get pipe fittings at cost as a favor to Bong."

Skip remembered her. "She the one holds the toy pterodactyl in front of tourists with Snoopy Rock in the background?" he asked. He felt confident Kuul only had one Korean-ex that drove jeeps, but he wouldn't bet money on it. Last week a forensic botanist from UCLA showed up for one of their hikes, another ex he hadn't met.

"Makes a great souvenir pic. You might want to talk with her. She was pretty close with Zebulon. Bong was his trainer. They spent hours riding together before he was certified to carry passengers. You get to know someone pretty good backing down Devil's Staircase in the mud."

They spotted Al coming down the sculpted Arizona cypress staircase beside the stacked stone fireplace with the hammered copper mantle. "Sorry it took so long fellas, I must of left Mary and Jane back in Malibu. How about Marlboros and scotch out by the pool."

• • •

The Director was reading an email from a collector he dealt with in Shanghai, another very specific order with a tight timeline. The collector had anticipated his response, offering a substantial bonus if he could meet the buyer's requirements.

Legal limitations on removing artifacts from public and tribal lands dated back to the 1906 Antiquities Act. But on private land all bets were off. Since forty percent of land in Arizona was publicly controlled, the Act ensured unscrupulous and unfettered digging wherever and whenever an undocumented ruin was discovered. If a find wasn't on private land it was usually at least close. The Director had long ago overcome his professional ethics. If he didn't, someone else would. At least what he stole ended up secure and protected.

His career had gone well up to a point. He hadn't had much of a home life growing up; in fact, almost none at all. He spent his early teens in the foster system after his parents died in a car crash and no other family had been willing to take them in. The Director was the more focused of the two boys: his younger brother the wild one. They'd been separated when he was fourteen and his brother ten. He lucked into a good home on his third placing, which turned his life around. The Director went on to work his way through college, majoring in anthropology, and had followed it up with a graduate degree in museum management. With a lead on a job as an associate curator in a small museum, he had come west like Horace Greeley famously suggested. He'd spent his first few years in the field.

After ten years, his field experience earned him a part-time interpreter job with a larger museum. The pay was never stellar; he'd supplemented it with contracted digs and consulting gigs. He had even done paid lectures at Forest Service visitor centers and national monuments to make ends meet. When he landed his current directorship, he was finally financially stable enough to buy a twenty acre ranch in the middle of nowhere with no year-round water. He lived in a two bedroom condo in Sedona, but spent his free time at the ranch where he'd built a rustic cabin and cistern.

The Director's private collection started with arrowheads, metate stones, and pot shards he found on his own property. Sure, there were also items found just outside his boundaries on public land, but that was harmless enough. Everybody did it. When he discovered an ancient agave pit and small one-room ruin in the adjacent National Forest he'd first thought of lobbying to have the artifacts staged as an exhibit in his museum. Before making the call he had a few beers with a junior colleague who knew some wealthy collectors.

That's how he began smuggling; small-time at first. There were more local collectors with deep pockets than the Director could count. His business grew from there as his name got passed around inside the shadowy world of stolen Native art. The closest he came to getting caught resulted from the 2008 Operation *Ceburas* raid in Utah. The Feds had rolled up an antiquities broker and rounded up over thirty collectors and dealers, more than a few of whom the Director had dealt with. Fortunately, his name didn't come up. He spent the next few years lying low.

The exploding Asian market changed everything. Scavenged antiquities became an international business with secretive import/ export networks set up to move goods. In recent years the trade had evolved from selling what was found or stolen to filling orders. The orders were becoming more and more specific. The money the crazy Asians would pay was ridiculous.

It was way too easy. All one had to do was drive around Arizona to realize how remote and undeveloped the land was. With human occupation going back over thirteen thousand years, the number of ruins and ancient sites was endless. There were places they were built on top of each other. The treasures were inestimable and still just lying around. No way could authorities patrol and protect them all. The Director had gotten back in business five years ago. He was even recruiting his estranged brother. The brother had a history of involvement in illegal activities and a record to prove it. *Little bro would come in handy.*

The Director reread the email from the Chinese broker. He had foreign buyers looking for Hohokam pendant necklaces, Mogollon pottery, and White Mountain Apache headdresses. There were so many suppliers now the brokers had created an online bidding system. The Director submitted bids on the necklaces and pottery. The Hohokam and Mogollon were all dead; he didn't want to mess with the Apache and their code of revenge.

11

KOREAN PTERODACTYL

BONG WAS FILLING THE THERMOS STRAPPED ONTO HER PINK Jeep and making sure there was an emergency first aid kit on board. The typical tourist was the clumsiest creature in the forest. Her pet pterodactyl was hibernating in the front pocket of her pink fanny pack. It was all about the tips.

She was scheduled to leave in a half hour for the Broken Arrow tour with honeymooners from New Jersey. Bong knew from experience it was 50-50 if they showed up. You never knew with honeymooners, they tended to sleep in and cancel at the last minute. In the competition between post-breakfast coitus and bouncing around in a jeep, the former typically won. It was a last-minute booking; she didn't get the call until after eight o'clock last night. She was hoping for a cancellation; her new boyfriend had been promoted to head of the paint department at Ace and had the day off.

If they cancelled, Bong could grab a quick coffee at Canyon Breeze with Skip and Lilac and spend the rest of the day painting rings around the monkey. Kuul had called last night and sweet-talked her into letting his friends ride along.

Balthazar had a bewitching hold over her. She swore it was a crazy Mayan spell; she just couldn't say no to his preternatural charms. Their marriage had lasted six months. One morning after a rousing tussle in the sheets, *Sweet Buddha, the man knew his way through the erogenous zones*, he had patiently explained it was time for them to continue their spiritual quests for enlightenment. Their stars would always be aligned, and their souls would be bound throughout their life journey. They'd keep in touch.

"Hi, are you Bong?" the girl asked, she was banding her tussled hair into a tight pigtail.

So much for the morning off Bong realized. "Bangers from New Jersey?"

"That's us," the girl said. She wore a sleeveless summer dress printed with Klimt's *The Kiss* in the front. Her new husband's hand was on her bare shoulder and the other patted her bottom. She turned in his arms and gave him a kiss; both hands clasped his backside. "It's our honeymoon."

"That's *so* nice," Bong smiled, thinking it was going to be a long trip. "I just need you both to sign these waivers," she said, noticing the new Mrs. Banger's feet. She wore white deck shoes, no socks. "You don't have another pair of shoes, do you?"

"We could go back to the room?" the husband suggested, his hands sliding around to the front of his wife's hip and kissing her neck. Bong waited to hand over the clipboard with the waiver until they finished smooching. *He better be a big tipper.*

She filed the paperwork in her pack. It was ten minutes before they left for the two-hour tour. "We're waiting on one other couple, so you've got a few minutes." The jeep had six seats in the back, two-person benches on each side and across the rear. "Take your pick of seats, you'll be sliding all over each other on the sides and the ride's extra bumpy in the back. Let me know if you get car sick, we can move you to the passenger seat."

"We'll take a side bench," Mrs. Banger giggled. "We're going to find some bottles of water, we'll be right back," Mr. Banger grinned.

"I've got free bottles in the cooler," Bong offered

"No bother, we'll get our own," Mr. Banger said while nibbling his giggling wife's earlobe. They smiled and ran off. "Five minutes," Mrs. Banger yelled over her shoulder.

Jin jja, seriously, Bong said to herself in Korean, *they should have stayed in their room*. Maybe they'd cancel yet. All the hands and kissing had her thinking of her boyfriend home alone. She hopped in the back and checked the seatbelts and whether there was any trash jammed between the benches from the last tour. Drivers were supposed to clean up after a tour, but they weren't the most thorough in their inspections. She found another water bottle for her collection and a hiking pole below the seat.

"More stuff for Craigslist?" Bong heard a familiar voice say. Lilac Williams was standing by the passenger door. Skip was talking with another driver prepping a different jeep.

"Craigslist's too dangerous; you never know who shows up. I save it all and have a garage sale every few months."

"How you doing Bong? Thanks for letting us tag along."

"Good. No problem. Asshole Mayan said you wanted to talk about Zebulon. He was a great kid. I've missed him; we were a good tag team. And I can use the company! Wait until you see my other couple."

Lilac laughed. "We've all got our assholes," she said, pointing at Skip who was saying goodbye to the other driver. "What is it that won't let us let them go?"

"*Mildang*, push and pull girl, we're all flaky when it comes to romance. The other couple picked a side bench. I suggest you and Skip take the back. They're newlyweds; you can keep an eye on them. Skip might even learn a thing or two," Bong winked.

Bong loaded the newlyweds and wound through the split, Sedona's busiest travel circle, heading south on Highway 179 to the Broken Arrow trail. The trail was named after the 1950, Jimmy Stewart, Jeff Chandler, movie about the friendship between Indian Agent Tom Jeffords and Cochise. The sixtyish Stewart marries an Apache woman, sixteen-year-old Debra Paget. The teenage Paget later dies saving her elderly husband in an ambush. The towering Elephant Rock formation was the backdrop to the climatic final scene, and now loomed over the entrance to the trail. Pink Jeep maintained the dirt "road" for the Forest Service in exchange for an exclusive right to take their tours there. The views were dramatic and in-season they'd run twenty or more jeeps thru each day.

"Hang on to your hats!" Bong shouted over the mic. "We can't stop on the highway to get them."

The newlyweds introduced themselves to Skip and Lilac as Turk and Serendipity Banger. It was the fifth day of their wedded bliss and sexual awakening. After ten minutes of watching Turk banging and bouncing up against Serendipity, Skip had whispered to Lilac that they reminded him of Bam Bam and Pebbles. Bam Bam's club having noticeably poked up once or twice after Pebbles had landed in his lap. *Bam Bam!* Lilac gave him a nasty look and shushed him.

A mile off the highway, Bong slipped into four-wheel drive as they bounced into the U. S. Forest Service road. Serendipity seized the opportunity, launching herself onto Bam Bam for the umpteenth time. They hadn't even gotten to Devils Staircase yet. She might as well just stay there Skip thought. Lilac gave him a harsh glare as he opened his mouth to say something smart. He shut up.

"We'll make two stops today," Bong said. "One at Submarine Rock and the other at Chicken Point. Otherwise hang on!" Bong gunned the engine and Bam Bam grabbed a twisting Serendipity from behind, pulling her back against his muscled chest. "Whoops, I meant to hit the brake. Ha!"

"How long have you been driving jeeps?" Skip asked, setting her up.

"*Jjorep*, beginner, it's my second week. Ha!" Bong joked. It was a standard gag with the drivers. Being Asian helped her differentiate herself and she played to the stereotype. "Koreans are bad drivers, guys. Ha!"

"There are the twisted sisters," Bong said, pointing at two junipers with intertwined trunks. "Not the band, the trees. Ha! The vortex does that, if you folks start to levitate, grab your partner. Ha!"

"I'm levitating," Bam Bam said. He grabbed Pebbles around the waist, his hands sliding up to her chest with the next bounce. Pebbles snuggled in, "I'm levitating too, ooh," she squealed, slinging a bare thigh over his hip.

"Ha!" Bong laughed looking at the coupled couple in her rearview. "You two look too comfortable. No hanky-panky back there," she said, swerving the jeep left and right rocking Pebbles atop Bam Bam. "Ha!"

Lilac was holding onto the rubber hand grips hanging from the crossbar above her head. Skip stretched his arm across the back of the seat and scooted against her to stop their sliding back and forth. "You gotta hold her tight," he shouted to Bam Bam, who was holding the bouncing straddling Serendipity by both hips.

"How long to a stop?" Lilac asked. She shot Skip another hard stare and he moved his arm.

"Five minutes. We're on the hunt for Red October, the submarine. Ha!"

From atop Submarine Rock, the panorama of geologic wonder is inspiring to nature lovers. It was Skip's favorite place to take tours that wanted big views with little effort getting there. The jeeps might be the exciting way in, but the hike to the same spot is short, and on a beginner rated trail. The 360-degree views of soaring red rock formations and sandstone cliffs are breathtaking.

Bong had led the Bangers to the conning tower of the submarine. From a distance, the sleek formation looked like a nuclear sub with the tower at one end and smooth fins at the other. The outer hull between the sculpted tower and fins was flat, the length of a football field. Serendipity was twirling around like Julie Andrews in an alpine meadow. Bam Bam was videoing her dance.

"Let me have your camera. I'll take a picture of both of you," Bong said.

Bam Bam handed over his phone and joined his wife. Bong lined up the shot and Serendipity raised a leg while they kissed. Bam Bam bent her over backwards like the famous photo of the sailor kissing a girl on VE Day. "One more," Bong said.

Pebbles jumped in the air and Bam Bam grabbed her waist pulling her into a 1950s sock hop scissor pose. Pebbles leaned backward and waved at the camera. "Hold it," Bong said. She pulled out the pterodactyl and held it in front of the camera to look like a giant flying dinosaur coming at the love birds, taking different angles of the Mesozoic scene. "Here, take a look."

Bam Bam swung Serendipity around his back to finish the move and she ran to see Bong's pictures. Skip and Lilac had walked the length of the hull and were sitting on an edge overlooking the Broken Arrow trail.

"We weren't ever like that were we?" Lilac asked. Serendipity was squealing in the background. She squealed a lot. "They're in their own little world. Wonder how long it'll last."

"Another two weeks," Skip said. "Bam Bam will get bored."

Lilac studied the manzanita and acacia below and pointed to more jeeps making their way up the road. "We might have some company." They watched the jeeps bypass the turn off to submarine rock. "Looks like they're going to Chicken Point first. Bong probably radioed them she had honeymooners."

Skip watched Lilac pick up a pointed rock and start scraping at an indentation in the sub's outer shell. He guessed she was thinking about their past. "I don't think we would have wanted to be like that. *Ditsy* never fit either of us, together or alone."

"If you'd hadn't disappeared so often and opened up more maybe we'd have lasted. A little ditsy is not a bad thing."

Skip stayed quiet longer than he should have, his head turned away from Lilac, watching the honeymooners amble hand-in-hand down a trail. Bong headed their way; she was still four or five first-downs away.

"Case in point," Lilac said to the back of his head. "You've got nothing to say for yourself, even now that it doesn't matter. One of these days you're going to have to let go of whatever it is that holds you back."

Skip faced her and smiled, "Well, when I do, I have your number." He'd said it hoping to lighten the mood. Her deepening frown showed it hadn't. Fortunately, the Korean dinosaur trainer was closing in to save him.

"You turned the children loose," Skip said to Bong.

"They asked to walk down the trail away...alone. I gave them a lecture on rattlesnakes and fifteen minutes before we're out of here. The Forest Service has us clocked and we still have to get to Chicken Point. They said they'd be quick. *Pumjeollyeo doeda*, newly married," Bong sniggered.

"Zebulon Ballsy. Kuul says you two were close," Skip said, changing the subject. "They found remains out Jacks Canyon and Zula swears it's him. She had a vision."

"You can bank on her visions," Bong said. "I trained him and when the schedulers could they booked us together. He respected my experience, and his local history and archeology knowledge always got us good tips. He'd stand up on that rock over there and give an off-the-cuff ten-minute lecture on all the ruins around here and the people who lived back then. The tourists ate him up. Too bad if that's him they found."

Lilac shook her head, still not understanding how it could happen. "Still doesn't make sense he fell. It's rare for a seasoned biker to have that bad of an accident, especially alone when they're extra careful. It's the beginners and vacationers we're always pulling out of trouble."

"Careful driver, too. Another reason I liked working with him. We get a lot of cowboys that do some crazy stunts out here but not Zeb, he was more thoughtful...he..." Bong hesitated and frowned.

"What?" Skip asked.

"The kid treasured where we are. It was like he was part of the land. He was serious about his studies, but it went beyond that. He liked -- *no* -- he valued the past." Skip could see she was picking her words carefully as if she was trying to explain an inconsistency. The Korean hesitated again and sighed, "It's probably nothing and I hate mentioning it, but when I heard about the body, I remembered some rumors that floated around after Zeb had disappeared. Not surprising that people made stories up, his disappearing and all. They just want to make sense of it, karma you know."

"Stories," Lilac said, glancing at Skip as she spoke. "Imagine that. Rumors and hidden stories."

Skip usually didn't know what she was thinking, especially when it came to him. *Was her comment intended for him?* No, he was probably being too self-absorbed. Another thing she commonly accused him of being.

Bong noticed the tension and broke it. "I heard a driver, he's long since gone, say Zeb was friends with a friend of a friend who was mixed up with artifact smuggling. Made me mad and I called him on it. *Geukyeom*, disgusting. He shut up and didn't say anything further. Just a nasty rumor about someone that couldn't talk back, you know."

Bam Bam and Pebbles appeared at the other end of Submarine Rock and waved. They had been gone for about twenty minutes. The image of the Klimt Kiss that had been on the front of Serendipity's dress was now on the back and her hair was out of the pigtail. They started dusting themselves off at Bong's jeep.

"Looks like it's time to saddle up," Bong said.

"It seems they already have," Lilac said cooly.

12

FERTILE FLUTE PLAYER

DAVID OGLESTAR WAS A RECENTLY DISCHARGED ANTHROPOLOGY professor from the University of Tennessee. He was still in his fifties and had bounced around SEC schools his entire career. His professional skills were top notch; he published regularly, and was well known and respected by his academic peers. The 3.9 rating on ReviewMyProfessors.org was not spectacular, but solid enough. True, he wasn't Margaret Meade or Herbert Gans, but few were. Everyone liked David, but that was never enough. The tenure track always eluded his grasp and went to a younger up-and-comer. His culpability had been an unwillingness to engage in the political games within his departments. Refusing to give passes to UT's football stars had closed his prospects in the Volunteer state.

When David's contract expired, and he had to move on from Knoxville, he decided to semi-retire and accepted the Directorship of the Verde Valley Archeological Center (VVAC). He had done his dissertation on *The Role of Navajos in the Pueblo Revolt.* Pre-

Colombian southwest civilizations had become his professional focus. He'd visited the VVAC on past sabbaticals and studied some of their small but impressive collection of *Sinagua* artifacts, including items on loan to the Sharlot Hall Museum in Prescott, Arizona. Because of the visits he had made key connections in local circles that paid off with the job offer. With his darker complexion, he wondered if his last name, suggestive of Native heritage, hadn't influenced the VVAC's search committee as well.

He spent his first two months training new staff, which consisted of a full-time office assistant, a part-time intern from one of the public universities, and a host of volunteer docents. The VVAC was pretty much a one-man show...the David Oglestar show. The old staff had left or been let go by the Board when the previous Director had been unceremoniously canned. His vividly explaining to a group of fourth graders from West Sedona Elementary School the roles of semen ingestion and menstrual blood in ancient fertility ceremonies around the world had been the last straw.

The Board hired David mainly due to his expertise in human excrement. It seemed obvious, but he had to explain in his interview, how his interest in shit was different from swallowing semen. Although an interesting intellectual pursuit, he'd told the blue-haired denizens that drinking jiz and/or female flushes were not appropriate topics for anyone under the age of eighteen. They suggested twenty-one and put it in Article I of his contract. The Board Chair had made it very clear that within certain bounds, digestion was fine, ingestion was not.

For an anthropologist, scat was the mother lode when it came to understanding the daily lives and diets of peoples who did not leave a written record. Thanks to the arid desert-like environment of the Southwest, David had dug his way through a lot of ancient poop and garbage piles looking for good shit. He could tell the dried defecation of an Anasazi from that of a Hohokam by the remnants of undigested corn kernels. From that he could theorize agricultural production and technology, trade partners and hence trade routes, common medical problems and disease, and life expectancy. The VVAC had acquired a trove of human and animal scat found on property donated by a developer who had uncovered a prehistoric burial site and several ancient pit houses. It all needed scooped, carefully dissected, sent out for lab work, catalogued, and exhibited. Oglestar was the man for the job.

· · ·

Skip parked the Bronco two blocks from the Verde Valley Archeological Center in the gravel public lot off Camp Verde's Main Street. VVAC was the local expert on ancient ruins and ongoing archeological studies in the valley; if anyone did, Skip figured they would have insight on reports of smuggling in the area. He left the driver's door unlocked and a key on the seat in case someone wanted to do him a favor and take the bucker off his hands. It was a hot day, and he exchanged his Stetson for a wide-brimmed straw hat and calico rag to keep the sweat from running down his back. The Bronco's freon once again had better places to be. The cold AC cranked high for the exhibits would be welcome.

He promised to come to Camp Verde for Zula and had wanted to meet the new Director, killing two birds with one stone. Business at the Sand's was picking up and Zula wanted an old wagon wheel to dress up the retreat's entrance and advertise SOB specials. She'd sent him to Marty's Streets of Laredo Antique and Tack Shop where prices were half what they were in Sedona. She had designed a sign in the shape of a Chuck Wagon, mounted on a wooden wheel outlined with blinking blue Christmas lights. Skip said it sounded like a gaudy Vegas sign and wished her good luck passing the sign ordinance. The old showgirl had accepted the challenge, adding a neon margarita glass to the wagon covering.

When Skip walked into the VVAC, David Oglestar was restaging a petroglyph display of clan signs and journey symbols in the VanDyck Exhibit. VanDyck had been a world renowned painter of Plains Indians. He worked out of his ranch in nearby Rim Rock where he discovered a remarkably intact cliff dwelling of three rooms; one of the few that hadn't been looted. *They were still out there.* After his death, a friend convinced his son to donate the father's collection of wooden and woven artifacts to the center.

"Babies or seeds?" Skip asked, standing behind the new Director, contemplating the Kokopelli figure etched into the red stone tablet.

Oglestar turned and did a quick assessment of the curious stranger. The straw sweat-stained cowboy hat said he was a local; the Director was still meeting VVAC regulars. And the man knew a little about the Kokopelli deity.

"Depends," he said. "You're right that it's a fertility symbol. Procreation or agricultural, or both, is the question, right? Most think the character's humpback is full of seeds and songs. He'd show up with his flute and the people would sing and dance to ensure a good harvest."

"Except the Hopi," Skip said. "They're always different. They believe he carried babies to be dropped off like a stork." He pointed at the figure, "That one doesn't have the protruding phallic. According to legend, maidens hid when they saw him coming."

"Some tribes think he was an Aztec trader, and the hump was a bag full of trade goods. I guess traveling salesmen with loose morals have been around awhile," the Director laughed. "I'm David Oglestar, the new Director here," he said, extending his hand.

"The Music Man meets unmarried Marian the Librarian," Skip chuckled, shaking his hand. On first impression he liked Oglestar. "I'm Skip Rhodes from Sedona. I run Sedona Chi Tours and bring groups here sometimes. I was on an errand and thought I'd introduce myself."

"Let me guess, Montezuma Castle and Well, stop for lunch up the street, and visit here if time allows?" Oglestar asked. VVAC's guests had typically just come from one of the two nearby National Monuments.

"And *Tuzigoot.* I only do small groups, so depending on their level of interest we may also drive out to *Palatki* and *Hohanki.*" The last two were smaller *Sinagua* ruins accessed only by a dirt road in good weather. Last count, there were over seventy habited sites documented along the Verde River and its tributaries. Tens of thousands of people lived in the valley hundreds of years before the first European came looking for gold and slaves. Every day some object they left behind was being found.

"For the hard core," Oglestar judged. "Come in the office. I have coffee on."

Oglestar's office was a cubicle behind the front desk with eight-foot partition walls. Except for a battered desk and a folding table that served as a credenza, the space was jammed with filing cabinets and stacked boxes. There was no door, just an opening between panels. The Director poured coffee into two cups that said, *Donate to the VVAC – We're Ruined if You Don't.* Skip squeezed past a cabinet and took the only other chair. He assumed the duct taped X on the vinyl seat indicated where to sit.

Oglestar softly blew in his cup, "So, I don't know what the last Director did, but I'm happy to talk to your folks whenever you bring them in. The more people we educate about the past the better off we'll all be tomorrow. It's a big part of our mission. No charge, just give me a half-hour or so heads up."

"Thanks. I didn't bring anyone here before unless they asked. Maybe I'll start. Your predecessor wasn't the friendliest. In my opinion, he didn't like the public much." Skip had gotten tired of correcting the past Director's mistakes to his customers. He hadn't been back since the man had explained to a Dentist and his family that the Sinagua treated tooth abscesses with locoweed. He'd gone on to claim the Spanish introduced early dental hygiene to indigenous populations throughout the southwest.

"That's what I'm told," Oglestar sighed. "We're doing better."

"To be honest, I did come by to meet you, but I'd also like to pick your brain a bit," Skip said. Oglestar refilled his cup and looked at Skip's. Skip took a drink and stuck it out. "It's good, thanks."

"Twenty-five years in drafty university offices, you learn things along the way. What can I help you with?"

Skip wasn't sure how to broach the subject of artifact smuggling. He hadn't thought that far ahead. Sitting across his desk, he realized the man didn't know him from Adam. He knew what he'd think if a stranger showed up at the Sand's and started asking suspicious questions.

"My landlady owns a retreat off Red Rock Loop Road - the Sand's." *Everybody knew Loop Road.* "She had a great nephew that disappeared three years ago and..."

"And she thinks he was the biker found last week," Oglestar finished his sentence. "Another reason I trust my boots for getting me into and out of excavation sites. My students liked to ride bikes out to remote digs too. Feet might take longer, but they're easier on fragile environments and you find more along the way."

Odd he was so quick to pick up Skip's direction, but it had been on the news and in the paper. "Right," Skip said. "The kid was an archeology student. Good kid, he had actually interned here." Skip studied Oglestar's expression. Last thing he wanted was to start ringing warning bells.

"We've heard rumors that there were looters working in the valley back then. I thought if that was true the VVAC would likely have been aware of it." Skip didn't share the rumors involving Zebulon's connection with the suspected smugglers or that Zula suspected his death wasn't an accident.

"Well, I've only been here a few months, but it's no surprise that artifact smuggling was happening. I'm sure it still is. Looting is on par with selling shoes, they're both small peas, just servicing a customer. The market for selling looted items is the bigger problem. It's a worldwide issue. In the last few decades, the Chinese and Russian economies have created extremely wealthy business people, many without scruples when it comes to sheltering their money from their governments. Art has always been a way to do that; a Picasso, Louis XVI inlaid dresser, a Cambodian statue, or an Anasazi headdress or *Sinagua* pot from right here. Financially, they're safer bets than Boeing or a condo development in Miami. Little regulation, unenforced laws, political payoffs, and the attitude it doesn't hurt anyone, all make antiquities from looted sites popular investments."

"So how does a Russian mob guy sitting in Moscow find a ruin site in the Arizona desert ripe for picking?" Skip asked.

"A chain of thieves ending with some local jerk with a flashlight wrecking in a night what an archeologist would spend twenty years excavating and cataloging. It doesn't matter if something precious is lost forever, as long as they have beer money for a month," Oglestar said, taking a breath and letting it out. "I'd help you more if I could; I just haven't been here long enough to get wind of any rumors.

"Any idea who could?"

Oglestar thought for a moment and opened his laptop. "Maybe, give me a second." He pulled up his contacts, trying to recall the name of the tribal archeologist he'd met last week for lunch. "Bass, Sams, Cass...Sasse," he mumbled, "*SASSE*, that's it, Trey Sasse. He's the Director of Archeology for the Yavapai Apache Nation. All reservations have to have one under the federal Antiquities Act. I met him last week at Cliff Castle Casino. Seemed like a smart guy and he knew everything about the history of the area before *WE* came," Oglestar said, pointing at his white arm. "You might try him. Let me know what you find out."

Oglestar topped off his own coffee and reached for Skip's. Skip had met Sasse at a workshop on Ethnobotany at Yavapai Community

College. The archeologist had talked about making soap from yucca root, and its use in cleansing ceremonies before big hunts. He had grimaced, *hopefully not noticeably*, when Oglestar suggested him. Sasse was fine and Skip should have thought of him first, but his office was on the Yavapai Apache reservation, which he did his best to avoid. Skip Rhodes wasn't on their *Welcome with Open Arms* list.

"Bring your people by anytime, Skip. Anything else I can help you with?"

"You wouldn't know where to find a cheap old wagon wheel would you?"

"Yeah, Streets of Laredo. Ask for Marty."

13

CHURCH OF ASTRO DEPARTURE

T HE LAZY SOB, TRUE TO ITS MONIKER, WAS NOT BUSY. THE WAY
Skip preferred it. The regulars had left after the end of Happy
Hour leaving only a handful of Retreat guests seated around a table.
Skip was heeding the nightly call for a pink Don Julio. Zula was
serving. He'd already downed a *cerveza* at his cabin before deciding to check in on her. Whether to share the rumors he'd picked up
from Bong had been wearing on his mind. How the high kicking old
dancer reacted to unpleasant news was never predictable. On the
other hand, maybe she knew more about Zebulon than she was letting on. Skip was normally on the right side of her moods, but not
always. The last thing he wanted was his glass rim coated in salt
instead of sugar.

It was past nine, the sun had set earlier while he was relaxing
in his hammock. The ebony stained wood of the century old bar
and the halos cast from the ruby glass wall sconces reminded Skip
of El Tovar Lodge at the Grand Canyon. They both matched the dark

warm ambiance of a Bavarian hunting lodge, customers decked out in lederhosen and green felt hats drinking double bock in front of a roaring fireplace with an Oompah Band playing *Roll Out the Barrel*. The *SOB* even had mounted elk and javelina heads above the counter; Spike, Zula's pet, refused to go any farther than the front porch.

Instead of the lederhosen and plumed fedora crowd, the *SOB* had Dr. Reginald Landish and his crew. The lederhosen had been replaced by zany patterned leggings and soiled cut offs; the fedoras, by hoodies, stocking caps, and knitted reggae beanies. No *Roll Out the Barrel* but Johnny Paycheck was singing *I Fell Off Barstool Mountain* on Zula's 1980s Panasonic boombox sitting on the shelf next to the line of Whiskeys.

Landish's groupies included the girl named Sky, who Zula had said was a decent enough sort, the aluminum foil kid, and four other interchangeable new age hippies. They were seated around two tables pulled together and drinking from pitchers of Zula's homemade Sangria. Skip doubted she had added the drizzle of dark Myers Rum like she did for her regulars.

"The crazies are in full force tonight," Zula said from behind the bar, handing Skip his sugar rimmed sweet drink.

Skip swiveled his stool and looked over his shoulder at Landish and entourage. Landish was espousing the gospel of alien apparition and the rest were *Amening*, except for the girl who made and held eye contact with him. She discerningly smiled and Skip turned back to Zula.

"How long have they been at it?" Skip took a bite of lime from the plate Zula had set beside him and a big sip of Don Julio, the sweetener on the rim complementing the natural sugary taste of prickly pear fruit.

"About an hour, maybe a little less. You wouldn't believe the crap comes out of that man's mouth. Back in Vegas his kind ended up in a soundproof basement room with a cattle prod poking their sphincter, if you know what I mean."

Skip noticed Zula's Smith and Wesson .38 Bodyguard strapped on her hip and decided not to further agitate her by bringing up Bong's rumors. Zula didn't know Bong and she didn't care for Koreans, north or south. Tony Two Ballsy had been with the 1st Provisional Marine Brigade. Better to let the rumors lay. Why she was carrying the pistol with a 12-gauge handy below the counter he didn't know; then again, multiple bodyguards for a woman running a bar weren't a bad idea.

"Listen to him," Zula hissed, unconsciously patting her .38.

"...When they beam me onboard, I might be gone awhile. It will be a short time for me in the *Obiedinobido* Galaxy due to the temporal distortion, but for you it could be years before I reappear." Landish shoved a bite of a second double Whopper in his mouth, ketchup dripping over the foil wrapping onto his pudgy fingers. One of the acolytes handed him a napkin. "You will need investments to finance Church operations while I'm gone. Our meetings haven't raised enough. We need to kick the fundraising into hyper drive, maybe diversify our message as well," Landish was saying.

Skip was on his second margarita; added to the earlier *cerveza* he was feeling plucky. He smiled at Zula, stood up, and walked to Landish's table. He didn't have a plan other than to free associate and tap his inner Chewbaca orneriness. The girl, Sky, watched him cross the room. Skip added a bit of John Wayne swagger and stared back.

Landish had his back to Skip, "... my cousin lives here and can coordinate any interstellar tele-signaling I'm allowed to do. In my absence he'll maintain our accounts and pay..."

Skip tapped him on his shoulder. By this time the groupies facing his direction were closely watching his movements. "So, *WHO'S* your cousin?" Skip asked in an accusing tone, pointing his margarita at Landish as he turned around. "Maybe I know him."

Landish pushed his chair back into Skip and stood up. A splash of tequila hit the floor. He had six inches and thirty pounds on Skip who stood his ground and coolly slugged the rest of his drink.

"Who's asking?" Landish frowned, "this is a private party." Aluminum Foil handed him two purple Skittles he popped into his mouth. The big man obviously didn't appreciate the intrusion, or Skip's not so subtle intimation he might be lying. Chewing gave him a moment to think.

Skip saw a dark look in his eyes not befitting a friendly, benevolent preacher. He was seeing the man's true self. "You spilled my drink," he said sternly.

Sky interjected, "I think he lives here. He's a friend of the owner," she said, speaking to Landish, hoping to deescalate their confrontation.

Landish's scowl slowly eased into a fake smile and he thrust his hand out, "I'm Doctor Reginald Landish. Sorry about the drink. You were a little too close, partner." Skip refused the handshake and the man's paw went awkwardly back into a suit pocket. He glanced at his group, "We're with the Church of Astro Departure. I'm the pastor and these are our deacons."

Under the freeing influence of a Don Julio buzz, Skip snickered, *"Partner? Deacons?"* He deliberately eyeballed the group, settling his gaze on the man who hadn't yet stepped back. Skip could smell the greasy onions on his breath. "I *ASKED* who your cousin is. You said he lived here."

"Not here here, not in Sedona," Landish said, conspicuously avoiding giving a name. "I meant Arizona. He lives in Phoenix."

"He a Landish too?" Skip pushed.

Landish leaned slightly closer without moving his feet and took his hands out of his pockets. He gave Skip a hard look. Skip kept eye contact and reached his hand behind him placing Don on a table. He was already planning his first move. As close as they were standing, he didn't have room for a roundhouse to an ear. It was going to be an uppercut.

Neither of the men noticed Sky stand up. She stuck an arm between them, "Look boys, by the shape of things neither one of you has a big penis so there's no use comparing." Somewhere behind, Skip heard a guffaw from Zula.

Landish changed tactics and flashed a charming grin at Sky. He turned to Skip, taking a half-step back, "My - Mother's - Sister's - Son," he said, enunciating each word slowly. He still didn't give a name.

Zula had come around the bar with another pink Don Julio and put it in her friend's hand, "On the house. It's a nice night out. Why don't you and I go out to the porch and feed Spike?" Skip was still staring menacingly at her guest, who had glimpsed her loaded hip. She put a hand on Skip's shoulder, feeling his muscles ease after several seconds of tense silence.

Zula had only seen Skip Rhodes truly riled twice. The first was when a pot-smoking junior hockey player from Flagstaff staying at the Sands had tried to sell him a reefer. The failed transaction had ended with Skip putting him in a headlock, dragging him several hundred yards, and throwing the kid in the creek. The second was in Uptown when a drunken tourist kept bumping the Bronco's rear bumper because Skip wasn't moving into a busy traffic circle; after the fifth tap, she buckled up as Skip calmly slipped into reverse and stepped on the gas. Skip didn't have an uncontrolled temper; it was more deliberate than that. If pressed, he executed a violent response that was excessive for the situation. Zula could tell that's where his questioning Landish had been heading.

• • •

Spike was straddling the front steps of the lodge gobbling pieces of bacon from Skip's hand. The javelina had trotted across the sandstone walk when it saw them come out. Zula had gone back in to fix another batch of watery Sangria for the Church of Infinity and Beyond, leaving Skip to cool off in the night air. Starting with a third pitcher she always lowered the wine to fruit juice ratio to keep her guests drinking and spending. It was working with Landish's crowd.

Skip was surprised he let Landish get his goat. He'd been within a second of executing a *Grab the Tail off the Bird* move, slamming the backs of his linked hands up into the fat man's chin. If Landish didn't collapse, he was going to follow with his patented *Rip the Tail off the Jackass* move. Practice made perfect.

The anger within was becoming less frequent, but a blind fury still overcame him when the wrong person hit the right button. *Escobar, his mind needed to move on. He'd left all that behind.* Landish was bad, he could feel it, but not to that scale. Sedona was a revolving door attracting all kinds of new wave, spiritual, little green-men-chasing charlatans. For the most part they were harmless. Maybe it was the Whoppers and Skittles or brainwashed deacons, but Landish was just wrong. Skip's *Fight or Flight* Meter swung into red when he was around fake people. And he didn't like running. Still, he knew he had to exercise better self-control, especially with others watching. If the girl called Sky and Zula hadn't interceded, he would be relocating again.

Spike licked his lips a last time and trotted off when the screen door to the lodge squeaked open. The door was a thin frame of two-by-two pine held together by screen wire. It didn't have a latch or spring and bounced shut. Skip heard bare feet lightly padding on wood planks. He twisted at the waist and saw a slim-hipped Sky coming his way. Under the porch lights he could see she was older than he had thought; maybe late 20s.

"Need some company, cowboy?" she smiled. Skip had the Stetson on. His gray wasn't as noticeable.

Sky had stopped under a flickering bulb. Skip took the break to reassess his and Landish's referee. The long brown hair was braided on both sides and tied behind her neck, a striped reggae knit cap sat sideways on her head. Her big toe nails were painted sparkly pea green and the other nails were neon pink. The stretchy leggings with geometric shapes and a gold lightning bolt down the left leg were definitely too tight to be comfortable. The white peasant blouse with knitted lace from shoulder to shoulder and down the front was sexually suggestive.

"Need?" Skip answered. Sky took a few cautious steps and sat down beside him. In one fluid motion she went from standing still to walking down two steps and effortlessly sitting. He wished he had her young knees. She moved like a cat sliding through a bunch of dominoes.

"Beautiful night. The stars are coming out. The Milky Way's like a blanket here. I came out late last night to see it. The sky is so clear here," Sky said quietly.

Skip detected wistfulness in her tone. *Was she sad?*

"You can see Jupiter there and Mars at the top edge of that tree," she pointed.

Skip wasn't sure how long the astronomy lesson would last, but her sing-song voice was soothing. She made it seem as if nothing had gone on inside. As he sensed Landish was bad, he picked up an inner strength and goodness in this girl. You could see it in her face, her flowing movements, and the composed way she talked. He had learned long ago to trust his first impressions; there were few people he'd gotten wrong.

"What are you doing with the Doctor?" His own tone left no doubt that he disapproved. The question had come out harsher than he intended. He hadn't meant to sound threatening.

"You cut straight to it don't you? He's not perfect, but he's not that bad," the girl said defensively. "That's how you see everything isn't it – good or bad, black or white - no gray or in between? Your way or the highway. I've seen you everywhere I go."

Skip looked to the stars and didn't find any help. They both knew she'd nailed him. She surprised him by not leaving.

"That's the north star," Sky said pointing. "It guides us."

They sat quietly for a while until Sky said, "I met Reginald in New Mexico at one of his meetings. He promised his church offered a spiritual awakening. I was lost, wandering and looking for a change. We shared some peyote I'd gotten from the Native American Church in Farmington and discussed life."

"So, you were drugged. That would explain it," Skip said.

Sky ignored his cynicism, "He was interested in me and asked about the NAC. *HE* didn't automatically write it off as an excuse to get high." Skip accepted the implied admonishment and let her continue. "We had a shared interest in religion. He was open to exploring, at least intellectually, a religion that interweaves Native American beliefs and Christianity. The peyote is a sacramental ritual that touches your inner spirit, just like our substituting wine and crackers for the blood and body of Christ."

"I doubt it was your inner spirit he was hoping to touch," Skip cracked. He immediately regretted the insinuation; he could tell the comment bothered her. She pulled her long braid around front and twisted it under her chin.

"Sorry, that was a little sharp. I'm sure it was..." Skip was searching for the right word, "... academic." *It would have to do.*

"*We did not* have sex," Sky whispered emphatically, "he told me about the Church of Astro Departure and how we knew so little about ourselves and our feelings and could learn so much from the *Obiekinobi* people. They're millenniums ahead of us in understanding everything."

"Little green men," Skip chuckled. He couldn't help himself.

Sky's eyes narrowed and she studied him, deciding his aura was messed up but not mean. Far from it; she saw compassion and a soft melancholy quality behind the gruff wisecracking exterior. He hid a lot. With those types, she'd always found it better to cut to the chase and get her gorilla out in the open.

"They aren't green. They're sort of gelatinous and multicol-ored, like rainbow sherbet, with light strobes in their feet and brain." Sky had released her hair and punched his shoulder to make her point clear. "They. Aren't. Green. But they're real. I know. I was abducted. They held me, taught me how to meditate and extend my aura circle, exercise my demons, and live more harmoniously with whatever gods I choose. When it was time to go home they gave me hypermobility." She cracked her knuckles and extended her fingers. They seemed to grow an inch. "I wasn't born this way."

Skip had been in Sedona long enough to think he'd heard it all. Twenty percent of the population swore they'd been abducted or had alien DNA. Every time the clouds reflected moonlight there were forty or fifty reports of extraterrestrial spying and missing Chihuahuas. She would fit right in.

"Hypermobility?"

"Double joints," Sky said. "Of course, they didn't actually double my joints. I can just stretch my tendons and ligaments much farther than before. They helped me engage my full physical capabilities. Most people only use around fifty percent. I'm closer to eighty. See..."

Sky grabbed all four fingers of her right hand with her left and bent them backwards until they touched below the lime green macramé love beads tied around her wrist. Skip marveled as she then snapped her left thumb backwards to a 45 degree angle. He had a vision of a shadow figure that looked like Donald Duck with a broken bill and wing.

"Whoa," Skip said.

"Watch this." Sky sat on the ground at the bottom of the steps facing Skip with legs straight in front. She smiled and popped her hips out. She raised both legs, knees locked, toes pointed to the north star, and rotated them behind her back until they touched the ground. It was like rewinding the minute hand of a clock counterclockwise from 12:15 to 11:45. "The *Obiedinobidans* gave me this gift."

"That's a useful ability to have," Skip deadpanned.

Sky swung everything back in place and retook her seat on the stairs beside him.

"I make up my mind pretty quick about people," Sky said. "It's why I jumped in between you and Reggie." It's *Reggie* now, Skip noted. "I know you don't believe my story. That's Okay. We don't have to all think the same way. Diversity's a spice you know. And spices keep life interesting. Like you and me. We could fit because we don't fit."

With that she rotated her arms behind her, braced her hands on the porch floor, and somersaulted backwards to a standing position. "See you around."

Skip's eyes followed her to the door where she disappeared to rejoin her friends in the Lazy *SOB*. Beneath the zany veneer and the trip to outer space, he couldn't help but like her. There was something deeper there. If he was honest, he wished she hadn't left. He had enjoyed the company. Her directness without embarrassment and perceptiveness about his character and willingness to point it out was...*surprising, refreshing, stimulating*... he wasn't sure what he felt. You shouldn't judge a book by its cover he thought.

14

FALLING SKIES

I**T WAS LATE AND DARKER THAN USUAL WHEN SKIP WALKED** home. Clouds had rolled in and hidden Sky's stars. His only guides were a veiled moon and his own muscle memory. The girl was on his mind as he followed the trail along Oak Creek. The large sycamore with mottled green and gray speckles on white bark was his cairn, telling him to turn right. Off to his left, black water cascaded in low waterfalls over rounded river rock, beating like the steady tempo of a symphony. Sky had been right about how he saw things one dimensionally, but he had good reason. She was too young and had too few scars to understand.

He walked a quarter mile before turning away from nature's allegro to climb the worn stone steps up the bank. He crossed the clearing and stepped onto his porch. The front door was open. He'd left it that way with just the screen door closed to keep out the mosquitoes. The few spring rains they got brought them out. Their blood lust wouldn't be so bad once the dry summer weather arrived in June.

He grabbed a bottled water from the fridge and walked to his bedroom, stopping in the bathroom on his way. Calling it a bathroom was being generous; it was actually a converted closet with a chemical john and small porcelain sink. Skip liked the compact size; he could do his business and brush his teeth at the same time. Looking in the mirror he saw creases around his eyes and in his forehead from the anger he'd felt toward Landish. *Why was Sky with that man?* He splashed cold water in his face, running his wet fingers through his matted hat hair. It refreshed him but didn't help with the wrinkles. *Maybe they weren't from anger?*

Skip set the plastic bottle on his nightstand, next to the book he'd bought about the lost confederate gunship. He kicked off his boots and laid on the bed, propping the souvenir pillows Zula had given him from the Riviera behind his head and shoulders. Flipping to the dog-eared page, he picked up the main character and his sidekick motor boating down a river in Africa with bad guys chasing them. He read another chapter, and his eyes began slowly ping ponging up and down. It'd been a long day.

Long blond hair covered his face. The smell of lavender. The small of her back was smooth to his touch. He heard laughter that sailed into pink clouds. There was a band playing Hotel California by the Eagles. He could see the musicians' shadows. The floor tiles were spinning, and he held her tightly. Laughter, this time not hers. Spinning faster. The band had stopped. He heard birds. Hawks, flying into and through the clouds. They collided and fell to the ground fighting. Fingers stretching. She tried to hold his grasp. Spinning out of control. They were running. Green and yellow walls, dark beams. The smell of onions.

Skip's eyes flickered open and closed again. His eyes were rapidly bouncing behind their lids. His mind was trying to regain consciousness, but waves of black kept sending him deeper into his dream.

An old door carved with plumed figures. He was running. Blond hair flying around both their faces. Something crashed behind them. Screams and popping sounds. Running faster. His arm pulling her forward. The door so close. She stumbled. A hawk swung the door open. Intense light spilled over them. Tortured faces, wings, unattached arms reaching out of the door. They were running. Have to avoid the arms. Get to the light. More popping behind. Footsteps. Curses in Spanish. Holding hands, they leapt through the door. Light, falling. He watched the blond hair float away like a sheet in the wind. Get up, fly he tried yelling!

Beyond his mental grasp, Skip sensed he was wet. His brain was trying to process the cold sweat he felt. Subconsciously, he could see himself waking, and he could feel the soaked blanket below him. His eyes refused to open no matter how hard he fought. Drifting deeper inward, he gave in.

He lay motionless. Rocks, water, softness surrounding him. Stink, moldy musty smell covering his face. He struggled getting up and then ran. Green sky falling. Searching, searching. Looking through swinging trees he saw movement. Jump. He was running in air. Hot, terribly hot. Sweat was weighing him down. He could see her ahead waving. He kept running but got no closer. No! Behind her, Escobar. He tried yelling but nothing, no sound. Escobar was slowly skipping toward her like a schoolgirl. The band began playing. Running... he couldn't make out the song. A trumpet. Escobar stared at him, laughing. A machete flew over his head boomerang style. Blond hair floating. Blood on his hands.

Skip heard himself screaming as he startled awake. His shirt was soaked. He hadn't had that nightmare in months. It never ended differently, memories never do. It had all been his fault. What had set it off? Sky - her long brown hair - the tequila? Would the dreams ever end?

He staggered out of bed, stripping down and stumbling out back. Maybe a shower beneath the stars would help; they were back out. Maybe the girl was right, and they would show him the way. The water was ice cold, coming from deep down in the well.

The heat would arrive but in the meantime the cold woke his muscles up and restored his senses to normalcy. He stretched his hands, leaning against the back wall of the house, letting the water run down his neck and spine. As it turned hot, he let it massage the muscles of his back and shoulders.

After ten minutes, the memories had been pushed back, for now at least. He stepped out of the makeshift shower into the semi-darkness; the light from a window casting just enough glow to light the pavers to the back door. The arid Arizona air dried everything but his hair in a few steps. Skip heard a rustling sound at the corner of his cabin, and then someone or something running. He could tell by the gait the footsteps were human. He ran naked around the corner and past the end of the front porch, hopping because of the larger pebbles poking his bare feet. He'd run through worse. A shapeless shadow ran away down the path toward the creek. In his birthday suit and with no shoes, there was no use giving chase.

15

RED SPIRIT CANYON

SKIP AND KUUL WERE HEADED SOUTH ON INTERSTATE 17. THEY were in the AAA Plumber to the Stars van instead of Skip's Bronco; the old warhorse was in the shop being fed a bag of Freon. They had a meeting with Trey Sasse, the Director of Archeology at the Yavapai Apache Cultural Center.

"Did you finish the Godfather?" Skip asked.

"Have to put a seal down and reseat the toilet. The stars are aligned man; Al referred the Italian Stallion to me. The slugger was pouring rotten eggs down his kitchen drain and not running the disposal. The smell was so bad even his broken nose finally noticed. I had to replace it. I think he's a little punchy. Yo!"

"He cudda benuh cuhtenda," Skip said thickly.

Kuul exited the highway at Middle Verde Road. The Yavapai Apache Tribal Nation Seal, mounted in the middle of the traffic circle, announced they had entered the reservation. The seal's two white feathers rising from an Apache crown headdress symbolized the unity of the two different peoples. The next sign advertised the Friday night fish fry at Cliff Castle Casino's Mountain Springs Buffet, which loomed on the hill above the cultural center offices.

For three years, in the early 1870s, the first reservation had covered the entire Verde Valley. Not the entirety of the Peoples traditional homelands, but a good chunk, enough to make a living on, and most importantly, control the Verde River. Once the white ranchers moved in with their thirsty livestock, they hollered at their territorial representatives who hollered at Congress, and presto, the reservation was rescinded. To neatly tie things up, the People were soon thereafter forcibly marched 180 miles south and imprisoned at the main Apache Reservation at San Carlos. It wasn't until 1911 that they were allowed to return home and were granted a small, dry 500 acres for their own reservation, about the size of a Phoenix subdivision.

Skip often stopped outside the Cultural Center on his tours. He liked to show his *People* the statue of an elderly Yavapai man carrying his frail wife on his back in a yucca basket with holes cut for her legs. In the cold of winter, with the strap to the basket tied around his forehead, he carried her from that spot over mountains and across rivers 180 miles to San Carlos. The only times he would accept any help was when crossing rivers, because he was afraid of stumbling and losing her in the swift winter currents. After telling the sad story, Skip didn't have to explain the injustices committed against the western tribes; his *People* understood the west was really won not through exploration and settlement of an empty land, but through conquest and expropriation.

Skip and Kuul nodded their respects to the burdened Yavapai, entered the Center, and walked past the prominently displayed map of the revoked 1871 reservation. Trey Sasse's office was at the end of a long hall.

"Skip Rhodes. Long time, come in," Sasse said upon seeing them in the doorway. He turned off a video playing on his laptop.

"I'm working on editing an oral history of the Yavapai and Dilzhe'e. The Tonto Apache were called *Dilzh'I'dine'i'*, *People with high-pitched voices*, by their traditional enemy to the north, the Navajo."

"Maybe the heat made them crazy," Skip half joked. It was over 90 outside, hot for April.

"Actually, they lived in the cooler mountains, so its unlikely heat exposure affected their behaviors. Then again, the Chiricahua called them wild and senseless. The Western Apache used a name meaning wild and rough. So, who knows? Conquistadors named them Tonto in their journals, probably picking up on their neighbors' assessment - *Tonto* means silly or foolish in Spanish."

"Don't go there, Kemosabe," Kuul cautioned Skip. He could see his friend was about to say something stupid about the Lone Ranger's sidekick.

Sasse grinned, guessing what Skip was thinking, and continued, "Both of the tribes have very little recorded past. The Yavapai and Tonto Apache were two different Peoples with two different languages. They roamed the Verde Valley and the forest of the Mogollon Rim to the east during the same period. There was a lot of interaction, and even intermarriage between them. After we acquired the territory from Mexico, the U.S. Government didn't care to recognize the distinction," Trey explained. "If your policy is extermination it doesn't make much difference right?"

"Same old story," Kuul said solemnly. "Still, they ended up better than my Mayan ancestors did at the hands of the Spanish." Neither Sasse nor Skip cared to debate his point.

"Our treatment of natives is a living legacy in the Southwest; very personal even today. We are still arguing over who has the rights to what. *Trey Sasse*," he said, extending his hand to Kuul. "I don't think we've met. Mayan huh?"

Skip had neglected to introduce the two men. "Sorry. Kukulkan Balthazar -Trey Sasse; Trey Sasse - Kukulkan Bonifacio Balthazar,

Kuul for short." The Mayan and Director nodded, shaking hands. "We have something we want to ask you about."

"Interesting name," Sasse said, smiling at Kuul. "Kukulkan, the war serpent god of the Mayans; Bonifacio and Balthazar are Yaqui, right?"

"Kuul will do. A German mercenary is how my Yaqui great-great-grandmother ended up in Arizona. Granddad was a soldier of fortune and hired out to the Mexican government. The Mexican dragoons slaughtered a Yaqui village, except for the girl Grandpa Aldreich hid in a blanket. When he came north looking for silver, he brought her with him. Ten years later he married her."

"You have to be confused...genealogically speaking," Sasse laughed. "I'm seeing a joke in there somewhere; hope you're not offended." He thought for a moment, "Did you hear the one about the Mayan, Yaqui, German, and a snake that walked into a bar?" Sasse stroked his chin, not coming up with the punchline, "... I'll have to work on it."

Trey Sasse was a popular act in Casino comedy clubs. "Natives love to laugh at themselves, especially at jokes about their traditional enemies," he said. Kuul smiled in agreement. "Most of you have a well-developed, though reserved sense of humor. If I get a sly grin or *Oh, that's a good one*, it's like they're rolling on the floor in hysterics.

Skip remembered Sasse's ethnobotany lecture at the Community College. The Dean had been beside himself when the funny archeologist opened with *"Why do Native Americans hate April - because April showers bring May flowers, and the Mayflower brought white people."* He used the line as a lead-in to the medicinal uses of desert plants. The archeologist later joked about a senile medicine man that confused the diuretic properties of the creosote berry with the analgesic value of a cottonwood stem...*the patient had a toothache.*

"No offense taken," Kuul said laughing. "Have you heard this one? What do you call a Mayan snake god tied in a knot?"

Sasse, acting stumped, rubbed his forehead for show and then grinned, "*Pretzalcoatl*."

"This dude's good, man," Kuul said to Skip. "My brother Navajos would eat him up. Put him on stage at Twin Arrows and there'd be more *pickups* in the lot than a Saturday night in Gallup."

"I do a show at the Casino once a month," Sasse said. "And, according to the BIA and Christians they're *Convertibles*."

"True enough," Kuul snorted, shaking his head.

Skip didn't get the last joke and had a quizzical look, "Over my head."

Kuul grinned, "The Bureau of Indian Affairs sent Christian missionaries to *convert* us."

Trey didn't have his day job because of his jokes. The Director of Tribal Archeology stuck around because of his skills, his contacts in the state legislature, and the difficulty in finding experienced professionals willing to work for small reservations. According to the job description, if any sensitive sites or remains were uncovered he was the first on the call list. Because not a lot of building occurred on his reservation, it left a lot of time for special projects, like oral history and developing new comedy routines.

As a horny undergraduate with an undeclared major he had kind of stumbled into archeology. A very pretty American History major at Eastern Illinois State had recruited classmates for a Spring Break dig in Montana instead of a frenzied *bakkheia* in South Florida. Her light blue eyes had sparkled when she asked if he had plans. Trey liked the outdoors and blue eyes, and the rest was his history.

"Well, joking aside, we came out here to pick your brain about looting sensitive sites and..." Skip began.

"I wouldn't recommend it," Sasse quipped.

Skip smiled smartly at the interruption, "*And*, the mountain biker they found out Jacks Canyon was a relative of a friend, or at least she thinks he was. We've heard some rumors that illegal trafficking might have been involved somehow," he finished, throwing out a hook.

Sasse sighed, "Zebulon?"

"That's right."

It seemed like everyone knew the kid, Skip thought.

"Everyone around here in archeology knew him. Zeb did have some problems, but I think you're barking up the wrong tree. I'd be shocked if he was involved in looting. He probably just fell, like the news said. I know the spot where they found him, there's an old granary up on that ridge where the *Sinagua* cached corn, not much else though. They're all over these hills. Nothing valuable. Certainly nothing worth dying over."

Skip made a mental note of his saying Zebulon had problems; Sasse obviously knew about his family history. "Were there any illegal digs you knew about? I stopped by the VVAC and talked to their director, but he's new to the area. You've been around."

"That's true, I have been," Sasse chuckled. "Archeologists are fickle...we're always dating other people."

Sasse had started his career as a freelance archeologist specializing in Grand Canyon river digs. The expeditions were all on the up and up, sponsored by universities and legit museums. A tipped pontoon and a ruptured ACL had settled him down. That led to a more sedentary associate directorship for the Museum of Northern Arizona working with the Hualapai and Havasupai tribes west of the national park. A connection had been made with the Yavapai Nation when their previous archeologist had been caught banging the Casino manager's eighteen-year-old daughter. That stuff just doesn't fly in a socially conservative matriarchal society.

"There are thousands of archeological sites in the Verde Valley alone, tens of thousands in Arizona. Most are undocumented. Paleo cultures and people have been living here for 15,000 years. They all left a record on the land. Most ruins look like another rocky hill or outcropping to the untrained eye," Sasse said. "But you're right, there are always people out there looking to make a buck. They're small time, selling what they find to careless retailers or mounting a collection of arrowheads in their den."

"Balboa has a heck of a Clovis point collection," Kuul interrupted.

Sasse started to tell another joke but changed his mind. "Just two years ago, Forest Service rangers found a couple, man and wife, digging for spear points and other relics. They'd dug over two hundred holes without being found out. *TWO HUNDRED!* When they saw the rangers they took off in a pickup, crashed into a wash, and ran on foot to their campsite. The idiots are doing five years in federal prison on felony convictions. Could have been twenty," the archeologist bemoaned. "That's just one example; I could go on for hours."

"What about commercial scaled operations that cultivate a bigger market?" Skip asked.

"Have you ever heard of the Acoma Pueblo shield?" Sasse asked. Skip and Kuul shook their heads no. "It was a centuries old shield stolen from the Acoma Pueblo outside Albuquerque in the 1970s. It showed up at a Paris auction house in 2016. The seller claimed no knowledge of its history; he'd inherited it. But, to get to your question, that started a legal discussion over a loophole in federal law. Under the 1990 Native American Graves Protection and Repatriation Act, it is illegal to traffic certain cultural items within the U.S. It requires any recovered artifacts be returned to their respective tribes. The problem is the law did not prohibit their export to the rest of the world.

"That's nuts!" Skip said. "It sounds like they inadvertently created a foreign market for stolen relics."

Sasse frowned in agreement, "They're trying to fix it, but an act of Congress takes longer than an act of God. There's a Senate bill pending titled STOP, Safeguard Tribal Objects of Patrimony Act, and it's in hearing before the Indian Affairs Committee. Keep your fingers crossed. It would close the international loophole."

"That's good, but the traffickers are probably rushing to do more business before it does," Kuul observed.

"My guess is you'd be right, but we haven't seen an uptick that we can tell. Of course the international black market is much more sophisticated than the couple digging holes to see what they can find. That's pretty much where we stand; nothing specific, I know. But hopefully it helps."

"Thanks for the lesson," Skip said. "I didn't know him, but it doesn't seem like something Zebulon Ballsy would have been mixed up in." Sasse nodded and shook his hand.

"Good meeting you funnyman. I'll definitely catch your act sometime," Kuul said. "Maybe you can use this one...Neil Armstrong and Buzz Aldrin trained for their moon mission here in Arizona. They met an old Navajo and explained where they were going. The Navajo pondered their journey for a moment, and then asked if they could take the moon people a message for him. Buzz said *Sure*, and the man had them memorize a short sentence in Dine'. The NASA boys asked what it meant, but the Navajo refused to tell them saying it was a sacred Native American prayer. When Neil and Buzz finished their training, curiosity got the better of them, and they found someone to translate.

The old Navajo had taught them to say: *Don't believe a word they say, they have come to steal your land.*

They all laughed and Sasse promised to use the joke. He even thought he might close with it.

"One more thing," Sasse said as Skip and Kuul were leaving. "That box canyon where Zebulon hopefully wasn't found - there's a dark story to it. This isn't published anywhere, and the Yavapai consider talking about it a taboo. To them, that canyon is a holy site...a graveyard actually." Sasse had directed his graveyard comment to Kuul. "You know what that means, right?"

Kuul answered circumspectly, "Evil spirits and bad outcomes for anyone who disturbs it. Let the dead rest and don't interrupt their journey. It's why rangers at National Monument ruins never mention human remains – respect."

"It took me two years to get to the bottom of it, but part of the oral history I'm narrating includes a story about a group of Yavapai cornered in there and massacred by the cavalry in 1873," Sasse continued. "They fought to the last brave protecting their families. In the end, even the women and children fought and were murdered. The Yavapai call it *Red Spirit Canyon*."

"Red," Kuul said. "The color symbolizes the power within ourselves to lay down our lives for others, just as the ancestors shed their blood for us."

...

On their way out, Skip and Kuul ran into the Yavapai and Apache Cultural Directors arguing in the parking lot. Unfortunately, the Yavapai Director, Toni Wathatewa, knew Skip by sight. Wathatewa was a strikingly attractive Yavapai woman, taller than most Native women or men, with high well-formed cheekbones and round intelligent eyes. Statuesquely regal was the description that Skip used. Her lineage predated the official 1934 census roll, and her ancestors had survived the Long March. She was in her late 40's with silver streaks running the length of her long black hair. An eagle feather held a tight braid in the back. She wore a black pants suit with a three-tiered turquoise necklace and hammered silver bracelets on her right wrist. The Native man in jeans and flannel she was arguing with was her Apache counterpart, Sam Sanchez.

Skip's misunderstanding with Wathatewa involved her daughter, who he had taken to the Sonic twice for ice cream. Judy Wathatewa had been a blackjack dealer at Cliff Castle until the casino manager had accused her of helping her white boyfriend count cards. Skip couldn't even remember the multiplication tables. It had been an obvious excuse to settle an old vendetta with

Mama Wathatewa. She and the Chair of the Gaming Commission had duked it out, with Skip being caught in the middle of a political maelstrom he cared absolutely nothing about. Consequently, he was persona non-grata at Cliff Castle and with both Wathatewas.

To get to Kuul's van, Skip and Kuul, who, given his Navajo act, had his own issues with Native officials, had no choice other than to walk past them.

"Keep your hat on," Kuul whispered, an age-old western simile for *Watch your scalp.* "Sanchez is bad Indian." Skip rolled his eyes at his friend who responded, "I've got a lien on his trailer because he didn't pay me for installing a water line to his fridge."

"I've got my own problems with Toni," Skip whispered back.

Kuul smiled, "Love's a bitch, cowboy." Everyone in the county knew the story.

Skip caught the words, *"Blood Quantum,"* before Wathatewa saw him and ended her discussion with Sanchez. Blood quantum referred to the percentage of tribal blood a person had. One-quarter or more was needed to be a member. Their argument likely stemmed from a move to lower it or replace it with direct ancestry from a relative who'd been counted during the all-important 1934 census. Currently, either way worked. Aside from social and cultural reasons, *Keep the Community United*, blood quantum determined who was eligible for a year-end "profit sharing" check from casino proceeds.

"Well, if it isn't a member of the Jackass Clan," Sanchez said, stepping in front of Kuul. "How's the fake Indian business going?"

"Good to see you too Sam," Kuul casually said. Skip had always been impressed with the emotional calmness Kuul displayed in confrontations. It was another of the reasons why he liked having him as a friend. The Mayan's cool aloofness in a sticky situation balanced Skip's own tendencies to fly off the handle.

Toni Wathatewa's bright black eyes were boring a hole through Skip's blue ones. *The woman needed to let it go.* She knew damn well none of her problems with the Gaming Commission were his fault. He suspected it was the threat of his white blood that really bothered her. Toni's ex-husband was Tohono O'odham, so if Judy married a non-Yavapai Apache her grandchildren could be the last Wathatewa's to be tribal members. *She really didn't have to worry about him – it was just a Heath bar Sonic Blast!*

"I thought we banned you?" Wathatewa said, glowering at Skip.

"Just at Cliff Castle. You know I come through here taking groups to Montezuma Castle. I don't think you can keep me out of a National Monument."

"We'll see."

"How's Judy?" Skip wisecracked. Wathatewa harshly muttered a series of Yavapai words he didn't understand. He doubted they highlighted his better qualities.

Sanchez and Kuul were standing toe to toe with their chests puffed out. The hair on Sanchez's neck was bristled like the back of a dog's when it was readying to fight. The barking prelude started. Shouting verbal insults was the Native way. Degrading an enemy with words was a necessary Apache precursor to battle.

"Take your stupid *k-nymsaw-e* and leave, *Nda Yutaha'*," Sanchez snarled. *Nda Yutaha'* being the Tonto Apache desultory term for an Indian who lives like a white man, and *k-nymsaw-e* the word for white man.

"Your mother does laundry for drunkards and bends over for Comanches," Kuul hurled back. The laundry part sounded Mayan to Skip.

"You a blanket-ass fort injun who squats below ponies to drink," Sanchez sneered.

"*Glonni*," Kuul spat back. He tilted a thumb to his open mouth and mimed chugging a bottle.

Sanchez's eyes opened wide at the last insult. He hadn't missed an agency AAA meeting in five years. The Apache and Kuul took three seemingly choreographed steps backward and turned their backs to each other, a sign of disrespect. Sanchez headed back to the center past the statue, and Kuul across the lot to the AAA Plumber to the Stars van. They'd both saved face.

Skip followed his friend; the hostile Yavapai woman walked beside him in silence. She had been leaving the center and was parked near the van. The tension between the two was as flammable as an Arizona wildfire.

"What is it you really have against me?" Skip asked. Maybe she'd let her guard down after seeing the childish war between the two men. Maybe enough time had finally passed since the Casino incident.

Toni stopped and looked him in the eyes. This time she wasn't boring holes. She was studying what she saw inside. This *k-nymsawe* was an enigma; she saw good and ugly. Which was dominant she couldn't tell.

"My mother was a seer," she said slowly. "She had revelations that helped guide our people. The power's not as strong in me, but I do sense you've done bad things. I believe..." she paused, still searching his soul. "I believe you are a good white man, but you're not at peace or honest with yourself." Wathatewa nodded and walked to her Silverado pickup.

16

HOOT PASSES THE BUCK

THE BLACK AND WHITE PATROL CAR TURNED AT THE SIGN advertising Happy Hour at the Lazy *SOB*. House margaritas were five bucks from 5 PM to 8 PM; the second plate of skins was half-priced. Officer Dickie had hoped Captain Hooton would make the trip to talk to Zula Ballsy. He should have known better. Hooton wasn't about to reenter the ring for Round-Two with the disgruntled widow of a mob boss. As much as Dickie wanted to get back into the field, this wasn't what he imagined.

The Chuckwagon sign was new, and from his participation on the Joint Task Force on Beautification and Illegal Signage he knew he should write it up as a violation. There wasn't a lot of code enforcement to do in Sedona, so the Task Force, led by the eager beaver Chairperson of the Keep Sedona Friendly Committee, had cited everything from seven inch grass to Christmas lights left up past January. It all ended in a raucous City Council meeting attended by hundreds of aggrieved property owners chanting *Down with*

Tyrants. The eager beaver had his teeth capped and moved to Lake Havasu after death threats and having a diamondback left on his front porch. *Maybe he'd let Zula's sign go unreported,* Dickie thought.

At least Hooton had called Zula telling her he had the autopsy results, and was driving out to meet her. Of course he didn't move his lazy butt out of his leather office chair; he sent Dickie instead. It was payback for his still not figuring out the new phone system. He winced as he drove past the interfering juniper that had rerouted his dart toss. Zula Ballsy was standing in front of the lodge with her arms crossed watching his arrival.

"Hooton too lazy to move his ass out of the chair or too scared?" the old showgirl growled as Dickie got out of the squad car. He left the door open just in case.

"He has a meeting with the Mayor, Public Works Director, and the Chamber on that new traffic circle in Uptown. A tourist from Australia drove the wrong way, hit a Japanese tour bus full of businessmen out of Vegas, and now they're dealing with an international incident. The Chamber director wants to put in dual side-by-side circles, one going right and one going left."

"Do I look like I give a friggin' Tokyo damn, mate?" Zula barked. "What do you have on my great nephew? And keep your hands off that lawn dart set, I remember you."

The memory of Bootsy's whistling boobs was something Dickie wanted to forget. *Why wouldn't they let him?* "We've located his parents...well, sort of," he hesitated a little too long. Dickie wasn't sure how well Zula had gotten along with her wacky kin.

"And am I supposed to guess? Suck it up son! Don't pull a Hooton on me."

Dickie straightened his back and adjusted his holster. *Damn he'd left his pistol on the station counter.* He'd been demonstrating the safety catch to the Sweet Adelines; they had toured the department, and he wanted to impress the lead soprano. She was younger and had promised to show him her racy barbershop pole tattoo.

"According to an email we received from the State Department, the mother is somewhere in Cambodia with a female Swedish sex therapist and the father is working as a bookkeeper at a Panamanian rum factory. Captain Hooton tried contacting both, but no luck so far."

Zula shook her braided gray hair, cracked her knuckles, and kicked at the dust with her pointed steel-capped boots. She disgustingly stared at Officer Dickie, who desperately wished he hadn't been distracted by the tattoo – he'd feel better with backup.

"Autopsy! Cause of death!" Zula impatiently yelled. Dickie wasn't showing a lot of initiative. She wished Hooton had come instead; at least she wouldn't have to keep pulling teeth for each bit of information. She might not have been able to look bobble head in the eyes like she could Dickie, but he would at least talk.

"Ah, yes." Dickie stammered. "Captain said to tell you that dental records confirmed it was your nephew, and..."

"Friggin' knew that. Where's your gun Dickie?" Zula said, noticing the empty holster.

Crap, Dickie thought. "Locked in the glove compartment, per departmental regulations when notifying next of kin," Dickie lied. Zula Ballsy rolled her eyes but didn't say anything. She stomped her foot and motioned for him to continue.

Dickie cleared his throat, "Although it's still technically under investigation, the injuries...the ones the coroner could still inspect anyway..." he said hesitantly, expecting a blast of venom. None came, the old girl looked sad and defeated. "They were consistent with a fall; cracked skull, broken forearms, wrists, and collarbone. The Captain and Chief think Zeb got close to the top of the hill when a wheel hit loose gravel, or slid off a boulder the wrong way, causing your nephew to fall."

"So, what's next, Officer *Dickie*?" Zula's voice was quieter, but her disgust was barely under control. She knew after her meeting with Hooton that Zebulon's death would be declared an accident with no further action warranted.

Dickie looked at her with sympathy. Despite the gruff exterior, the one promising relative she had was now confirmed dead. He understood her anger and saw her hurt. But he still wanted to be done and get the heck out of Dodge before she blew up. He took a few steps back toward the open door of his car.

"Captain Hooton says once he gets the final death certificate from the Coroner's Office he's likely closing the case. He said as soon as that happens, you'll be able to collect the remains, since the parents are...unavailable."

Zula calmed down as the reality, and the pain of knowing her nephew's suffering, set in. Being mad at Dickie wasn't going to change that. "Thank you, Officer. I know you would have preferred to not come out here. I appreciate this not being a phone call. You've got a credit for a free one at the *SOB*."

"Thanks mam. Sorry for your loss."

"And tell Hoot to go smoke a pig fart!"

• • •

Skip agreed hiking to Red Spirit Canyon for a firsthand look might answer their questions. Zula asked him to take a picture of Zebulon wearing the medal for the bike competition he'd won and one of his archeology textbooks to leave as a memorial. Kuul volunteered to go along, telling his friend he didn't want him mucking around his People's sacred sites without supervision. Skip countered he wasn't going to the Yucatan.

Skip didn't have any tours scheduled, and Kuul was giving Al's tile a few days to set before installing the new gold-plated toilet. It was a cool day for late April, and a double digit breeze kept the bugs down. In another six weeks the blistering heat of summer would be edging thermometers up to 100 degrees. The crowds had thinned a bit on the trails; it was shoulder season between the end of Spring Break and before schools closed. Even locals were gravitating toward shadier hikes. Jacks Canyon was deserted except for hardcore backpackers.

They stopped to rest and eat lunch at the fork with the deer path. Two luke-warm beers and two Kind bars was all they brought, aside from a gallon of water each. They had been on the trail for an hour keeping a quick pace. The high seventy degree air was pleasant, but the sun was still hot and there wasn't much shade.

"You remember that redneck Florida cracker?" Kuul said, biting into his Cherry Chia KIND Bar. The Chia seeds in the bar had more calcium than a cup of whole milk and less than half the fat and calories. It was a superfood his people had harvested in the desert for thousands of years...until the Europeans showed up with herds of grazing cattle.

"Which one?"

"At PJ's Bar, the Dolphin fan."

"Which one?" Skip grinned.

Kuul crossed his arms and gave Skip a stoic Native stare. It was an old story they always fell back on. They both knew who he was talking about. It's how they met. PJ's was a local watering hole with multiple satellites that carried all the games. On any given Sunday during football season most states were represented in the small bar tucked into a shopping center next to a veterinarian office. The Vet had his own stool; he was a diehard Bears fan originally from Springfield. After a few cold ones he'd bark at every sack.

The Florida cracker was drunk on mojitos watching the Fins play the Washington Redskins. Every time Washington had the ball he kept slurring, *the only good Indian is a dead Indian.* Kuul had warned the jerk twice, before snapping when he called a female Washington fan in a Joe Thiesman jersey *Squaw Thunder Butt* and her boyfriend *Tepee Hugger*. But before the Mayan could touch his enemy and count coup, Skip had casually walked up to the blowhard Dolphin fan, called him a *Loud-Mouthed Sonny Crockett Goldfish*

Scum Sucker and knocked him off his barstool. That had set off a John Wayne styled bar fight between the Miami and Washington fans. Patriots' fans joined the Redskins and the yahooing Dallas Cowboys contingent teamed up with Miami. Kuul and Skip, who hadn't yet met, propped Sonny against the bar, shook hands, and with each grasping a shoulder, threw the loser out the front door. The Vet wolfed the guy's half-full beer.

After a few more Sundays at PJ's, Skip and Lilac invited Kuul to share a Navajo fry bread pizza at El Rincon. Kuul showed up with a red-headed podiatrist from Munds Park. His subsequent dates had been just as colorful; the purple turbaned Adra from Jaipur, Jaye Gray Wolf from Holbrook, who made headstones from petrified wood, and Rose Sweet Gum, a Shoshone herbalist most recently from Santa Fe. Sweet Gum left him for a timeshare salesman, and when Lilac gave up on Skip, Kuul started tagging along on Sedona Chi tours in her place. He was good for business. Skip reciprocated and helped him out with celebrity pipe problems, also good for business.

"Time to saddle up Skipper. It's a couple more miles to that ridge," Kuul said, finishing the power bar and judging the distance by how quickly the flanking red hills pinched inwards.

It took forty minutes to reach the end of the path and the beginning of the switchbacks leading up the ridge. The wind had picked up whistling through gaps in the side walls, swooshing the pinon pine and juniper. The lonely sound highlighted the canyon's seclusion. A thousand years ago the same noise, the same light on the rocks, even the same smells, would have been present. If not for the solemn purpose of their visit, Skip would have been mesmerized by the tranquility and timelessness.

"Looks like Big Bob's group stopped here. Lot of trampled sand and this rock's been brushed clean - someone sat here," Kuul said, reading signs at the base of the incline.

Skip gazed up the switchbacks, shielding his eyes from the sun that was directly overhead. "Would you ride a bike up there?"

"Do you know any of these white-line junkies? There isn't a challenge they won't try." Sedona was famous in mountain biking circles for a nine-inch ledge of white rock where risky riders tested their skills.

"Hmm," Skip was trying to picture controlling two wheels careening down the switchbacks. It looked incredibly foolhardy. "What about coming down?"

"Not me Kemo, be hard enough in a good pair of boots. It's hard imagining Zebulon attempting it. The kid was local and knew what to try and what not to," Kuul said.

"Yeah, but he did, or we wouldn't be out here." Skip was poking around a clump of manzanita bushes. He found a cross stuck in the ground fashioned from mesquite branches, probably left to mark the spot where Search and Rescue had found the remains. It seemed as appropriate a place as any to leave Zula's offerings. Kuul joined him, looking over his shoulder.

"Sad, man." Kuul knelt and touched the ground. "The earth is alive here. This spot is where his life-force transferred to our mother."

Skip leaned the framed picture against the cross, hanging the medal Zebulon had won on its arm. "Rest in peace." Both men took off their hats and stayed silent for a moment. It was a peaceful place, almost spooky. The wind gusted, creating a little dust devil from the sandy path.

"Spirits," Kuul said as they watched the devil spiral upwards and dissipate.

"Let's see if we can find the bike. Lilac said the search team found it by a group of boulders, which is where they left it. It wasn't worth the effort packing it out," Skip said, shaking off the eerie feeling. "If the Police had come, they'd have taken it as evidence. Zula's right about Hooton."

They scrutinized the area, spotting a likely group of Volkswagen Beetle-sized boulders that had eroded and fallen down from the slope. Sure enough, the Santa Cruz Tallboy was lying crumpled behind. Skip pulled it free from the bush that had grown through the wheels.

"Sure looks like it had a rough ride down," Kuul observed.

Skip was cleaning sticks from the bike and placed it on a knee-high rock for a closer inspection. It was in one piece, but beat to hell. The handlebars were twisted like a pretzel, and the seat post was bent. The wheel rims were badly buckled but still intact. The front wheel was the worst; it had probably taken the brunt of hits on the way down. From the looks of it, the bike had hit bottom with tremendous force. He hated thinking of Zebulon absorbing a similar impact.

Skip studied Tallboy closer and noticed that several spokes were snapped and several more bent all at the same height and in the same direction, like something had been...

The exploding sound was unmistakable.

The shot ricocheted off a rock between the two friends, the bullet thudding harmlessly into a pinon. Skip and Kuul instinctively dove behind two boulders. A second shot landed in the dirt behind them.

SADDLE UP

SKIP LOOKED AT KUUL.

"*Are you okay?*" he mouthed.

Kuul nodded. They were hunkered behind separate boulders lying as low to the ground as they could get. Because they dove in different directions, they were ten to fifteen feet apart. The shots had come from up on the ridge and whoever was there had a clear line of sight. They were pinned down.

Kuul motioned with his hand that they should stay put. The firing had stopped. Skip shook his head in agreement. They waited. After a few tense but silent minutes, Skip put his Stetson on a dead branch, raising it above his rock. Nothing. He held up five fingers, mouthing, "*Five Minutes.*" Meaning if nothing happened in five minutes they'd try moving.

Five minutes passed without any shots being fired. Skip held his hat back up and nothing. He waited another five minutes and did the same routine. Nothing. If whoever shot at them was gone there had to be another way down from the ridge. They would have seen anyone coming down the switchbacks.

"What do you think?" Skip whispered to Kuul.

"I think your hat is safe."

Skip peeked over the rocks. Still nothing. He counted to one-hundred and cautiously moved through the open gap separating him from Kuul. Nothing. "Looks like they're gone," he said, sitting down next to Kuul behind his rock.

"Or waiting for a better shot...I know what Geronimo felt like now," Kuul said. "There's some bad mojo in this place, Kemo."

"We need to get up there," Skip said.

"I'll watch the top and yell if they start shooting again," Kuul unenthusiastically said.

Skip spied a split in the ridge that dropped into a saddle over to a lower hill. The climb up to the saddle would be tough; it was a steep rock slide from where they were hidden. The ridge and hill had once been the same level; erosion between the two had created a slope of broken rocks ranging in size from the larger VW they were hiding behind to smaller basketballs. From the saddle it looked like he could climb to the ridgetop. Unless there was a path down the backside of the ridge to an unmapped trail, it was the only way up other than the switchbacks.

"I'm going to try climbing up through that saddle."

Kuul looked at him like, *Yeah, right, and your ancestors were clever enough to beat mine?* He frowned, "You aren't Teddy Roosevelt and that's not San Juan Hill. Good luck, you have any next of kin I don't know about."

Skip stood up; still nothing from up top. "Give me a head start. When I'm halfway to the saddle you start working your way up the switchbacks. If they start shooting again, head back to town."

"It's time to *vamonos,* my crazy brother, we both need to head back the way we came."

Skip ignored him. "Remember, when I'm half-way up you start. We'll flank them if they're still there."

"Flank with what, rocks?" Kuul grumbled.

Skip crept off, and Kuul stayed put, watching the ridge as his risky friend picked his way over and around the rocks and boulders in the arroyo. Once Skip started up the slide, he knew he'd be exposed. It had been over a half-hour since the shots; he felt confident whoever was up there was gone. If they had really wanted to kill them, they would have kept shooting. His only other option was to turn tail and sneak out. Skip wasn't the sneaking type.

Halfway up the saddle he thought he heard voices; he hid behind a pile of rocks as best he could. *Maybe it was the wind playing tricks?* Nothing happened, and he didn't hear anything more. He looked down the slide to Kuul, motioning for him to stay behind his rock. Kuul signaled a big *okay* sign with his fingers. After three more minutes listening, he started again. He moved as quickly as possible from one group of rocks to another. No sounds or shots from up top. He waved at Kuul to start up the switchbacks.

Skip was breathing hard by the time he made the saddle. His knees and elbows were scraped by the sandstone he had been hugging during the climb. The next section was steeper but less broken up; there were scattered trees to dodge behind, and the angle made it hard for anyone up top to get a clean shot. There was one tricky ledge; he'd had to grasp the edge with his hands and twist his body, swinging his legs sideways and up. The rest of the way had been relatively easy. He crested the ridge several hundred yards from where the last switchback began. Kuul should be close to the top.

He saw Kuul in the distance and made a circling motion, telling him to skirt the path instead of going through the thick acacia bushes, he'd move along the ridge in the opposite direction. He clasped his hands and pointed to a rock wall; they'd meet there. Still no sounds and he hadn't heard any more voices. Fifteen minutes later they met; it was clear the shooters had left. How, Skip wasn't quite sure.

They were standing in a small clearing, with thick, overgrown, catsclaw between them and the rock wall. The flat ridgetop extended in both directions, Skip and Kuul had approached the clearing from opposite ends. The backside slope of the ridge was obscured with shrubbery and several low hanging junipers, except for where Skip had climbed. Kuul was searching for footprints or scuff marks in the dirt from the shooter.

"Did you see anything?" Skip asked. They were both scanning the top of the ridge they had just circumnavigated, confused, but quietly glad they hadn't found anyone.

"Nothing. You?"

"Nada. I thought I might have heard some voices, but I'm not sure. Probably the wind."

"There were a couple of small faults they could have gone down. But I should have seen them down below," Kuul said. "Ghost people. You remember what Sasse said about the massacre and this being a sacred site? There are spirits here, brother, Zeb's got company. It wasn't the wind you heard. It was their cries."

"Spirits don't leave these," Skip said. He held up two shell casings he'd found on his side of the ridgetop. "These are .22 long rifle casings."

"Yeah, well, whoever it was magically disappeared. Maybe the ghosts are shooting back this time. Fair is fair." Kuul kept glancing over his shoulders as he spoke.

"Did you see the granary Sasse said was up here?"

Kuul shook his head, "Too busy keeping my eyes open for snipers. Let's get out of here and take our time hiking out, maybe go cross-country in case they double back on us. I've seen enough granaries."

• • •

The Shanghai collector had made serious inroads into the Russian black market. The owner of the largest pharmaceutical plant in Moscow had requested a particular type of Puebloan necklace for his mistress from Kiev. The collector smiled upon receiving the order, things hadn't changed much since the Japanese savages had held his mother; powerful men taking what they wanted from powerless women who were just trying to stay alive. What had changed was the Chinese collector being the one taking advantage of their greed and avarice.

Twelve-thousand years ago Paleo-Indians in southwestern America began making jewelry for ornamentation and eventually trade. Shell and stone were chipped into smaller pieces, those pieces were carved into beads, and the beads transformed into beautiful primitive pieces of work. Animal and fish bones were sculpted into lavish pendants used to decorate ceremonial clothing. In some fortunately located communities, surface minerals such as quartz, obsidian, and turquoise were mined and hammered into ornate designs to be worn by priests and important warriors.

The Russian had ordered a special kind of necklace called a *heishe*, the bigger the better. The collector smiled again. Of all his clients, the Russians had the most easily satisfied tastes and overpaid the greatest.

Heishe necklaces originated with the Kewa Pueblo people and spread through southwestern tribes. Elaborate *heishes* were made from thousands of handmade beads shaped into thin tubular discs strung in colorful patterns. Because of the jewelers' dedication to perfection, they doubled as highly-prized trade goods, exchanged for equally valuable items produced elsewhere. *Heisha* necklaces during that early period held the same value in trade as several safes full of gold in the courts of contemporary Europe.

The drug czar was staying in the Ritz Carlton penthouse suite with his Ukrainian whore. The Russian had flown to Shanghai in his Learjet Liberty with his mistress and two of her long-legged modeling friends for a two-week orgy and shopping spree. The necklace had just arrived and was ready to be picked up, completing its circuitous illicit route.

The collector had toured the Russian and his girls through his private gallery and shown them the androgynous figure with its penis extending through the glass case. He had laughed to himself, watching the Ukrainian bitch rub the wealthy Cossack's genitals while her friends had stroked the exposed turquoise tip of the figure. Seven million for a special night had been an easy sell after that. The two-million surcharge was for an extra-large czar-like bed imported from Moscow and a powdered, highly skilled, Japanese geisha. The geisha had been the girlfriend's request. The collector's mother would have appreciated the irony.

The Shanghai collector was reviewing the taped version of the Nippon-Soviet encounter when his phone rang. He took the new order over a secure line while watching the geisha and the Kiev mistress each work on the same Russian missile. The collector laughed, *it was good to see different cultures getting along so well.* The order was not unusual; *Mogollan* and *Sinagua* artifacts were always popular. He knew just how to procure their acquisition and delivery.

18

CLARKDALE ART COOPERATIVE

"**Y**OU SHOULD USE MOUNTAIN LION *SCA-SCA-SC*AT," SUGGESTED Winslow Crane. Crane was a balding bird of a man with a long neck containing an Adam's apple that bounced two inches whenever he said a word starting with *sc* or *sh*. The extra movement caused him to stutter the sound, particularly if he laughed.

"Every Tom, Dick, and Harry uses coyote *sca-sca-sca-sc*at," he chuckled to Kulkulkan Balthazar. "Mountain lion *sh-sh-sh*it is what you *sh-sh-sh*ould use." Crane explained, his Adam's apple bouncing up and down, "It's more marketable. You can charge more. Any amateur *scru-scru-sc*rewball crafter can find and use coyote *sca-sca-sc*at. It's not unique, it's not art."

The Clarkdale Art Cooperative was sponsoring a collection hike out Sycamore Canyon with Sedona Chi Tours...Skip Rhodes. As usual Skip had brought Kuul along to have someone who could talk shop with the small group of natural material artists that had signed up for the tour. Skip's Bronco with its balky AC had made it to the end of the dirt and gravel road where they had parked and hiked the trail down to the Verde River. The Coop members were looking for fresh scat, feathers, yucca twine, fur, dead wood, berries, iron oxide, sand, river rock, and whatever else of interest they could find to use in their locally sourced art. Skip's job was to make sure they found all the shit they needed.

"Fresh *sca-sca-sc*at at 11:00," Crane pointed out. "Where's my *scu-scu-sc*ooper?" he said to himself rifling through his plastic lined zipper bag. "I'd lose my head if it wasn't *scru-scru-scru-sc*rewed on," he chortled. His thyroid cartilage was getting a serious workout. "The juniper berries *sh-sh-sh*ould still be intact," he said scooping it up and sniffing to identify its source. "*Sh-sh-sh*it, it's just javelina, I *sh-sh-sh-sh*ould have known better" he said, laughing and throwing it away. "*Sh-sh-sh*oddier than coyote, nobody wants to buy rat *sh-sh-sh*it.

"You do mobiles with your *sca-sca-sc*at, right?" Crane asked Kuul.

"And fetishes," Kuul absently replied, transfixed by the bouncing ball on his throat, wondering what kept him from swallowing it.

"Fetishes, hmm. Maybe you *sh-sh-sh*ould fashion some turquoise beads to look like juniper berries and use them to balance the wheels. That might increase your profit spread. *Sh-sh-sh-sh-sh-sh*ow me the money!" Crane laughed uncontrollably.

"You could tie feathers or use agave membrane," another member offered. "The more natural materials you incorporate the more distinctive and unique your work will be.

"Also think about using multiple types of scat," another suggested. "That's one way to appeal to a broader more sophisticated clientele."

The other three Coop members on the hike were Dale "Rattler" Bowman who worked with snake skins, Mary Beth Trimble who was a natural fiber weaver, and Carla "Sandy" Littlefoot who did sand paintings with red Tanager feathers and lava pebbles.

Winslow Crane was an accomplished cat scat sculptor, mountain lion and bobcat. The four Clarkdale artists shared a studio in downtown Clarkdale across from the Copper Museum and had concessions at the Verde Valley train depot gift shop. The Sedona galleries demanded too high of commissions.

Rattler Bowman had wandered a little off the trail toward the river having noticed a promising sunny spot, "I found a sidewinder trail, you can see it in the dirt over here," he yelled. The other three artists rushed over to inspect his find.

Sandy Littlefoot studied the markings, "The Hopi god *Palululkang*. The Snake Clan's been here, eh Kukulkhan," Littlefoot said winking, referring to the serpent origin of Kuul's Mayan name. Littlefoot looked like a desert queen with her wide colorfully patterned Hopi skirt and red blouse, her long peppered hair tied with a blue calico braid. She and Kuul had been flirting since the first step of the hike.

Kuul shook his head in agreement. *"Palululkang* was a snake-like God of the Hopi Snake Clan. The myth tells the legend of a Hopi boy named Tiyo who journeys to the meeting of the Colorado River and ocean," Kuul explained to Skip. "There he finds an island inhabited by the *Kikmongwi*...Snake People. They don snake costumes and turn into dancing slithering snakes. Tiyo ends up marrying a *Kikmongwi* maiden and returns to Hopiland starting the Snake Clan. But the maiden gives birth to rattlesnakes which bite Hopi children. Tiyo is forced to take his snake children back to the Snake People and from that point forward his wife bears only human offspring." Kuul grinned at Littlefoot after reciting the myth, "He should have married a good Hopi girl."

"A Hopi and Mayan would make beautiful children," Littlefoot slyly grinned. "I'd grind cornmeal with you anytime, Kuul."

Kuul rolled his eyes at Skip, away from Littlefoot. It was the first time Skip had seen an Indian blush. "You asked for it," he whispered to his purplish friend.

"Seems Tiyo didn't return all his children," Rattler held up a molted skin, saving Kuul from awkwardly responding to the cornmeal offer. Bowman was standing in a sandy delta area by the river. "This little one will get me thirty to forty easy as a hat band."

"You could triple that in Santa Fe or Scottsdale," Mary Beth Trimble chimed in. "I do their art festivals twice a year. Any of my weavings with fur or yucca thread go faster than hotcakes." Mary Beth's weavings were highly prized. In addition to only using natural fibers and animal fur, her colors were hand-dyed by native saps, pitch, and berries. "If they only let me set up at the Governor's Palace like Sandy I could retire."

Tiyo's story and Trimble's observation started Skip thinking about the archeologists' lessons on artifact thieving and how illicitly obtained relics could be sold. He didn't have a clue how much an old snake costume or sacred ceremonial rattle would go for, but he guessed it might be worth the risk. Santa Fe and Scottsdale were full of wealthy collectors attending art shows, spending money, and lounging poolside in fancy country clubs.

"Do you ever see any ancient artifacts being sold at those festivals?" Skip asked offhand. He didn't want the Clarkdale Art Cooperative thinking he was involved in an illegal trade. They had a nasty ironworker member from Humboldt he wouldn't want to cross metal with.

"Illegally? I'm guessing you're not talking about arrowheads. Truly rare artifacts would be criminal and major trouble for the sponsors. They're usually put on by Chambers of Commerce or City Art Commissions," Mary Beth said. "Not the place to move anything stolen from protected sites." All four artists shook their heads confirming her opinion.

"Besides, the legitimate dealers would turn them in," Rattler added. He was carefully placing the molted skin in a protective baggie and putting it in his canvas backpack.

"Most festivals and outdoor shows are just mom and pop venders. Artists like us," Sandy Littlefoot added. Now the *art* galleries, they can be a different story." Skip noted she said *art* derisively.

"What do you mean?" Skip asked.

"There are fine art galleries and then there are *art* galleries. Usually, the distinction is just decimal points on the price tag. The fine art galleries, with very few exceptions, are on the up and up. There are too many experts and artists doing business with them. But some of the *art* galleries, the cheesier ones in particular, aren't real picky when it comes to buying collectibles off the street and marking them up for a quick resale to unknowing tourists."

"There are too many of those and their inventories turn too quickly to adequately police. The only way to catch them would be by random inspection, and there aren't enough inspectors," Mary Beth said.

"And most of them can't tell a Native prayer *sh-sh-sh*awl from an afghan anyway," Crane added.

"Any shops or sellers in particular?" Kuul asked, picking up on where Skip was heading. If they could get a line on the go-betweens they could try tracing a sale. He had gathered a wild bouquet of late blooming desert lupine and Mexican poppy, handing them to Littlefoot. Maybe they could skip the Hopi cornmeal bridal cere- mony and go straight to praying over the morning sun.

The four artists thought about the question, but it was clear they didn't have an answer. "Not really," Crane said for all four. "That market's not our *sse-sse-s*cene, but everyone knows it happens."

• • •

Taco Charlie's was owned by Charlie Valdez and his wife Inez from Oaxaca. Charlie was the head waiter and chief bottle washer, Inez the cook, and their daughter Julia ran the register. Their quirky five-table restaurant was located in an Uptown Sedona strip center, sandwiched between a commercial blood lab and an herbal teahouse specializing in manzanita-infused lotus leaves. The cuisine was *Oaxacan*, but they also grilled a darn fine burger. Lilac died for Inez's banana leaf-wrapped pork tamale with grasshopper and tiny avocado filling smothered in mole'. If she was with Skip, Charlie always ran upstairs to their apartment for his own bottle of Don Julio - *Only for Mister Skip*. Kuul was so-so on their tacos but got a kick from ribbing the amiable owner about his Aztec ancestors.

After the Clarkdale Coop tour, Skip, Kuul, and Sandy Littlefoot met Lilac at Charlie's for a late lunch. Skip wanted to run a theory up Lilac's flagpole. Her connections in Phoenix might be able to answer some questions. He had begun to think that Zebulon Ballsy just might have gotten himself mixed up with the wrong people, or stumbled onto something he shouldn't have. Most rumors had a basis in fact.

"*Quetzalcoatl*, my friend!" Charlie grinned, welcoming Kuul. *Quetzalcoatl* was the big god of the Aztecs, a feathered serpent. Snakes and serpents seemed to be a recurring theme. It was a jibe at Kuul's name, Kukulkhan, the warrior serpent god of the Mayans.

"So, what's good from your swamps today?" Kuul needled. Aztecs had grown their food on islands and large lakes around today's Mexico City. They had arrived in Mexico later than Kuul's ancestors, the Mayans, who had lived in Central American jungles. "I'd like something that isn't rotted," Kuul joked. Mayans had been more traditional farmers. The differences were similar to those between a farmer from Des Moines and one from the Delta.

"Inez has started cooking *Huitlacoche* tacos and frijoles just for you, my friend. I know how you like the earthy pungent flavor of fresh mushrooms."

"Corn smut," Kuul responded. *Huitlacoche* was very much about the texture of the cooked fungus. *Not for everyone.*

"He'll have the blue cornmeal *Piki* bread wedding appetizer," Littlefoot added.

Charlie laughed, "Not on the menu today," and sat an *Oaxacan* pizza in the middle of their table. Lilac had arrived before the boys and hadn't waited to order. She'd already polished off her favorite tamale. The *Tlaydua* was layers of pork, refried beans, avocados, chilies, and chorizo, with tomatoes diced on top. It was big enough to feed Montezuma's army with a large doggie bag left over. Inez followed with a pitcher of pink margaritas.

"I know Mister Skip likes the prickly pear," Inez said while pouring drinks.

The next twenty minutes was devoted to moving the overflowing pizza from the pan to their mouths while trying to keep the dripping salsa off their shirts. They finished with a last round of margaritas while listening to an Herb Albert knockoff singing about a lonely bull over the speaker. Littlefoot's breezy red linen shirt was open a button too low with a chunk of red pepper lodged where her cleavage started.

"Whoops, let me get that for you," Kuul said, reaching his napkin toward Littlefoot's stain. She slapped his hand aside and picked the pepper off putting it in her mouth. "Not without stating your intentions and presenting presents," she scolded.

"And I thought this was one of the few places a girl didn't have to worry about being sexually harassed," Lilac said. Littlefoot nodded in solidarity. "I shouldn't have left the Glock in the jeep. Is that how you treat all your girlfriends, Kuul? What happened to the red head?"

"Redhead?" Littlefoot winked at Lilac while giving the Mayan a discomforting glare.

"Me good Indian, try to help," Kuul mocked himself. Both women rolled their eyes.

"It's been fun guys, but I have to get back to the studio," Littlefoot said. "I have a 4:00 class and have to lay out the basic circle and design on the sandpaper before it starts." She stood to leave. "Call me Kukulkhan and we'll smoke pipe." The unabashed

Hopi maiden lightly stroked the Mayan's arm and gave him a good-bye kiss on the cheek.

After Littlefoot had gone, Skip brought up his theory. Despite the harassment crack, Lilac seemed in a good mood, and if that changed at least he knew she wasn't armed. It was becoming fifty-fifty he'd say something to set her off without understanding why. He doubted they'd be smoking pipe anytime soon.

"You have a few gallery connections down in Phoenix, right?" he asked her. *Seemed innocent enough, no problem with that question.*

"Scottsdale. I helped the owner of a Zuni gallery with a paternity issue. He was born a she but had a sex change ten years before he hired me. Two women, former employees, both claimed they were pregnant and pointed to him. Exhibit opening, wine, little coke, experimental threesome – you get the picture. Little did they know!"

"TMI," Skip said.

"Sounds like the second world in the Navajo origin story," Kuul chuckled, "The ants from the first world messing around with the King's wife in the second world."

"Seriously," Skip said. "I'm not telling Zula this, but it seems possible that Zebulon might have been mixed up with the wrong people."

"Or he ran into them at the wrong time and place," Kuul added, thinking of their ambush. Kuul told Lilac the history of the massacre of Red Spirit Canyon. "There's still bad medicine there." Kuul told her about the shots and their not being able to find the shooters. "Ghost people were angry because we disturbed their sacred place."

Skip scoffed at the superstitions, pulling out the shell casing he found, "Not ghosts."

"No joke either," Lilac cautioned. "How many times have I told you to go fully loaded on your hikes and tours? People think Sedona is like Disneyland, it's all good and nature's a playground. Ten minutes from here you're in wilderness and there it's Darwin's rule."

"Agreed," Skip said, not wanting to argue with an NRA spokeswoman. He changed the subject, "We found the bike and you're right, something was off. Not only was it too far from the body, but it looked like it had been intentionally hidden. And the way the spokes were bent didn't look like it happened in the fall."

Lilac thought about it a moment. "Yeah, it could have been the fall. Who knows? Spokes can break a lot of ways we can't imagine. They could have caught a root or anything on the way down. Zebulon could have panicked when he went over, letting go of the bike." She didn't really believe that but in the absence of any other proof...

"Maybe," Skip said. He was about to voice another possibility. *Maybe the broken spokes were WHY he fell.*

"Or maybe he was looking for something," Kuul said.

Skip and Kuul told Lilac about their meetings at the Archeology Museum and the Yavapai Apache Tribal Center and what they had learned about artifact theft and trafficking. The Clarkdale Art Cooperative members had gotten them thinking about whether there might be a trail leading through galleries in Phoenix. They thought Sedona galleries were too risky for local looters. "We were hoping you could quietly inquire with any connections you have in... Scottsdale?"

Lilac had listened and been nodding along, but Skip noticed her expression inexplicably darken after he told her about meeting Trey Sasse at the Yavapai Center. By the time he ran through his conversation with David Oglestar her icy glare could freeze a scorpion. *The 50-50 odds had played out.* He didn't have a clue what had changed.

"So, you met with Toni Wathatewa?"

Skip looked at Kuul who looked out the window. The town's iconic Snoopy Rock loomed in the distance with his head down and tail between his legs. The sidewalks were busy, and his friend was pretending to watch tourists argue with their hot kids and out-of-state cars navigate the traffic circle. Skip wished he could join them. He had hardly mentioned their running into the Yavapai Cultural Director and that's what Lilac had focused on.

"Didn't meet, we ran into her and Sam Sanchez as we left. For Christ's sake, Lilac."

"You do know she was jealous of you and her daughter, right? Personally, I would have shot you if it had been my child."

"Child? She's twenty-eight and it was two dates!" Skip argued, parking the idea that the elder Wathatewa might be interested. "You want to help Zula with Zebulon or bust my chops?" he snapped.

Lilac switched her attention to Kuul who was still imaginatively studying nothing out the window. "What were you doing?" she asked, swiveling her chair and punching him in the arm.

Kuul shrugged. "Fighting Apache?"

19

FEMALE FIREPOWER

LILAC HATED DRIVING DOWN I-17 TO PHOENIX. HER RUBICON Jeep was great on Sedona's backroads, but at seventy-five the soft top, plastic windows, and terrabite Baja tires made it sound like a jet engine on a tarmac. She couldn't even hear Karen Carpenter on Fun Oldies 100.9. However, she had decided helping Zula Ballsy trumped doing the bidding of a two-timing ex-boyfriend. She had known Zula long before she even met Skip Rhodes. Sister camaraderie was thicker than male BS.

Mooney Zuni Gallery and Gift Shop was located a block from Old Town Scottsdale. The southwest tchotchke market was cutthroat, and attracting customers with schlocky sounding names and sidewalk sales was the name of the game; which only partially excused the politically incorrect painted wooden Indian wearing a Sioux headdress and holding a bowl of candies outside the front door. Lilac took a red and white striped mint.

The only authentic Zuni pieces in the store were those worn by Terrance Mooney, Teresa to his old friends. She was heading directly to Terry's back office but was stopped by the overly decorated salesgirl behind the counter. The girl had more lemon colored beads in her hair than a cholla had yellow buds, and a wedge of saguaro spine sticking through a hole in one ear. She looked to be maybe twenty with sunburned shoulders as red as a miner's pecker after an all-nighter at Miss Kitty's. Lilac smelled aloe in the air.

"Can I help you?" the salesgirl said in an aggressively loud voice to get Lilac's attention. She had stepped from behind the central counter and was eyeing the pistol strapped on Lilac's hip.

Lilac followed her gaze and decided the girl's interest was a teaching opportunity. "It's a Glock," Lilac said, patting the gun. "I wasn't expecting any trouble today so I packed light. The G19 is popular with women. I was able to customize the grip to my hand. As a 9mm it's on the low end in firepower, but hey, as long as I aim straight, right?" Lilac snickered at the girl's silence and turned to head back to the owner's office.

"I prefer the Kimber K6," Lilac heard the girl say from behind. She was back behind her counter holding a K6 snub-nose revolver. Lilac recognized it as the lightest Magnum, good for petite-sized women with firearm experience, but still a hole-blasting Magnum. "It feels good and smooth in your hands, kind of sexy don't you think. Little kick, but nothing I can't handle," the salesgirl said. "Anything I can help you with?" she smiled politely.

"Very cool," Lilac said. *A chip off the old block*, she thought. "Lilac Williams, I'm here to see Terry. He knows I'm coming."

"Betsy Oakley. Let's just check," the girl said cutely, wrinkling her nose like a contestant answering a question at a beauty pageant. She put her K6 away and walked around to join Lilac. "What do you need from Terry?" she said walking toward his office.

Lilac fingered her stress-relieving anti-anxiety chakra bracelet. It had been a while since anyone had pulled a gun on her, even just for show. It had only happened twice while she'd been on the force. She couldn't believe she let this little hipster get the drop on her. And now the questions…

"… Hold on," Lilac said, stopping. She reached her left arm up over her head to her right ear and pulled her neck to her left, then did the same move from the other side. It immediately relieved the tension to her shoulders and back. The girl, Betsy, had watched nonchalantly.

"Trapezius Stretch. I do Yoga too. Guns will do it, won't they," Betsy said. "If you need to do a Cow pose, be my guest. The floors are clean."

"Oakley? Any relation?" Lilac asked more relaxed, her root chakra balanced and adrenal medulla under control. *This girl was a pretty cool customer.*

"Great-great-great-great aunt," Betsy confirmed, smiling and counting her fingers as she raised them to keep track. Lilac chuckled. The sharpshooting niece knocked on a door with a nameplate that read Terrance Mooney. They heard alto-pitched grumbling and then, "Come in."

Terry Mooney, previously Teresa Mooney, sat behind a white French provincial desk with carved legs of naked cherubs entwined in play. His platinum hair was stretched tightly over his scalp with a long ponytail hanging over a shoulder. A pair of Buddy Holly glasses was perched on his head. He smiled on seeing Lilac, clapped his hands with polished long nails, and rose. "It's been a while Honey, I was happy you called. Betsy this is…"

"…we met," Betsy said. She shook Lilac's shooting hand and excused herself, "I think I heard a customer."

"Doubtful," her boss said.

"Business not good?" Lilac asked after the salesgirl and firearms expert had left.

"It's okay. It's just off season and a weekday. It picks up in the fall and stays that way through March while the snowbirds are here. You didn't tell me what you called about?"

Lilac explained she was on a fishing expedition about disreputable shops and any that might be buying stolen antiquities.

"That's why I don't buy from the streets or online unless they're certified and the item comes with papers. You working a case? I thought you'd left all that ugly business behind after that misunderstanding with the DA."

Lilac never liked being reminded of why she'd left Phoenix and the PI business. The philandering DA had pulled strings and had her license revoked for misconduct. He was now the Deputy Mayor, so any chance of returning to the "ugly business" had long since gone out the window. Not that she wanted to, she was finding Yoga and firearms training in Sedona much more lucrative.

"No, I've got a friend with questions, and I said I'd help. I mentioned I knew a gallery owner down here. My friend has a friend who had a friend who might have had friends mixed up with the wrong people." She couldn't have been vaguer.

"That's a lot of *friends*," Terry mused. "Well, let's see, disreputable shops huh? You might have more luck with pawn shops and trading posts, the latter all have Indian pawn sections - a holdover from the old days. Most are good places. But even the Met in New York and the Getty in California have repatriated items to original owners. It kind of comes down to what you call stolen. When you get right down to it most antiquities aren't that well documented. They are only in the public because at some time someone took them from somewhere without permission. The Elgin marbles are the poster boy example. Have you ever been to Egypt?"

"No, why?"

Terry gave her a sarcastic look, "How many mummies have you seen?"

"You know what I mean," Lilac said. "I'm not talking about legitimate museums or world-renowned galleries. I mean any local businesses that knowingly buy something obtained illegally or that just don't bother to document the origin and original bill of sale."

"Legitimate? What's legitimate? Take Indiana Jones, he was stealing, right? And teaching at Princeton...or was it Columbia? I know what you mean, I'm just making a point that it's sometimes hard to judge what's right when it comes to collecting artifacts," Terry said.

"Come on, Terry."

He sighed and continued, "Look, you can break the trafficking process down into three stages, each with a different set of players and different level of risk. It starts with the looter. Here in Arizona, the independent cuss with a shovel and compass. His risk is high, and he will eventually get caught. He's just too stupid to know it. And he doesn't make that much comparatively speaking. Whatever he finds of value he'll pass on to a smuggler who has almost an equal chance of getting arrested. The Feds and other agencies have gotten really good at breaking that stage up. They know if they break that part of the chain the other ends are out of business. The smuggler will clear a little more but not as much as you think."

"And the last stage is the buyer, right, the stage I've asked about?" Lilac interjected.

"Not quite, they're not really part of the *process*, they're the end. I'd classify the rogue shop buyer you've asked about as a smuggler, they're likely turning around and selling it to a wholesaler instead of a collector," Terry stated. "The last stage in the process is laundering. It's the best stage to be in. They're the wholesalers...or the upper middlemen if you prefer. Their risk is low. They buy for pennies from the smugglers, turning the goods over fast at fantastic prices to collectors and unsuspecting and hungry auction houses and museums in countries with few controls. They are almost impossible to catch. Which is too bad, because without them there would be no looters or smugglers...at least not to any scale."

"So, the local galleries, shops, trading posts - the dubious ones, they don't factor in?"

"I didn't say that," Terry said. "It's just not a big part of the problem. There are certainly those that buy without proper documentation, but they're few. The risk-reward equation doesn't work for any retailer that wants to be in operation for long. None I know of would display anything that wasn't legit, as you mean it. Whoever you're onto may be selling to a pawn or trader, but they're more likely working directly with a smuggler who's shipping elsewhere."

It sounded complicated To Lilac. "Why not consolidate the first three parts, the looting, smuggling, and wholesaling, or at least the first two? Wouldn't that be easier?"

"Yes and no," Terry replied. "It's probably happening, especially with the dark web. It would make sense for a looter if they were smart and technologically savvy enough – most aren't, again they're out there with a compass and axe. For a smuggler or wholesaler, adding the actual looting to their operation would just mean more risk and harder work for little gain."

There was a knock at the door, and Betsy poked her head inside, "We have a customer interested in the silver butterfly piece in the locked cabinet. You want to talk with them?" Terry looked at Lilac.

"Thanks, Terry. It's good to see you again and I appreciate the lesson," Lilac said standing up.

They shook hands and headed out with Betsy. Terry went to unlock the case and make the sale. The customer was an aging prom queen in her late forties with fake breasts, high heeled boots, and a feathered cowboy hat. Her elderly male companion wearing a blue Brooks Brothers blazer was sitting in a chair holding a portable oxygen tank...typical Scottsdale vacationers.

"I hope for his children's sake he has a prenup," Betsy commented. "All the wheezing, I was afraid he was going to croak before I got the chair out.

Lilac smiled, "You ever get to Sedona bring your Kimber and we'll see who's the better shot. I've got an agreement with a range outside Cottonwood."

"Look forward to it. I know that range well," Annie's niece winked and blew imaginary smoke from her finger.

· · ·

Lilac had an hour to kill before lunch and decided shopping was in order. Sedona was small and its businesses targeted wealthy tourists with expensive t-shirts, bike rentals, hiking gear, and jewelry shops; sure, there was a *Dahling It's You* in Uptown, but no Victoria Secret, no Dillard's, not even a Bed Bath and Beyond. Even a pistol-toting outdoor yoga instructor needed some soft things now and again at reasonable prices.

She was meeting a friend from her PI days, a Phoenix PD detective, at a trendy restaurant. Skip hadn't asked her to, *he wouldn't even if he'd thought of it*, but she planned on having her friend run a check on Zebulon just in case he had been mixed up in something. Even though she believed it unlikely, her law enforcement background had taught her to trust her instincts only after they were confirmed.

Hashknife Kitchen was the in-vogue place for brunch. On Hayden Boulevard, it wasn't far from where she'd shopped. Visiting Scottsdale was like rafting down the Colorado, around every curve there was something new; just like the Colorado dredged its banks so did the city of Scottsdale constantly widen its roads for more commerce. There were so many tired Californians priced out of the uber-expensive L.A. market that developers were calling Phoenix - Crane City. New condos and shopping malls were springing up daily on what had been open desert.

John Cooper, her PPD friend, was sitting at a patio table. It was a cooler day in Phoenix, meaning the thermometer was reading double not triple digits. Overhead misters were running full speed, the droplets evaporating before reaching the tables. Coop was dressed in a flowered Hawaiian shirt and smart dress slacks, wearing a smart straw fedora. Ever the urbane ladies' man, he stood up upon seeing her, placing the fedora on the table.

"Lilac, glad you called," he pulled out her chair, placing his hand on her shoulder with a gentle push as she scooted in. She didn't mind the contact; they'd certainly done a lot more.

"Slumming down here in the valley." Coop said more as a comment than a question. "I see you're prepared as always. You should have been a boy scout," he said nodding toward her glock.

"The scouts wouldn't let me in. I think I scared them," she joked. "A girl can't be too careful in the big city. How you been, Coop?"

"Haven't been shot lately," he said cagily. Lilac started to apologize, but he waved it off. They opened up menus with burned Hashknife brands on the cover, which in sleek nouveau Scottsdale was a Japanese Yoshihiro blade with two slashing flames from a spiraling phoenix.

Coop's comment about being shot was their version of reliving old times. Their professional relationship had evolved into casual sex when she had been working in Phoenix. Neither of them had wanted anything serious. She'd met Coop during his investigation of a robbery that dovetailed one of her divorce cases. Lilac had been surveilling the husband for her client, when the wife's nail shop was vandalized. It ended up being kids, but at the time the husband had been the primary person of interest. Lilac and Coop hit it off immediately, her volatile nature contrasting nicely with his laid back surfer style.

The waiter arrived and took their orders. Coop had the California Cool, hashbrowns with avocado and a side of melon; Lilac had the Southwest Burner with green chilies and spicy pork. The server refilled Coop's huckleberry lemonade, and Lilac ordered the mimosa flight. *What the heck, she wasn't on anyone's clock.*

"Seriously, how are you Coop?"

"It's been four years Lilac, *both boys are fine*," he whispered, scanning the other customers like he was revealing a state secret.

"I should have had the safety on," she groaned.

"Lilac, I'm good. Let it go. Are you here for lunch with an old friend or business?" Coop said changing the subject while mixing the huckleberry puree settled at the bottom of his glass.

"Both actually," Lilac said.

Their romance had ended during a partially clothed impromptu yoga lesson. Horsing around in Coop's apartment Lilac had suggestively demonstrated the Happy Baby pose by lying on her back and pulling her knees to her chest, feet in the air. Jeans and a sports bra were the only clothing she still had on. Unfortunately, she was still locked and loaded, and her gun had gone off as Coop playfully assumed a different pose on his knees in front of her raised legs. His shirt was on but no pants. The result had been an embarrassed, bleeding cop with only one good testicle being wheeled past his neighbors to a waiting ambulance. The EMTs had radioed in an officer down code, and half the force was waiting for them at the hospital. Physically he'd recovered with everything still functional, but the legend lived on at PPD.

"I'm all yours. What do you need?" Coop asked. His double meaning wasn't lost on her. She'd been the one to call it quits.

That was the problem with clever cops; their inquiries were more a series of verbal chess moves than direct questions. Lilac wasn't ready to go down that road again, at least not yet. Pocketing the personal offer for a rainy day, she explained what she *was* after. She wanted to check whether PPD or any other Valley agencies had a record of Zebulon Ballsy or knew of any trafficking investigations dating back three years.

"I don't expect you'll find anything," she said. "I knew him, and he was a good kid. I just want to make sure we haven't missed anything."

"Give me a few days," Coop said. "It won't take long to run a background, but I'll need to check with the FBI and Interior on the trafficking question. They're pretty closed-mouthed on anything that's open, so don't get your hopes up." Coop paused. "Wait, who's *'we'*?"

"Huh?"

"You said *'we'*. That's plural."

"Just a figure of speech," she said, realizing her slip and covering it up. She didn't want to get into telling him about Skip. They were both old news anyway.

Coop smiled, "Your business. But you do know Sedona's not that far, right. *We* should get together more often."

"How's your hash?" Lilac asked, downing the mini raspberry flavored mimosa and itching her nose at the bubbles.

20

JOYS OF HYPERMOBILITY

IT HAD TAKEN SOME CONVINCING, AND ENLISTING ZULA BALLSY, before Skip Rhodes caved and agreed to take her for a hike along Oak Creek. Doe Mesa had been Sapphire Sky's first choice. Skip had vainly argued it was unlikely they would see any mule deer...like that was Sky's point. "Then take me swimming out Oak Creek," she had countered. All she wanted was to get to know the big lunk better and escape from Reggie for an afternoon. Hopefully the extra two inches she'd trimmed from her worn cutoffs would make an impression.

Sky wasn't exactly conventional. She was always open to anything new, but Landish was increasingly pushing her ethical boundaries. The man could be shady, and, as she was realizing, insincere. She'd been stimulated by the cold way Skip had handled the Doctor at the bar. Despite her carefully crafted free-spirit façade, deep down Sky was attracted to the strong silent type; she sensed Skip walked the walk instead of talked. Even now, he'd hardly said three words on their hike toward Cathedral Rock along Oak Creek. The shorter cutoffs hadn't seemed to make a difference. His longest string of words had been *"How you doing?"* to an older couple of hikers down for the day from Flagstaff.

They reached a secluded spot where the creek made a bend. Storm water coming off Cathedral Rock had dug a wash, spilling tons of rocks into the creek bottom. The series of low waterfalls tumbling over the barely submerged polished stones created a romantic setting. The remnants of an old tire swing hung from a sycamore tree. Too bad it wasn't usable; Sky would have loved the freedom of swinging out over the water.

Zula had packed a lunch and they decided to eat sitting on a rocky shelf that overhung the corner of the creek and wash. With little rain, the wash was dry, and Oak Creek was lower than normal. Sky had taken off her shoes and was dancing her feet in the cold stream. Her nails were purple today with a fleck of pink sparkle centered in her big toes.

Rhodes asked her about Landish's plan. *At least he had asked something.*

"He plans to take his members up top Bell Rock, and we all leap into space. The *Obiekinobidoans* will be there in their ship to transport us aboard. Reggie planned on doing it on a solstice until he learned there are only two each year, and the next one isn't for another month. He says it doesn't matter, he can communicate the change of date to the President of *Obiekinobido*," Sky explained.

"And you're buying that?" Skip asked. He handed her a peach from Zula's bag.

Sky took a bite before answering, pink juice ran down her chin. She wiped it with her index finger and sucked it clean. "God, that's fresh! Perfectly ripe." She finished licking between her fingers like a cat, her eyes all the time on Skip.

"It's from her own tree. Zula has a small orchard at the retreat," he said, trying to ignore her sanitary work in progress. "You don't plan on jumping, do you?"

Sky lampooned his disbelief, "Why wouldn't I? I told you I've been up there." She glanced skyward. Skip didn't say anything, he just shrugged. She coyly smiled in return.

He handed her a peanut butter and honeysuckle jam sandwich, interested to see what she did with it. Her double-jointed abilities and feline hygiene demonstration had piqued his curiosity. She ate her sandwich, sucking the peanut butter from her lips like she was applying a heavy coat of Revlon, and finished with her tongue licking the oily residue. She saw he was watching her, so she twisted her arm with her palm facing her back and handed him the empty plastic baggie.

"I'd heard of Reggie before I met him. To be honest I went to New Mexico looking for him. I'd been in Kanab at a silly UFO convention and ran across a member of his Church selling subscriptions to his online Atmospheric Interpretations newsletter. I was looking for a change and to get out of Utah."

"What's wrong with Utah," Skip asked. "It's pretty up there."

"It is," Sky said, staring at him intently. Skip felt she was deciding how much of her personal story to trust him with. She flipped a switch and the stare turned back to a twinkling gleam.

"After my abduction and change, my parents and our friends couldn't accept it. They felt I was possessed. Even though they're Church of Latter Day Saints and my father is convinced he's going to heaven to live like a King when he dies, he didn't believe me. He kept demanding I marry a Mormon caterer in Moab. He'd arranged it. I refused, things got tough between us, and he threw me out when I told him I believed in reincarnation and had been a gay Black Rabbi in my previous life."

Skip couldn't help but laugh, "A gay, Black Rabbi. Were you a democrat, too?"

"I made that part up...the Rabbi, not the reincarnation. That I do believe. But it was the last straw for Dad."

"And *Reggie* is better?"

"He doesn't judge and that's big."

"How did he decide Sedona was an intergalactic hub?" Skip asked, hoping a shared scientific reference would make things more comfortable. It didn't.

Sky frowned. *He was patronizing her.* "He talks to them. And the cousin that you don't think exists told him about Sedona."

"Okay, then who is he...the cousin?" Skip asked.

Sky was fishing in her bag for the last avocado chip. "Haven't met him. According to Reggie, he's not a believer, a bit of a loner. But he knows about Native culture and magic ceremonies. It's where Reggie gets his local mumbo jumbo as he calls it."

"What's he do?"

"The cousin?" Sky thought about it a minute. She wasn't sure why Rhodes was so curious about someone she didn't even know, not even his name. People had relatives all over. "Not sure, maybe he's a guide like you," she teased. She hadn't brought him out here for a test...at least not on Landish and his family.

Sky was tiring of his questions. Dusting her hands clean she stood up facing him. She raised and twisted her knee, her foot touching her smooth belly. *He was paying attention to her now.* She grasped the bottom of her purple T-shirt with her matching-colored toes. His jaw dropped as she pulled the shirt over her head revealing plump enough breasts to strain her skimpy bra. She quickly slipped off her cutoff jeans. "Time for a swim," she laughed at his open mouth and high school blush, sure that he was studying her from behind as she turned and tiptoed into the water.

Skip watched her wade into the middle of the creek, the water knee deep, with only the bra and black bikini panties between her and the great outdoors. "Oooh, it feels wonderful! Come on in!" She stepped into deeper water and floated into a pool downstream. Skip watched her go under and come back up. Buoyancy didn't seem to be an issue. She untied her long hair, swinging it back and forth, water droplets catching the rays of sunlight coming through the trees. *What a strange girl,* he thought.

•••

The Director hung up the phone. His wholesaler had called with another order from an Asian collector. He'd just sent off the Hohokam necklace and several pieces of Mogollon pottery. The latter came from a remote site outside Payson, Arizona. The Mogollon People had made their homes in the higher elevations of eastern Arizona and western New Mexico over a thousand years ago. Like the *Sinagua* and *Anasazi*, they had disappeared by the 1400s, leaving their ruins to be pillaged by whoever found them. The later tribes, the Navajo, Apache, and Yavapai had left them alone, afraid of the ghosts. Unless someone stumbled upon the Director's find, which had happened with his site in Sedona, there was enough there to fill pottery orders for years.

Business was picking up. The orders and requests for bids were becoming more and more specific. He had explained to the wholesaler that his risks and costs increased if he had to discover and excavate different sites. So, he needed to charge more. The Director also needed more help if the orders continued to grow and increase in frequency. Without extra assistance he would have to be pickier about the items he bid on. His contact had assured him more money would not be a problem.

The Director had convinced his little brother to enter the business, at least tangentially until his other scheme played out. He had hoped to persuade him to keep a lower profile, but the two siblings who had grown up apart had different personalities. His kid brother was more brash and employed a more slash and burn system. He had never lucked into a stable situation like his older brother had with his last foster family. The younger brother had been on his own since he was fourteen. With no formal education or support he had scammed and conned his way through life by making fast money and skipping his scenes.

The brother's current swindle was to take collections for his terrestrial Church, and make his followers believe he had disappeared from a vortex on a journey through space and time. The Director had begrudgingly admitted it was a brilliant scheme for Sedona but had argued the high profile and vanishing would negate his future earning potential in the area…and his usefulness to the Director's business. As a compromise they decided he would relocate and start an antiquities franchise, the Director liked to think of it as such, somewhere in New Mexico. The loot from the naïve alien worshipers would set him up. That would help solve the Director's inventory and cash flow problems; there were more than enough orders to fill for both of them.

They were still discussing a solution to another problem. Skip Rhodes and his girlfriend were poking around and asking questions about antiquity trafficking after Zebulon Ballsy's remains had been discovered.

That kid had been a pain in his ass that he thought he had taken care of three years ago.

The Director knew Rhodes, not well, but enough to understand the man was stubborn and capable of fixating on a bone like a starved wolf. If Rhodes kept it up they would have to terminate his snooping just as he had ended Ballsy's. The man had already been given two loud warnings that could easily have been more harshly applied and still hadn't backed off. Time would tell what further action was required.

21

RIP THE TAIL OFF THE JACKASS

TEQUILA MOON, **THE MONTHLY PARTY AT THE SANDS, STARTED** inside the Lazy *SOB* before sundown. The revelry usually ended at the outside fire pit whenever the last person left. The warmth of a fire corralled guests once the sun set; the air outside turning cool and crisp even in mid spring. The relaxed gatherings were popular with Zula's friends; an invite was needed from the showgirl or one of her close friends. Visitors staying at her retreat were welcomed. Tequila Moon was a time to kick off the boots, chill in good company, and put the world's and one's own troubles aside.

Skip intentionally arrived late, waiting until after sunset when he knew the party had moved outside. A crowded bar with well-lubricated customers wasn't his scene, and most of his friends likewise chose to come later anyway. Outdoors was a good way to end a day, with the stars overhead and the breeze cooling the dry air. Being mesmerized by a crackling fire with orange flames lighting the inky Arizona darkness relaxed him. A sweet Don Julio margarita stuck in the cup holder of a camp chair made everything seem just right. He even enjoyed the diverse company that gathered at Zula's. *Once a month for a few hours*. And if he didn't it was easy to wander off unnoticed whenever the spell broke.

He could tell by one look that tonight wouldn't deliver the serenity, peace, and comradery he sought. Sure, the fire was blazing, and there was the usual cast of characters: people he knew and was used to. He scanned the small crowd. Agnes Speer, the librarian, had taken him up on his invite and brought Mustang Timmy. Apparently, their date had worked out. They were sitting in molded Adirondack chairs below the lotus tree talking with Zula. Mustang had his feet propped on his walker and was using a stick to scratch something in the dirt beside his chair. Lilac was on the porch steps with Kuul and a surprising visitor, Toni Wathatewa. Toni and Lilac, together, spelled trouble, though not with as big of a T as Landish and his groupies standing around the fire pit roasting hot dogs.

Skip was planning a smooth retreat when Zula caught his eye and waved him over.

"We found him here," Skip heard Mustang explaining as he walked up. Mustang had drawn the trail into Red Spirit Canyon and etched topo lines illustrating the switchbacks and ridgeline. "Never would have found him if Puddles hadn't wandered off to take a pee. That man wouldn't have survived Inchon, all that water, the Chinese would have shot his pecker off sure as shootin'. On shore you couldn't take a piss without getting blown up by a landmine."

Agnes Speer patted Mustang on his good shoulder to calm him down, acting like they were an old married couple. The other shoulder was still in a sling from his fight over the last piece of chess pie at the Sedona Winds buffet. "Mr. Speer had a urinary frequency problem too. He had to carry an empty Dr. Pepper bottle whenever we took a road trip...even to Walmart. I told him for years he needed to have his prostate checked. The humidity in North Carolina doesn't help...keeps you full of water. My goodness the man got to where he was up four or five times a night. I sure got tired of cleaning up his misfires in the dark. We finally installed one of those LED lights beside the toilet you could step on. Changed my life."

Zula rolled her eyes at Skip and politely nodded to Agnes. He could tell she'd heard enough of Korea and male incontinence.

"Agnes here was telling me about your meeting at the library," Zula said, hoping to open up a new avenue of discussion.

"I like to read," Skip quipped. "I can attest to that," Agnes confirmed.

"What do you read into him?" Zula said, pointing to Landish and his crew. "It's a nice peaceful night, hope you don't continue the lesson you were teaching him in the *SOB*."

Skip took a long pull of his pink potion, "You never know, some people just don't learn as easily as others."

Mustang had followed their looks toward Landish whose broad back was silhouetted against the campfire. "That the sidewinder Kempdinger was talking about? The one planning to fly off Bell Rock?"

"One and the same," Zula said. "I'd kick him out of here if it wasn't for the money he's spending."

"Mr. Speer never had two nickels to rub together," Agnes lamented. "County extension officers don't make squat. Not like Gladys' husband, God rest his soul. He sold suppositories to prisons. Made a killing. That's why they could retire to Sedona."

Skip had been ignoring the smart conversation and focusing on Landish. The fat man was holding two hot dogs in one hand and gesticulating to his minions with the other. The pimple-faced kid with aluminum foil accessories was trying to squeeze mustard on the dogs, but Landish kept flapping his arms, the mustard squirting all over. The good Doctor hadn't yet noticed the yellow stripes on his jacket. Maybe, Skip thought, he should go over and clean up the mess.

"I think I'll go check out the fire. It doesn't look hot enough," he told Zula. She gave him a harsh look. Skip wasn't sure whether it was a warning to lay off her customer or irritation at being left alone with Agnes and Mustang.

Sky was standing by Landish and had watched Skip talking with Zula Ballsy and then head toward the fire. She could tell by his look he was coming to finish what he had started the other night at the bar. The strong silent types never went around when they could go through. Straddling the fence between the two men wasn't where she wanted to be, but that's where she was. Once again, a strong man was forcing her to make a choice, just like her dad. Landish was spellbinding his children with his planned exploits to *Obikenibeduo. Nothing new.* She slipped away to head Skip off. He saw her coming and stopped.

"Nice night for a moonlight swim," Sky whispered leaning close and looping her arm through Skip's. "Unless you want to introduce me to your friends at the porch?" She had seen the big Native and tall red-haired woman around and knew the three of them were close. *How close?* The attractive Native woman she hadn't seen before, maybe she was here with Skip's friend.

Skip glanced at Lilac and Wathatewa. He didn't know why Toni was here other than she was friends with Zula who donated regularly to the cultural center. He doubted Kuul had brought her, but the big Mayan did have a reputation as a player. He remembered Lilac had intimated Toni was interested in him. *Maybe she'd invited her.* The Yavapai woman had noticed his glance and subtly tipped her beer to him; hard to tell what she was thinking. Toni was confusing, but she certainly looked good in a pair of jeans and western-style shirt. Whatever the reason, introducing the younger Sky to the Yavapai elder and Lilac wasn't a place he cared to go.

While he was swapping gazes with Wathatewa, Landish had turned and was calling Sky back. *Maybe she had the fat man's Skittles.* With his back to the fire, there was just enough light to see him wipe his paws on his jacket. *What a pig.* The impatient demanding voice beckoning Sky grated him.

"Bring your friend. I'd like to talk to him," Landish yelled.

"Let's go see what he wants," Skip said in a cold voice. Sky watched his eyes narrow as they turned their attention to Landish. She could sense his body tightening.

"You do what you want. I'm heading back to my room," Sky said, ignoring Reggie. The two would have to settle their differences themselves. "Why don't you join me?" she asked, taking a last shot at breaking up the storm. Skip had already released her arm and was moving toward the fire.

Landish was standing with his hands on his hips waiting. He'd taken off his stained jacket and given it to Aluminum Boy who was dabbing it with tonic he'd poured from a bottle. Skip guessed the sloppy man spilled a lot; he planned on finding out soon enough. The rest of the "Church deacons" were scattered around the bonfire roasting marshmallows and drinking margaritas from plastic cups. A girl who looked even younger than Sky was rearranging the logs into a tepee with a poker. The flames were bouncing, and sparks were popping upwards.

The two men met halfway from where Skip had left Sky. Landish had decided to match Skip's aggressiveness. "Did you say something wrong?" Landish smirked, referring to Sky's leaving. "She can be difficult."

Skip wasn't in a mood to jerk around. "I tried looking you and your cousin up online. I couldn't find a thing, except for a Batman Landish who planned to jump off a battleship in his shorts. That wouldn't be you, would it?" Skip let the accusation hang in the air a moment. "Jumping off a boat...jumping off a rock, it sounds similar."

"And who are *you,* Mr. Rhodes?" Landish countered. "You've only been here a few years, right? What did *Skip Rhodes* do before h up from nowhere and offering tours?"

Skip realized he hadn't been the only one doing background research. Landish had been poking around his history as well. That wouldn't do, even though his chances of finding anything out were nil.

"The Church of Astrological Departure appears to be new. I didn't find much on it either, other than a few notices in Utah and New Mexico for *Awakening* meetings. I'm asking again, nicely, who are you?"

Skip had moved squarely in front of the Doctor and tapped his flabby chest.

Landish didn't back off. He locked eyes with Skip and raised his voice loud enough for everyone to hear, "How was your hike along the creek? I wouldn't pay much attention to whatever *she* told you. Did the skinny dipping cool you both off?" Landish cocked his head triumphantly. He intended to embarrass the man before his friends. "She's a sweet kid. Kinky in a loose kind of way. And the contortion tricks...a pleasure to be around. But you know that, right?"

Skip's right fist moved fast and hard, sinking deep into Landish's hot dog filled gut. The Doctor doubled over expelling a blast of stale pickle relish air. Skip reached his left arm across the front of the sputtering man's chest and whipped the back of his clenched fist up into his double chin. He followed that with a solid punch square on Landish's bulbous nose. Blood splattered on both of them. The acrid smell of fresh blood and the fury deep inside him had taken hold. It had been a long time since he'd lost control. Before Landish could fall Skip drove a knee into his groin. He grasped the screaming larger man by his neck holding him up. Landish was gagging and bleeding profusely. One of the deacons stepped up to intercede but quickly backed away when Skip stared at him with eyes that could only be described as demonic.

Skip was keeping Landish upright with one hand and pulled his other elbow back preparing to transfer his full force onto the man's already mangled nose. Done correctly and keeping his forearm rigid he'd drive cartilage and bone into softer brain matter. He wanted to kill him.

As his fist started forward his arm suddenly stopped, and his legs were taken out from below. He crashed to the ground with an unconscious Landish landing on top and then rolling off. Before he could jump up Kuul had sat on his chest, grabbing his arms and pinning them to the ground. Lilac was standing over them and threw a drink in his face. Skip thrashed, swearing and threatening them both, but the stoic Mayan didn't move or say anything. It wasn't clear to him whether Skip even knew where he was. Lilac helped the cowering deacons and Aluminum Boy get a groggy beaten Landish to his feet. They led him away, holding him up with his arms draped over their shoulders.

"Next time it won't be so easy," the Doctor moaned.

Finally Skip stopped struggling and his heart rate slowed. Lilac was wiping his face with a wet towel, he felt feverish. She was trying to talk him down, but it was clear he didn't understand her. When Landish's crew was out of sight, Kuul let him up but clasped him in a bear hug as he stood. Skip's eyes were wide and darting around, like an animal sensing danger. He was only vaguely aware of where he was and not of what he'd done.

Toni Wathatewa was standing off to the side studying him, "That doctor's right about one thing...*who are you?*"

• • •

Later that night Skip sat by the creek in front of his cabin. Kuul had brought him home. He hadn't asked Skip anything, just walked him to his cabin where they'd sat on the porch without speaking. After an hour, Kuul had asked if he was okay. When Skip nodded, the Mayan explained what had happened to his muddled friend. All Skip remembered was throwing the first punch. The Mayan had told him, *"Get some sleep brother,"* and left.

Instead of sleep, he knew where that would take him; Skip had gotten a cold six-pack from the cabin, putting the beer in the stream to keep it cold. He tried washing Landish's blood from his shirt, rubbing it on a wet rock in the water. All it did was diffuse the bright red drops to pink splotches. He was on his third *cerveza* when his memory of the fight and how viciously he had responded returned. Landish was scum and the man had been stupid insulting him and disparaging the girl, but those weren't excuses for sliding back, not an excuse to lethally attack. *If Kuul and Lilac hadn't stopped him...*

He needed to uncover what Landish was really up to and expose him, but there were better ways to go about it.

Skip was reluctant to revisit his past, but he didn't see any other way to quickly get the reliable intel he needed. He glared at his phone, it was an unwelcome reminder of who Skip Rhodes had been and there'd be a price. He wanted to throw it in the creek, raising his arm, but instead dropped it on the ground – the lighted numbers he'd been entering staring up at him. *There might not be any going back.* He gave in; completing the sequence of numbers he knew by memory, listened, pushed another set of numbers and then waited until the electronic tone stopped. Static followed and then five short clicks.

"It's been a while," said the voice on the other end of the satellite feed bouncing through a series of impossible to trace connections. "You entered a system yellow code. I'm sure you remember that."

Skip stared at the phone. At first, he didn't say a word, knowing he'd made a mistake, knowing his troubling dreams would revisit him when he fell asleep, "I need some information. Reginald Landish, but that's probably an alias..." he began explaining what he needed.

"Give me a few days. Are you coming back?" the scrambled voice replied after Skip finished.

The man hung up before Skip had a chance to answer.

22

BREAKING BAD

"**P**ISTOL PRACTICE AND YOGA?" THE SLIGHTLY INEBRIATED tourist from Salt Lake City was reading from the business card. It wasn't yet noon and she was at the bar ordering a third round of drinks. She and her girlfriends seated beside the pool table were on their annual Mormon Moms' Away Weekend. Suzy homemaker had struck up a conversation with the local seated on a metal stool chatting with the bartender.

"Sure. They each satisfy different parts of the inner being," the local explained. "The human psyche has a lot of parts, and they all need to be exercised from time to time. There's a metaphysical balance to life in general, and our individual lives in particular, that needs to be consciously maintained. Ignore one part and it eventually forces its way out. That's not healthy."

Suzy thought about her husband Roy, exercising, and certain parts being ignored. The boys and little Suzy kept her maternal parts busy, but the rest was left to chance. Lately, the chances hadn't been that good. She was hoping for a little excitement, maybe guns and stretching would do the trick, or else she might have to take a closer look at the friendly bartender.

Lilac was meeting Skip at PJ's Bar to update him on her trip to Phoenix, but as usual the big lug was late. At least he had called and explained he had another of his bad nights. When they were partners in arms, he would have a nightmare at least once a week. He refused to tell her what he dreamt. He'd say, *I can't remember*, and roll over. It had been maddeningly obvious he didn't want to break the seal around *his* inner being and open up. His silence was the reason they were now just friends.

David the bartender delivered five more house margaritas to the curious tourist from the shining city on the lake and a diet Coke for Lilac. "You should listen to her, Miss. Last month we had a German lady climb up Thunder Mountain in flip flops to practice Yoga. She couldn't find her way back down and her phone was out of juice. Luckily a hot air balloon tour saw her and notified the Fire Department, otherwise who knows how long she would have been up there."

Suzy liked being called "Miss". Roy called her "Mom" at home. "I'm missing your point," she said, slurping the premade frozen slush David had poured from a repurposed milk jug. She tickled the straw with her tongue and batted her eyes. *A little flirting was harmless enough,* she told herself.

"Well," David continued, "if she'd had a gun, she could have at least fired a shot that someone would have heard." He winked at Lilac; helping regulars was part of his job description. She also advertised on the back of PJ's menu.

"It does sound fun. What else do you do for kicks around here?" she grinned at David. "It's kind of outside what I'd do at home with the kids, but what are vacations for? Let me talk with my girlfriends. It'd be great if you could fit us in this afternoon," she said to Lilac. "We were going for a hike, but these margaritas are going to our heads. I'd hate to get lost like Frau Flip Flop and have to call you for help," Suzy giggled at David, then headed back to her table carrying cinco margaritas between her fingers.

Lilac wasn't sure about their mixing alcohol and firearms, but she had bills to pay. "I offer a group discount," Lilac called after her. The woman turned her head and yelled back *Thanks*, sloshing half the margaritas on her hands.

"Thanks for the plug, David," she said as the woman delivered the drinks to her friends. "Looks like I might make some decent dinero today," she said nodding at the excited group of *Mormon Moms Gone Bad* talking by the pool table. "I'm guessing their conservative husbands won't be happy when they return home with an amateur firearm rating. That kind of thing is reserved for the boys up there, right?"

"Not a problem, just remember your tab. And you're right about women's rights in Utah."

Partying at PJ's before lunch said a lot about the kind of weekend the Tabernacle ladies were after. A little on the seedy side, for upscale Sedona anyway, the owner took pride in the sticky concrete floors, plastic encased menus with dried salsa stains, his collection of antique neon beer lights, and his fondness for hiring waitresses with colorful hair and big tattoos. Wednesdays were Harley Night for bored business execs playing Easy Rider in their retirement. Most everyone else, including Lilac and the next door veterinarian, came for the buck-fifty Bud lights. Not exactly Studio 54, but for the Mormon ladies colorful enough to let them brag about their walk on the wild side to their King James Bible study compadres back in SLC.

Technically PJ's was in the unincorporated community of the Village of Oak Creek, VOC in the local vernacular, fifteen miles from the overpriced chimichangas and t-shirt hawkers in Uptown Sedona. She was meeting Skip there because VOC was the gateway to Jacks Canyon, off of which Zebulon had been found. Despite the "success" of their last visit, *they got out alive*; the twin idiots had decided to revisit the shooting gallery again for a more thorough investigation. That is if they ever showed up.

Right on cue Skip walked through the door, waving as he spotted her. It had been two days since Tequila Moon when he'd blindly beaten the daylights out of Landish. First impression, he looked like hell. As he got closer, she apologized to those in hell. His blood-strained eyes, matted hair, and the stains on his shirt, the same shirt he'd been wearing when she last saw him, said he'd suffered more than just losing a little sleep. Self-recrimination is a bitch. Kuul, the faithful companion, followed close behind, probably to catch his friend if he fell. Lilac moved to an open table and the two boys joined her.

"You look like a Pomeranian that slept with a bobcat," she said.

Kuul headed to the bar to order a couple of Bloody Marys. He chuckled hearing Lilac's diagnosis, "More like a scared hunting dog that ran away from a grizzly and spent two days licking its emotional wounds, howling at the moon, and draining a bottle of tequila."

Even David the bartender, who'd overhead, laughed. Skip leaned his chair back on two legs, opening his mouth to make a pithy rejoinder. His iffy equilibrium sent him backwards crashing onto the concrete floor. Fortunately, he landed on his shoulders, not his head, which was still pounding from Kuul's prematurely waking him from a drunken slumber.

"Jesus, are you okay?" David yelled.

Skip had righted himself and was inspecting the chair. "You ever mop this place? What's wrong with this chair?"

"Once a month and nothing," David answered, seeing Skip was no worse for wear...and he sure was worn.

"Legs not that steady today?" Lilac teased. Skip's peppermint candy eyes didn't react to her taunt. No cold stare or charming grin this time, just a sad look, and she guessed a rolling stomach and foggy brain. It wasn't hard to see he'd spent the last two days regretting his loss of control with Landish. *Still...there seemed to be something more bothering him.*

"What'd you find out in Phoenix with your gallery contact?" he brusquely asked. Kuul set a Bloody Mary in front of him with sliced jalapenos floating on the top. Lilac wanted to tell him to get his act together and they'd talk, but she bit her tongue. She shook her head as he emptied half a bottle of tabasco into his glass and downed a third of the drink.

"Feel better?"

"Getting there," he said, then downed the rest of the drink and started fishing out the peppers. "Phoenix?" he growled, blowing hot stale air between his teeth as the jalapeños hit home.

Lilac's empathy meter was crashing. She was ready to slap the moron and storm out. Then she thought about Zula and Zebulon and the whole point of her trip south. "I didn't find out much, but my contact provided a 101 on artifact trafficking." She coolly relayed what she had learned about the smuggling process. Skip seemed to not be paying attention, showing an astonishingly poor display of hand-eye coordination as he tried to fork the last soggy pepper.

She gritted her teeth and grimaced at Kuul, "If Zeb did run into someone, it was probably a local looter selling whatever he found to someone who immediately passed it on to a bigger fish. If that's what happened, and that's two big ifs, our chances of tracking them down three years after the fact are pretty much zero. And Terry said it's doubtful any galleries or shops would have been involved."

"So, a dead end?" Kuul said. Neither one of them knew if Skip had followed what she said. He was now spooning leftover jalapeno seeds from the bottom of his glass.

"Maybe," Lilac said thinking. "From what he said it does seem possible. Maybe even probable that Zeb stumbled on a looter or something he shouldn't have. Especially given the granary Sasse told you about. It just doesn't make sense he was out there riding for fun and slipped. There are too many problems with the scene; the placement of the bike, the broken spokes you two found, pot shards around his body, and the fact he fell to begin with. Not to mention you guys being shot at. There are too many questions."

"So, Zebulon might have been involved in something?" Skip finally spoke, making a baseless leap from "stumbling onto" to "being involved."

Lilac hadn't planned on telling him about her lunch with Cooper, at least not unless Coop's checking turned something up. Skip and Coop hadn't met, but he knew about him, and that they were in a relationship that ended when she left the valley for Sedona. She stared at Skip; he still looked like a mangled lap dog. *He deserved it.* Since he'd been so rude, she decided to go ahead and torment him a bit more.

"I met with John Cooper and asked if he could check on any investigations into smuggling in the area," she said matter-of-factly. "We had a delightful lunch in Scottsdale," she added.

She saw a flare of suspicion in Skip's eyes, "How's he doing? Still wearing baggy pants?" Lilac had made the mistake of telling him about the unfortunate yoga incident. She remembered thinking she should at least warn him.

"He's doing great. Everything is working just fine. He's going to ask around about Zeb and any ongoing investigations. We made a date to hook back up."

Skip turned a yellowish green and burped; the jalapenos and tomato juice had taken their toll. Lilac pushed her chair back as he blurted out, "You shouldn't trust him. You ever think he might have been the one that tipped off the D.A. and got you run out of town? His case was screwed too and the whole force was laughing at him. There are a lot of dirty cops in Phoenix, Lilac!"

It was Lilac's turn to glare. She looked at Kuul, who was doing his best to ignore the physical world and the crazy white people warring amongst each other. *Damn Indians*, she thought, they're able to disappear whenever and wherever they want. The Mayan avoided her eyes as she got up and stormed around the table to confront Skip.

"I hope you told someone else you're heading out to that canyon this afternoon," Lilac said, pointing a finger at Skip. *"BECAUSE IT WON'T BE ME WHO REPORTS YOU MISSING IF YOU DON'T COME BACK!"* she barked.

"So, you're coming with us?" Skip smirked.

Kuul accurately assessed Lilac's change of mood from pissed to *Where's My Gun* but was a step too slow to stop her. His friend deserved what was coming anyway. Looking down at Skip's pasty face, Lilac hauled off and punched him in his left eye. She grabbed a jalapeno from Kuul's glass and yelling, *"BURN, BABY, BURN!"* crushed it in Skip's other eye, seeds and all. A group of well-dressed ladies sitting by the pool table started clapping wildly and cheering, "You go, girl." Lilac gave a thumbs up and stormed out the bar.

Kuul watched her peel her jeep out of the mostly empty parking lot. For a jeep that meant she popped the clutch too quick shifting into second, the tires didn't really squeal. It was more a grind. His friend was face down on the table groaning. He couldn't tell whether it was from pain or remorse.

The Mayan patted him on the back, "I think she still loves you, Kemo."

"I can do without the affection," Skip mumbled.

23

DRUM CIRCLE

DESPITE LILAC'S WARNING AND ANOTHER ROUND OF VODKA-spiked V8s, Skip and Kuul headed to Red Spirit Canyon. The bruised purple halo forming around Skip's battered eye would match the Sedona sky in a few more hours; by midnight they'd both be coal black. For the time being he could still see through the swelling, but things were a little blurry. The jalapeno infused eye had stopped burning but was still weeping uncontrollably. His head was pounding like a drum circle at a powwow. But his feet worked, and the hair of the dog had steadied his legs.

He was in no mood to talk, but his loquacious Mayan-Yaqui-German wannabe Navajo friend hadn't shut up since they hit the trail. Skip quietly accepted the chatter as part of his punishment.

"That Hollywood director and his girl Friday, the two you introduced me to...they're renting my Hogan for ten days."

Kuul's Hogan was a reconstructed multi-sided Navajo dwelling he'd bought for a song at auction. Skip had helped him disassemble the circular structure on the reservation and rebuild the stack of logs and timbers by hand on ten acres Kuul owned west of Flagstaff. They'd put it up and taken it down twice before getting the door facing due east and the morning sun. The authentic Hogan was listed on several online vacation rental sites and was making a killing. Kuul blacked-out one weekend every month for youth of all races to come stay and learn about the Native way of life from a Mayan plumber in a traditional Navajo home.

"They've hired me as a consultant for the film they're making. I have to be back up in Flag by nine o'clock. They plan on sneaking into Walnut Canyon to shoot a moonlight scene at the ruins. Actually, I think all we'll get are some night stills of stacked rocks they can dub in later, but I didn't want to spoil their enthusiasm."

"This the L.A. porno king and the Instagram girl?" Skip asked. His head was splitting from the vodka and Lilac's pugilistic accuracy. He didn't care about Kuul's cinematic career, but moving his jaw a bit eased the pain.

They had already hiked for nearly two hours covering only several miles. Kuul insisted they take a roundabout route away from the main trail and reconnoiter the whole entrance to the canyon before charging up the deer path. Given their previous experience it had seemed like a good idea. Skip wasn't so sure now. His head felt like the drum circle had added a flute and brass section. With another three miles to go, it'd be his luck the Phoenix Symphony would join in as backup. That would teach him.

"Same dude with the aviator shades," Kuul said. "Definitely west coast nut jobs, but they cut me a ten grand advance: not including the four-fifty a night I'm charging for the Hogan. Movie's called *Bare in the Saddle*. Blondie says she wants a red pommel, bigger the better to keep her from sliding off."

"Glad I could set you up," Skip grumbled as he just missed twisting his ankle in a packrat hole.

They walked for another hour until reaching the west edge

of the canyon. It was still a quarter mile to the deer path leading to where Zebulon had been found. Avoiding tripping hazards with one good eye, the one he was constantly dabbing dry with his bandana, had been treacherous. Kuul hadn't seen any signs indicating they might have company, but they had stayed off the main trail.

"Let's just find the path and follow it to the switchbacks like we did before," Skip said, squinting at his friend.

They had stopped for a breather in the shade of a pinon. Skip was draining his second gallon of water and in no mood to suffer another two hours getting to and up the ridge where the shooter had been. That's where he wanted to poke around for any evidence and find the *Sinagua* granary Sasse had told them about.

Kuul shook his head, "No, we're going to zigzag across this canyon, Kemo. I'll cross that path several times along the way and should be able to tell if there's anyone out here. You want to play Custer and charge into another ambush, be my guest."

Without a word, Skip slugged another quart of water, wiped his wet eye, and walked in a straight line toward where the path should be, leaving Captain Reno behind to attack from the rear. He felt like upchucking a bellyful of tomato juice but didn't want to give Kuul the satisfaction; it'd wait until the Mayan was out of sight.

Kuul yelled, "Suit yourself. Wait for me at the bottom." He was sticking to his original scouting plan. The Mayan figured he'd at least get an advanced warning if someone started taking pot shots at his stubborn hungover friend.

Skip found the path fifteen minutes later and stumbled to the base of the switchbacks in another hour. The tomato juice didn't make it. He hadn't seen Kuul, but after spying fresh boot tracks in a patch of sand, he was pretty confident his friend had seen him. Skip collapsed on the same rock bench Mustang Timmy had found. Fifteen minutes passed... a half-hour...forty-five minutes...still no sign of Kuul. He was about to say screw it and head up alone when a stick tapped him on the shoulder.

"Coup, brother," Kuul whispered in his ear. The Mayan had been tracking him all the way. "Why don't you just ring a bell announcing we're here? Get your scat together, man."

Skip growled, "You're right. You want to do this like the last time? I'll climb the slide?"

"Naw, you'd never make it. As long as you keep your head out of your ass, let's both take the switchbacks. I haven't seen any new signs and I've been half way up the s-backs already – you just didn't notice."

. . .

The climb was uneventful. Once up top they headed toward the rock wall they'd seen on their last visit. That's where the animal path led so it made sense to explore there first. Kuul stopped and started poking around a slightly sunken area covered with dark stones. Skip kept walking to the edge overlooking the rock slide he'd scrambled up before; it would be a good place to unload the jalapenos he'd been burping.

"Hey, come take a look at this," Kuul called out. "There's an old agave pit here."

Without the jumping jalapenos, the rhythm in his head had settled down to just low beats on a hoop drum. He felt better. Kuul was turning over blackened rocks covering an area the size of a small room. They looked like rounded pieces of basalt. He flipped another one over and there was an oblong rounded depression in its underside.

Skip took a closer look, "Mortar."

"Close Kemo, but no cigar. This is a *metate* stone. The groove's longer and shallower than a mortar. Our women rolled another smaller stone back and forth to mill beans or corn. With a mortar the depression is rounder and deeper because they pounded more than ground," Kuul explained. "You find both out here, mostly *metate*. They're all over, man. The ladies just turned them over when they broke camp. That way they looked like any other rock and would be there waiting when they came back. Pretty smart, huh?"

"You wouldn't want some out-of-towner coming by and stealing your copper chef cookware," Skip added. He had discovered broken pieces of pottery outside the blackened area. "That pit's big, looks like it was used for a while. They probably cooked the agave to feed themselves while they harvested mesquite and pinon nuts up here. Stored them in the pots."

"You're learning, Hoss. You see anything by that rock face?" Kuul asked, walking that way.

They both started exploring a sandy plaza-like area in front of the red wall. Kuul was searching around the perimeter of the plaza and Skip was poking in the thick acacia and manzanita bushes growing out from the wall. He noticed a narrow gap between two large bushes; their tops and other sides were wild and overgrown. He pushed through. From a distance this part of the wall had been obscured by overgrowth. Up close, what had looked like a loose pile of stones from ten steps away were actually the remains of a once mortared wall. There was a short square opening in the mortared stones. He ducked inside and was in a cave-like room, no larger than six square feet. Not thinking the ceiling might be low he bumped his head. *Drumming again.* The roof was blackened with smoke like a Mary Coulter fireplace.

"The granary." Kuul was hunched overlooking through the opening. He had seen Skip disappear in the bushes. "It's where they stored their grain. This is *Sinagua*, man, long before the Navajo or Apache."

Skip's eyes were adjusting to the darkness. "There are piles of grain and corn in here, no containers." There was also a petroglyph pecked into the black ceiling, a winding circle with a dashed line leading to a square.

Kuul was squatting inside the doorway. "That drawing says the artist's ancestors had been on a journey. That's the circle. The dashes may mean it was a long trip. The square says they found a home here. This granary wouldn't have been far from some kind of settlement or village. The people would have stored their surplus grain in here, built these walls, and then started a fire right inside." Kuul was scratching his foot in a dark spot on the floor.

"The fire was here, see? It's why the ceiling's black." He bent down and ran his hand through chunks of black coals that crumbled into dust. "Once the fire was going, they would have started mortaring the opening and then waited to close the top as the fire went out. It created a sealed vacuum. The corn still being here means the People never reopened it."

"Smart to have a backup plan, especially if you lose a harvest due to drought or bugs," Skip observed. "I'm guessing since those coals are still here, the air was locked out until recently."

"12th Century technology, my friend. People had been living in cliff castles and five-story pueblos here in the desert for centuries, before your ancestors built Notre Dame. My Mayan fathers had calendars, astrological clocks, space observatories, and stadiums seating thousands when most Europeans were living in mud huts."

Skip stepped back toward the opening where it was lighter. "I tell you what's not 12th Century. These shoeprints with boot treads. Three sets it looks like." He hadn't noticed them coming in but was now able to follow them out the doorway and into the bushes. They ended where a wavy pattern of thin lines began in the red dust.

"Hmm. You thinking what I'm thinking," Kuul asked, joining his friend and studying the markings. "They've been brushed to hide the tracks."

"Our shooters didn't magically vanish or disappear down the cracks on the backside...they were hiding in here when we weren't twenty feet away."

"I don't like this Kemo. There are too many taboos here, too many spirits, good and bad," Kuul said, shaking his head. "This place should be left alone to heal."

"They weren't ghosts, just robbers, flesh and blood," Skip said. "Lilac was right. Our friend Zebulon could have been up here for a reason... and it might not have been a good one."

24

BALLET FOLKLORICO

*C*INCO DE MAYO, **THE MOST FESTIVE DAY OF THE YEAR IN SEDONA,** a town that has more festivals than a hermit's cabin has fleas. Cinco de Mayo is the anniversary of Mexico's independence from Spain, and next to *Dios de los Muertos* the biggest date on the Chamber of Commerce calendar. Adopting Mexican culture and national holidays is politically acceptable if doing so comes with tequila, handmade tortillas, outdoor dancing, fireworks, and *mucho dinero* from hefty sales tax receipts. The absurdity of showcasing Spanish flamenco dancers and guitarists is overlooked in the interest of having a good time.

The queue of cars on Highway 179 was only marginally shorter than the line of locals and tourists on sidewalks. They were all heading to Tlaquepaque, Sedona's ritzy outdoor mall masquerading as a poor Mexican village. Winding pedestrian alleys flowed into small picturesque plazas with wisteria covered arbors, bougainvillea draped balconies, and drink stations tucked in shady alcoves. Colorful red, green, and yellow banners decorated each square with blue Mexican tiled water fountains. Skip counted at least twenty Frieda Kahlos with flowered headdresses and heavy eyebrows strolling beneath silver wind chimes and Paper Mache piñatas. It was a bigger costume party than Halloween.

Each square had entertainment; Flamenco performers, Mariachi bands, folk dancers from Guadalajara, the Scorpion jazz band, Gladys Knight with Eddie on the ukulele, and a whistling Bull snake whose owner painted rings around its tail to pass it off as a diamondback.

Tlaquepaque's central cobblestoned drive was shoulder to shoulder with people sampling Cinco de Mayo's iconic dish - American Chili. The street was barricaded at both ends for the Chili Cook-off, the hotter and greener the chilies the better. Plywood booths and plastic tables lined a Camino Inferno past the Chili con-testants; restaurants, bars, hotels, resorts, and elected officials all dishing out their special spicy concoctions. The Mayor and Fire Chief had an annual bet on who placed higher, almost always won by the mayor. The last Chief who won had been forced into early retirement.

Zula Ballsy's dried El Guapo peppers stuffed with her secret recipe five-alarm gum-peeling, tongue-melting chili always finished in the top five. Skip's cheeks were streaked with tears from the rising fumes. The spoon hadn't even passed his chin.

"It's an old recipe from Buddy Greco. Juliet Prowse put it in her book, which pissed us all off," Zula said. "I've added a special ingredient this year," she whispered to Skip, handing him a napkin and tissue.

Zula was in her usual spot found between *Tamaliza's* and *Javelina Cantina's*. Sky was dressed as a fetching Frida, without the thick unibrow, serving condiment sized cups of the sliced peppers topped with Buddy's chili. She'd also crafted the cardboard Sands Motel sign with blinking LED lights affixed atop the booth. The two women, despite their many differences, were fast becoming good friends.

"Have you seen Lilac?" Skip asked the older woman. He needed to apologize for acting like a jerk at PJ's. He'd been out of line about her friend Cooper. If he survived the apology with no loss of blood or broken bones, *he'd* consider it forgiven.

"She has a tour with a group of Utah ladies. Might be here later, might not," Zula cryptically answered as she plopped home-made garlic sour cream on each of Sky's cups. "I'm not her social secretary...or your manners teacher."

Clearly, she'd heard about their argument. He turned to Sky hoping for a better reception. She had painted her face to look like a pale emaciated zombie with black circles around her beautiful eyes, similar to his own shade. "Nice outfit, you know its *Cinco de Mayo* not *Dios de los Muertos*, right?"

"Got me, I was going off an online picture for Mexican holidays. It looked so cool. I figured when would I have another chance. You're the first one to point it out. Thanks," she smiled sweetly.

Was that sarcasm?

"Why don't you quit critiquing her face and show the poor girl around," Zula ordered. "I can handle things here; go have fun Honey," she said smiling at Sky. "*YOU* don't be an a-hole," she warned Skip.

"I would like to see the Guadalajara dancers," Sky added, leaving the booth and hooking her arm in Skip's elbow. "Lead the way," she said pulling him in the direction of the circus tent set up in the roundabout at the end of the drive.

The Ballet *Folklorico* was a choreographed story based on Guadalajara culture that started every hour on the hour. Since it was between performances, Skip and Sky wandered through the rest of the chili stands. Sky laughed as Skip asked for seconds after trying the Fire Chief's Butt-Burning Ten-Alarm jalapeno-infused tabasco-smothered white bean elk Chili. She made a note that when she cooked for the man, and she would, it needed to be extra spicy.

By the time they reached the roundabout, the University of Guadalajara student dancers had already started. Sky tightened her grip on Skip's arm out of excitement as the women gracefully swirled, flaring their colorful skirts while suggestively gesturing to their male companions with intricate lace fans. The music picked up as the men in their black vaquero suits with silver *concho* buttons and black felt sombreros strutted onto the floor; the ladies flowing to the back, kibitzing and playacting like Southern belles at a Mississippi cotillion. The men began rhythmically stomping their boots as one by one they took turns spinning on one foot with their bent arms held wide. After a while the women joined them and they twirled in pairs, beckoning the admiring crowd to join in.

Sky tried dragging Skip into the dancing crowd. He gave in when she held his hand up, curtsied, lifted her skirt out from her hip, and began pirouetting on her toes like a Spanish ballerina. He mimicked the stoic pose of the Mexican vaqueros as their women danced around them. Stoic he could do. Sky placed his hands on her hips, her lower body twisting right then left in time with the music, her flirty green eyes fixed on him the entire time.

When the music stopped, she led him across the parking lot to the shaded bank of Oak Creek. They were both sweaty and flushed. Skip glanced around to see who was watching in case she stripped down for another swim. In her own way she was as unpredictable as Lilac was in hers, just more peaceful. He was relieved when she sat on a bench. She scooted over, making room and patting the space beside her.

"What's your real name?" he asked after a while. *Not the smoothest of lines,* but it had been on his mind since she'd talked about her father.

Without warning, Sky kissed him on the lips. Skip felt his hand tighten around her waist and pull her closer. She opened her eyes, and it was clear she didn't want him to stop. Confused, he released her, not sure what he wanted. Sky smiled and laughed quietly.

"Clara Skyline."

"What?" Skip was still trying to understand the kiss.

"My real name. You asked me. It's Clara Skyline. Everything else I told you about me was true. The name is too, I just changed it to something I like better." He eyes were still on him but studying now. "I doubt your parents named you Skip."

Skip let the veiled question about his own identity go. *Why would he tell this neurotically enchanting girl who he was when he didn't tell anyone else?* "And the baker from Park City?" he asked, redirecting.

"Caterer from Moab and we'd known each other since grade school. Our fathers' plans, not ours. Arranged marriages are still pretty common in traditional LDS circles. When I came back from being abducted Dad pushed. By that time, I was old enough to make up my own mind. I still keep in touch; I didn't actually run away. They knew I had to leave."

"And did Clara Skyline kiss me or Sapphire Sky?" His question changed her expression. Her flattering *I'm interested* look became an informed *Why am I bothering with him* stare. She was probably guessing how old he was.

Sky started to stand. Skip gently touched her forearm, "I'm sorry." She sat back down and turned toward him. Skip thought he detected an, *I can't make my mind up about him* look. He'd take it.

"I told you they're the same, Clara and Sky," she said. "What can you tell me about Skip Rhodes...if that's your name?"

Skip thought she was perceptive before, and he was confident of it now. *And so young.* He wondered what exactly she was reading from him. And how? Was it those *Obdobokidoans*? Maybe they had given her super psychic powers. She sure could peg him.

He lied to her about how he'd been to Sedona years before and decided to relocate when the time was right. Everything else he told her was true; clearly, she had cast an *Okidobubido* spell with that kiss. He explained how he'd met Zula and ended up renting the O'Bryan cabin. He talked about his business, Sedona Chi. He told her about his friendship with Kuul and even his breakup with Lilac. He also explained the Zebulon Ballsy story and how he was looking into it. The girl didn't ask anything during his whole monologue. She just sat with her hands crossed in her lap and listened.

Finally, she cut him off, "Let's get back to Zula, she probably needs a break. When you're ready to tell me about *Skip Rhodes*," she said his name like it was something he had made up, "I'd like to know him."

Sky kissed him again, only this time longer with her arms around his neck. Her mouth slightly opened and he could taste a hint of hot sauce. When she finished she took his hand and led him back to the festival. Befuddling, puzzling, bewildering; Skip couldn't decide which word best fit the girl's effect on him.

"How were the dancers?" Zula asked as they walked up to the booth.

"Interesting," Sky said.

"Confusing," said Skip.

"Well, good." Zula sensed neither one of them were talking about the Ballet *Folklorico*.

"How'd you score?" Skip asked.

Zula frowned and disgustedly threw her apron in a box. He noticed she had packed almost everything while the other cooks were still serving lines of customers salivating for the free chili.

"They closed me down. It's that new health inspector. The tricky coyote bastard," she spat. "Cousin to the new Mayor. Same old government graft. The boss says *how high,* and the cousin jumps right over here and gives me a citation for a health code violation instead of a trophy. Despotism, that's what it is."

Skip and Sky wanted to laugh but knew better. "What for?" Sky asked.

"My secret ingredient. Hell, it grows all over town! The Happy Hipster Café uses the distilled oil on their bacon flapjacks."

"Not marijuana?" Sky whispered, guessing Sedona's new wave spiritualism had to be aided and abetted by something.

"No Honey. Jimsonweed."

• • •

Later that night Skip was alone at his cabin with his good friend Don Julio. He was out of prickly pear, so the drink wasn't as sugary. The day had been too syrupy sweet anyway. He'd realized Sky hadn't asked him what he did or how he lived his life or who his friends were. Don gave him a sour bitter know-it-all look. She'd asked *WHO Skip Rhoades was*. He'd gotten good at not answering that question. It wasn't something he wanted to own. Sky had seen right through his cover story, what everyone else accepted at face value. *I'd like to know him,* she had said. Well, that wasn't going to happen.

He felt a vibration in his pocket. Gas from the chili, he thought, before remembering it was where he had put his phone. The screen read *Unidentified Caller*.

Skip thumbed the accept button and a series of tones followed, the sounds stopped for ten seconds, and then another series of tones. He entered a twelve-digit code and pushed the accept button again.

"At least you haven't forgotten the sequence in your retirement," a voice said.

"I wish I could," Skip answered.

"You called us."

"What'd you find?"

"Regarding your inquiry, not surprisingly the church is bogus. Surprisingly, there were twenty-two religious institutions with similar names in our database. Seems to be a popular option for extraterrestrial revenue," the voice smirked. "Your subject's not particularly original."

"Maybe that's the point," Skip pondered out loud. *No, that would be giving Whopper man too much credit.*

"Maybe."

"Reginald Landish?" Skip asked.

"Real name is Arnold Landon. Small-time grifter. Nothing violent that we can tell. Did serve time for fraud in Illinois. He was selling timeshares to a non-existent condo property in the Everglades to the Polish community in Cicero. He was into them pretty good until he hit a mark with a son in the Department of Interior."

"Last known?" Skip followed up.

"Utah - with the aforementioned church. The IRS has it on their radar, but its low priority. The last thing they want to do is step in the mucky sludge of Church and State. Your guy's got a good thing going."

"He'll get too greedy."

"They always do," the voice said. "Landon grew up in the foster system. The records show he had a brother, but they got parceled out. Sad. Even we can't access the records on him. Despite what you hear in the news, we don't control everything. Unfortunate."

"Thanks for the intel," Skip said.

"You owe us a favor now," the voice said. "It will be right up your alley."

Skip heard a shorter series of tones as the voice ended the call. If it took doing a disagreeable favor to get Sky, Clara out of this mess and away from Landon, it was a price he'd have to pay.

25

FRED THE FORNICATOR

EVERY TIME A SHOT WAS FIRED A LION ROARED. LILAC WAS AT home, Smokin' Joe's Gun Range on Highway 260 in Camp Verde. It felt like home; Joe's and anywhere deep in the red rocks were where she was most comfortable. Free to stretch her long limbs and plug holes in wooden bad guys. The last time she'd been at Joe's was a few days earlier with the girls from Salt Lake City. They'd showed up in sexy sundresses with beach colored flip flops and each paid her going rate of $89.99 for an hour shooting lesson, ammo included. They passed on the yoga; too dull, they said. To her surprise all five women were crack shots. Come to find out they were wives of DEA agents; while the men had been elk hunting in Colorado, the girls had come to Sedona to play. They complained Phoenix was too hot and Albuquerque...well, Albuquerque was still under a DEA dark cloud due to the whole Breaking Bad connection. By the time the girls ran through their mags the African lions had gone hoarse.

In a land use conflict that would have driven Jane Jacobs batty, Smokin' Joe's was located next to Out of Africa Safari. OAS was a drive-through Wildlife Park in the middle of the Arizona desert stocked with lions, zebras, giraffes, and other bush animals not endemic to the North American continent, unless you went back to before the last ice age. Word was they had a couple of hippos on order. Not a black bear, bobcat, mountain lion, or antelope in sight. Out of the entire Serengeti menagerie, the African lions were the most neurotic as their exhibit was located closest to Joe's.

"Right in the nut sack, hot damn!" the octogenarian yelped, raising her polarized copper Ray Bans for a clearer look. "Nailed that old fornicator! Lilac, I want that target. I'm going to frame it and hang it in my bedroom."

For personal reasons, Lilac had been hesitant to mount the target Camilla Sudsapper had brought. It was a picture of her dead husband, a set of plastic genitals glued in place with red target rings outlining the offending anatomical features. Lilac had been taking Camilla shooting for the past six months ever since Fred's funeral. She hated charging her given their current mutual dislike of the male species, but business was business. She had offered her a twenty percent senior discount following their third lesson which Camilla turned down. She'd said, *you need the money more than I do sweetheart. Go buy something pretty.* Lilac bought a polished wormwood gun rack for her jeep with elk horn hooks to hang her yoga blocks.

"I told Fred I'd cut them off with a bowie knife if he ever stepped out on me. Then the coward went and died of syphilis without giving me a chance to follow through." Lilac nodded in agreement as the old lady lowered her glasses and opened a hole in the pubic region with a single shot from her Glock.

"Lower and to the right," Lilac reported looking through the mounted scope. Camilla fired two rounds in quick succession splitting the penis in half. "Nice," Lilac said high-fiving the jilted wife. Rusty the Lion was roaring in empathetic pain.

The eighty-two-year-old sharpshooter reloaded. "Watch this." She put a round in her husband's mouth. "That'll stop his lying. Sixty years we were married, and I didn't have a clue until the funeral." Camilla put a 9mm through his forehead. "What was he thinking? I knew he'd been meeting Lou Ann the spiritualist once a week for the last ten years, she put him in contact with his mother. At least that's what Fred said. He'd been boinking her brains out."

"Give me the AK Lilac."

"You sure you want to keep blasting at the past?" Lilac asked. "Maybe it's time to aim for something else?"

"You're right. Time to put this up." Camilla gave Lilac another poster, this one of Lou Ann. "I'm gonna blast her to hell. She can talk to Fred in person, no crystal ball necessary. Spiritualist my saggy rear-end; the woman was a mean-spirited slut!" Lilac switched targets, and her client set the selector in the automatic position and let her rip. At 600 rounds per minute Lou Ann's red teddy nightgown was obliterated in less than ten seconds.

"What the heck, take her head off," Lilac shouted, getting into her client's mood.

"Settle down darling. You get too emotional." Camilla aimed and fired two short twenty shot bursts to give Lou Ann and Fred matching patterns. She put the AK down and pocketed her Ray Bans. "I feel better Honey, thanks for setting this up. Why don't you come by the house later, I made a nice white cake with lemon curd. Fred's favorite."

Lilac wheeled the last target in, rolling what was left of the torn sheet, handing it to her client. "Here, you can hang her next to Fred and shoot them both whenever you want."

The client crossed herself and said, "No way, Lou Ann's already haunting me every time I get my extra-large sterling silver vibrator out. The bitch stole Fred and now she's got me scared to use Herbie."

Lilac returned the AK to Joe and paid the discounted fee for tour guides. Camilla packed up her Glock and joined her in the

Smoking Gift Shop. Lilac suggested stocking up with a case of 9mm cartridges. Smokin' Joe's had them on sale, buy one case and get the second case half off. Like all seasoned guides Lilac got a ten percent credit for any purchases by her clients. It had been over a year since she'd paid for any personal ammo. Between Camilla Sudsapper and the Latter Day Saint gals she was probably good through summer.

"Camilla, you given any more thought to my suggestion? It's been six months, and you're still going through six hundred rounds a week. You can't keep that up, it's not a good way to find your inner peace," Lilac broached the subject on the way to their cars.

"I already have a polyethylene prosthetic in one hip, and the Doc wants to replace both knees with some new plastic gadget. Honey, my old bones can't take the stress. Yoga's a young girl's game, seventy-five tops, after that it's best to warm up with Herbie."

Lilac laughed and decided to not argue the point. If the choice was between yoga and a sex toy, she had to admit it was a slam dunk. But she hadn't meant a yoga regimen. "I meant my other idea - a séance at the Palace of Way Beyond. I think it'd help to clear the air with Fred."

"I heard Fred clear enough air through the years – No Thank You."

"Same time next week," Lilac confirmed, giving up.

The girls reached their cars and Lilac was helping Camilla into her used Dodge Bighorn Ram 2500 4x4 pickup she'd bought with Fred's insurance money. She'd had to sue when they found out he'd been hospitalized for a sexually communicable disease, but the official cause of death was listed as kidney failure which carried the day. Camilla reached her foot to the block she'd attached to the accelerator and fired up the 6.7 liter diesel engine. A cloud of black smoke blew out the back.

"Honey, I've been thinking about your trip to Phoenix. You know Fred was into making jewelry his last few years - probably for that gin guzzling genie Lou Ann. When you said you were checking out artifact looting, it got me thinking about the necklaces Fred made with old beads and broken pieces of pots."

Lilac was standing beside Camilla's truck holding the driver's door open until her friend got situated. If the big door snapped shut before she was ready Camilla would need another polyethylene hip. "Where'd he get his beads and shards?"

"That's what I wanted to tell you. Probably nothing, but he got most of his junk from a kid he knew over at the Verde Valley Archeology Center. I never met him, and Fred never dropped his name that I recall, just always said he was a good kid."

"Thanks," Lilac said. She didn't want to get ahead of herself in guessing who the nice kid was. "Save me a piece or two of cake, Camilla. I've got some running around to do and I'll stop by."

26

BUDDHA BELLY YUCCA SUCKERS

"**M**AGIC MOUNTAIN?" COOP REFLECTED WITH A SLY SMIRK. "Wasn't that the couple's yoga pose we tried that weekend in Santa Fe?" Cooper had the report to share with Lilac and had called to make a date.

"No, it was the Seated Cat Cow," Lilac corrected. She couldn't help smiling to herself. "Your not-so-subtle innuendo isn't earning any brownie points. Magic Mountain's a Kama Sutra pose, which I'm sure you know, which we never did nor will. A half-clothed Gee Whiz is what got you in trouble."

"Not the points I want," Coop said. Lilac was unsure whether he meant a different kind of points or her. As usual, you had to try to read the tea leaves or trick him into saying what he meant. It was the cop in him. She found it too much work to do either. As frustrating as Skip could be, Lilac preferred a bull and a straight arrow.

She had told Coop to meet her at the Montezuma Well picnic grounds. He was making a trip to Flagstaff to run down a lead and the Well was on the way.

She offered a weekly yoga class for the stressed-out park Rangers from the Well and Montezuma Castle, the nearby cliff dwellings. From the start they christened her Puebla Moonbeam and named their class the Buddha Belly Yucca Suckers; Lilac didn't care to know. Four rangers had attended her first class, three months later she routinely stretched out ten to fifteen Yucca Suckers, not including the volunteer staff from Tuzigoot National Monument, thirty minutes away, who took to calling themselves the Mesquite Shiva Sap Lappers. They had a bowling league on Tuesdays. Moonbeam was rethinking the deeply discounted, as in *free*, rate she'd offered.

Generally, the Buddha Bellies despite their name and the Mesquite Shivas were in good shape, the habitual physical problem being their backs from standing on concrete floors. One ranger, Rooster Beatty, from the Castle ruins had bursitis in his shoulder and a frozen neck from pointing up for hours at a time. Lilac chose to focus on vertebrae issues for the younger full-time rangers with a series of Great Seal and Half Lord of the Fishes poses. She had tried the One Legged King Pigeon at their first session, but all four had toppled onto their faces. She'd come back to it later. With Rooster, she taught chin tucks and neck tilts; by their third session he had advanced to Threading the Needle and Supporting the Plow, even though his size thirteen steel-toed boots never got closer than two feet above the ground, and he had to really focus on not passing gas. For the volunteers, who were all over seventy, she employed the easier Butterfly and Upward Facing Dog poses. The Butterfly had split several pairs of olive khakis.

After the stretching and moaning, the Suckers and Lappers worked on stress relief with breathing exercises and a meditation period. The volunteers who ran the Junior Ranger program were always the most receptive to meditating. To keep it simple, their mantra was *Attendance Up* when they inhaled and *Attendance Down* as they exhaled. The whole squad, led by Puebla Moonbeam, sat in a campfire circle chanting for fifteen minutes, cross-legged, eyes closed, palms up, forefingers and thumbs pinched, brown ranger hats in their laps. Except for Rooster, who crossed his arms behind his head with fingers resting on the dangling hat hanging down his back while chanting, *I'm sending out good vibrations* from the Beach Boys. Moonbeam had never seen a rooster that didn't make a spectacle of itself.

Coop walked up just as Moonbeam initiated a traditional closing Namaste, posing her hands in a sacred Mudra gesture over her chest, the location of her heart chakra, joining the left and right hemispheres of her brain and completing the unification of her ying and yang. The Rangers did the same, slowly bowing their heads and upper bodies in gratitude and respect for their instructor. Except for Rooster, who placed his hands on his forehead searching for the rays of peace and harmony emanating from his third eye.

• • •

"And I thought I'd seen it all, Yogi Rangers," Coop joked after the rangers had left. Lilac was rolling up the prayer pads and putting them in the back of her jeep.

"You think dealing with criminals and snitches is stressful, try shepherding hot and sweaty tourists and snotty school groups around all day. You'd be yearning for inner tranquility and not making jokes," Lilac said. She pulled a paper bag out of her front seat. "I brought lunch."

They followed an old *Sinagua* irrigation ditch to a worn picnic table next to the entrance to the nature walk. "Walk before lunch?" Lilac asked.

Coop smiled but shook his head no. "I have to be in Flag in an hour. This is cutting it close the way it is. Sorry."

"Your loss," Lilac said, unwrapping a turkey-on-rye with Havarti cheese sandwich. "How about a pistachio seaweed cookie while we talk." She held out a chunky green wasabi colored lump of...something.

"I'll pass," Coop said, eyeing the hunk of algae. "I checked with a colleague in Vice about your friend's nephew. He was a minor character on their radar before disappearing. They were part of an election year taskforce looking for a rumored ring of looters working in middle Arizona. The kid was associated with some possible suspects. They couldn't give me anything solid and wouldn't disclose names. The case was closed after a sting in the valley nabbed a few traders working out of Payson. And there was no rolling up the chain afterwards; priorities changed following the election, and their unit was moved into a higher profile drug case involving the Mexican cartel."

Lilac pulled a piece of wilted lettuce from her sandwich and threw it by a tree for the squirrels. She stuck the whole slice of tomato into her mouth. "Sure you don't want a sandwich, I've got two?" she garbled, starting to work on a dill pickle.

"I'm good," Coop answered. "You have any Cheetos in there?"

"Soy chips and dried cholla buds?" she said rummaging in the bag.

Coop ignored the offer, "My colleague's best guess was your friend Zebulon either skipped town or, as was known to happen in the business, tried looting from the looters or going out on his own, which would have got him killed."

"Hmmm. Not much help Coop. No leads on the ring, huh?"

"Like I said, nothing my guy was willing to share. But it sounds like they just let it die. The Vice guys are action junkies you know, fraudulent artifact sales don't click their triggers like drug busts and sex trafficking. It was all for show anyway. Unless it reached the Feds, they had bigger and better to do...and before you ask, he said they never had enough to bring the Feds in."

Lilac had hoped for more and was disappointed but there wasn't much she could do. "Well, thanks for checking John. I appreciate it."

"Glad to help." He hesitated. "Lilac, I've been thinking and remembering how we got along pretty well. I want to see you again next time you're in Phoenix. I know you're not attached at the moment. It's gotta get boring up here in the sticks."

Attendance up, attendance down, Lilac repeated the mantra to herself before answering. "Not on my cosmic radar right now. Sorry. But if things change here or I *want* a change I'll let you know." she said, wondering where he'd got his attached/unattached information from. "We'll do lunch again," she added, noticing the look on his face and wanting to let him down easy. No use burning bridges she might decide to cross again.

27

18 MULE'S MISTAKE

SKIP WAS BALANCING A BEER STEIN FILLED WITH WINE ON THE arm of the glider on his front porch. A recent client had given him a case of 18 Mule's Mistake, a blended red pinot from Page Springs Winery, instead of a tip. Not a bad trade. He had picked the blond man and his Scandinavian wife up at Sedona airport for a Verde Valley wine tour; they were from St. Paul and tired of milk. Six hours later he had dropped them back off. The pilot of the small charter plane to Phoenix already had a full load of imported *Zapotec* rugs stacked in the cargo hold and couldn't spare the weight, hence Skip's unexpected gratuity.

He had thought about taking the wine to the Lazy *SOB* for Happy Hour, but it'd been less than a week since his performance with Landish. Better to lay low and avoid any chance of a repeat run-in, especially given what he'd learned about Skittles Landon. When he confronted him again it wouldn't be in front of a crowd.

He'd have a tannin fueled headache in the morning. Despite being dulled by the wine, he heard her coming long before seeing her. *Training and Instincts.* It wasn't surprising Sky would come find him when he didn't show at the retreat. He'd been avoiding her since their kiss. The girl was becoming too attached and he wasn't doing enough to scare her off. *Another thing to add to his To Do List – Scare off beautiful young girl.*

He caught a glimpse of red hair and long legs thru the leaves. She turned at the creek and hesitated before advancing up the stone stairs into the clearing. It wasn't Sky. No wave, but their last meeting hadn't been his finest hour. Lilac had her ponytail undone, waves of scarlet hair splaying over her shoulders. She wore a faded pink and blue flannel shirt with the sleeves rolled above her elbows and a pair of women's khaki shorts that hit mid-thigh instead of at the knees like a man's. If not for her scowl she was a picture of the woman of his dreams.

"I thought I'd see you at the party," Lilac said, climbing the porch steps.

Skip motioned to the empty spot next to him, thinking of a safe way to say hello, wishing he had a sparring helmet. "Wine?"

She looked confused. "I'm good."

Lilac sat down in the camp chair next to the metal glider. Skip handed her the stein and she looked in. "Wine," she said, surprised he hadn't been kidding. She took the glass, swirled the wine, and held her nose to the edge. The aroma was smoky with a whiff of prunes. "Mule's Mistake?" She took a sip, followed by a *not bad* look and a longer slurp like a perfectly suntanned Greek oenophilia goddess. That's the image that passed through Skip's mind anyway.

"Still no stemware?" she commented, taking another sip. The red pinot left her lips deliciously moist and rosy. She smiled. The goddess was toying with a mere mortal.

"It was either this Oktoberfest commemorative stein or a chipped pilsner glass. I went all in."

"Since when did you start drinking wine?" she asked.

"It was a tip," he said. Lilac nodded, took another drink, and kept hold of the stein.

They sat in silence watching the last of the light leave the sky. Lilac wasn't giving up the Mule, so Skip had gone inside for a cold beer. Just as well, the wine wasn't his cup of tea. He heard the screen door rattle and turning from the fridge saw Lilac curling up in the end of his sofa. "It's getting chilly," she said. Skip sat next to her with his Modelo, his free arm relaxing behind her across the top of the sofa.

"Cooper and I met, he gave me an update on what he'd found out about Zeb," Lilac said, assessing his reaction out of the corner of her eye.

Skip tensed almost undetectably, but she noticed. The slight frown and sudden change to his usual unemotional gaze gave him away. A romantic spark Lilac had seen there a moment before had gone dark.

"I bet he did. That all?" He pulled his arm down and shifted away.

Lilac detected a hint of hurt in his tone. The wine, the unspoken truce on the porch, and a rum punch at the *SOB* had lowered her defenses. Normally she would have barked back at his cluelessness, but not tonight. She wasn't in the mood for an argument.

"John checked with a colleague and Zeb was on their radar before he disappeared. He was somehow associated with a suspected smuggling ring, but nothing solid enough to bring anyone in. They think he might have got himself killed. Their investigation ended when they broke a ring down in the Valley. It was a political thing and all they were looking for was a win and they got one. Zeb's disappearance was left to the Sedona PD."

"You buy he was part of something? It doesn't seem to fit with what everybody up here thought of him." Skip's tone and the stony look had softened.

"I don't know. Maybe. I don't want to think about it now."

Lilac turned, kicking her size nine sandals off, she was a well-grounded girl, and rested her feet on his thigh. *Like old times*. She finished the wine, watching the confusion grow in Skip's face. Her glassy teddy bear eyes stared at him with a glint of expectation as she wiggled her toes. He had rubbed her yoga calloused feet more than a few times, but not for a while. When he just sat there not sure what to do she poked him with a bare foot just above his lower brain. That woke him up, in more ways than one she noticed.

He started with the ball of her big toe, rubbing hard, stretching his fingers outwards to get the balls of her other toes in on the action. First one foot then the other when she let him know it was ready. He worked both thumbs together down the cleft of her underfoot to her heel and then sent each thumb probing and massaging the soft outsides of her feet.

Skip had repeated the same sensuous rub over and over for ten minutes before she scooted down, the back pockets of her short khakis pushed against his lower hip. He was transfixed by how soft her inner thighs looked inside the gaping shorts. "Knees," she said, bracing her well-kneaded feet on his opposite thigh while raising her knees to in front of his chest. He lightly traced small figure eights on the underside of her knees, knowing what she liked from past experience. It brought out her first low moan. After the knees were loose, he straightened one, holding it prone and running one hand down the inside of her smooth thigh. Inside her shorts he could feel a rising heat. He slid his other hand down her calf to her ankle, holding her leg suspended in the air. With his lower hand he started tickling his fingers up and down her leg from the taut tendons high inside her thigh all the way to the bottom of her foot. Lilac looked up at him and scooted even closer, almost onto his lap, her legs spreading a bit more, his hand moving lower. She closed her eyes, another moan escaping her moist lips.

"Shhhh," Skip whispered. "Be quiet."

"I don't think I can," Lilac's thick voice uttered as she lifted her hips, shifting her left foot around the right side of his neck, her right leg straddling across his lap.

"Shhhh," Skip whispered again, this time harsher. He grabbed her leg and pulled it off him, sliding her bottom back onto the couch as he stood up in a crouch. "I heard something outside."

Lilac was still collecting herself as Skip slipped out the kitchen door. By the time she was up she saw him flash past a window toward the front of the cabin. She raced out the open front door onto the porch just in time to see a shadowy figure disappear down the steps into the dark toward the creek. Skip was trailing fifty feet behind. She ran after them, losing both in the gloom. It had been a cloudy day and the moon was nowhere to be seen. When she neared the creek, she heard noises down the trail in the opposite direction from the Sands.

Then she heard the sharp crack of a shot.

Most people run away from gunfire, but not Lilac Williams. Even though she wasn't armed, she tore down the trail after Skip. She heard another shot. It sounded like a 38 special. A picture of Skip lying ahead dead in the dark with the shooter waiting for her crossed her mind. She knew Skip wasn't carrying and ran faster, hoping she didn't tumble over a root, an unfortunately placed rock, or something much worse. She couldn't imagine anything happening to him. She prayed that *what she didn't know about him,* but suspected, would keep him safe.

Five minutes passed and Lilac was gassed. In her condition, she could run forever, but fear, anxiety, and too many stumbles had her breathing heavier. The initial adrenaline surge had worn off. She stopped to catch her breath. She hadn't heard anymore shooting, which could be either good or bad. It was dark in the wooded area along the creek, *really dark*; she couldn't see five feet ahead of her. She heard a noise next to her and screamed as two hands reached out from beside the trail grasping her shoulders.

Lilac instinctively swung at where a head would be. Missing, she dove into a yoga side plank position at a forty-five degree angle to the ground and drove her left foot up in a whipping kickstand move. She felt it connect between her assailant's legs and heard a cry followed by, "Fuck, Lilac, it's me."

"You scared the crap out of me! Don't do it again!" Lilac said punching him in the shoulder, not caring he was doubled over with waves of pain wracking his family's jewels. This was not what she'd planned for when she'd left Zula's party and walked to Skip's cabin. Was it some pathological unconscious anger that always seemed to have her incapacitating her would be lovers the same way in the same place?

"What happened, I heard shots?" she sharply asked.

"Some lunatic kicked me in the scrotum," Skip choked.

"You won't need it. You should have told me it was you!" Lilac was frustrated by how things had ended in the cabin. "At least tell me you saw who it was?"

He'd been shot at for Christ's sake, why was she mad at him. Whoever spied on them got away. He had wisely chosen not to follow in the dark after the second shot splintered the trunk of the tree he had been hiding behind.

"Who'd you piss off this time?" she asked not so nicely. *This was his fault not hers.*

Skip had managed to straighten up and assume a protective posture, one hand covering his still aching balls. "All I can think of is we're asking too many questions, and someone doesn't like it. We need to keep our eyes open from now on."

"This is the second time you've been shot at," Lilac said looking around. "You're right. Someone's sending a message."

· · ·

The Director had given his brother a simple enough job: poke around and see if he could discover what Skip Rhodes knew. That was all. After the call they'd just had he was reconsidering the New Mexico franchise idea. His brother had taken it upon himself to spy on Rhodes and nearly been caught in the act. If not for his misguided sibling having a gun, Rhodes would have. And then where would they be? Thank God he hadn't shot the man. That would have really brought unwanted attention.

The idea of his brother crashing through the woods in the dark would have been comical if not for the implications of what he'd found out...which was that Rhodes and Williams were going to be a problem. The woman had apparently even been in contact with authorities outside Sedona's complacent police chief. The Director realized he'd have to do something to get them off his track.

His brother had been ready to walk until the Director talked him down. The man simply wasn't made for any work that required any kind of malevolent exertion. He was too soft and that wasn't going to change. The Director had listened to his complaining that he already had an easy thing going and didn't want to blow it. Three times he had whined, *you shouldn't have gotten me into this, I've got enough on my mind.* The Director had yelled back at him, *you can walk and chew gum at the same time can't you?* The brother had idiotically answered, *I prefer Skittles.*

28

RUSSIAN BARBARIANS

THE SHANGHAI COLLECTOR WAS NOT HAPPY. THE DELIVERY on one of his latest orders was overdue, and the St. Petersburg client had warned he was ready to take his business elsewhere. In this trade, that warning meant more than a simple refund. The client expected a full return on his investment plus fifty percent interest since he had already fully paid for the rare collection of Hohokam shell artifacts and an intact polychrome ceremonial pot with a painted map of their intricate canal system. The collector had no choice but to pay. He knew better than to cross the ex-KGB henchman-turned-billionaire industrialist. Incorrectly handled, not only his whole operation was threatened, but his life along with it.

The Collector had begun thinking about liquidating his inventory, except for his personal collection, and retiring or at least finding a new line of business; something that wasn't so heavily dominated by the Russians. It had been a mistake to expand outside the old world European and polite Asian markets. The Russians were too new to wealth and the barbaric new world they were creating carried too much risk.

What they hadn't learned was there were too few players in the collector's field to alienate anyone if you wanted sustained access to world treasures. Even the composed and vulgar Japanese, as much as he hated them for their historic transgressions, understood that international trade amongst the world's richest individuals couldn't get personal. But they had become like the West, overly regulated and policed, not to mention their conglomerates and leaders were no longer earning the outrageous profits they once were. Unfortunately, the arc of disposable wealth had bent toward ruthless men like his St. Petersburg client.

The Collector wasn't a young man any longer. He had more than enough money to last several well-enjoyed lifetimes. He could keep the fertility effigy, it was a money maker. There was a never-ending string of warped customers from Germany, Turkey, and Asia, especially Singapore and Malaysia. Super wealthy sex addicts caused very few problems, and if they did, all he had to do was send them a copy of his private taping. He might even tap into the international human trafficking business; they dealt with a similar target market and he already had the contacts.

The more he thought about leaving the "antique" business the more he liked the idea. It would take a while to phase out the antiquities line and ramp up a high-dollar sex operation, maybe a year or two at most. He was a patient man; his family's past trials and his present bank accounts had already taught him there was, to quote his Hindu clients from the sub-continent, a cosmic karma to the universe.

In the interim, the collector still had orders to fill, and cancelling without cause wasn't a good business model, even for a business he now planned on closing out. And then there were the half-dozen purchases he had already accepted payment for from additional Russian clients, including two others with ties to the Russian mafia.

29

MAN WHO RUNS WITH THORN IN FOOT

"**L**OUSY CALIFORNIA DEVELOPERS," AL SAID. "JACK WARNED ME about them. He had the same problem in Malibu, but out there you can just go whiz in the Pacific. Here there's a goddamn snake under every rock. But watch out for Brolin. Jack and Leo were partying after *The Departed* premiered, flipped their weezers out to whiz in the waves and up walks Barbra and Brolin. Brolin beat the shit out of the drunk bastards. Hey, you fellas want a cognac?"

Kuul and Skip were back replacing a hot water heater for the famous actor. Kuul had just explained the heater had a cracked liner despite only being three years old. It also hadn't been sitting in the required pan with the proper overflow drain.

"Panned out, you might say," Al punned, snickering at his own joke. "You know, I've been thinking about that case of yours, the stealing pots caper. Serpico cracked a deal like that – inside job. I think it's that Cheers dude and his Hippy wife Steinburger. They've got the hots for Native art. They have more arrows in their house than a Sedona roundabout."

Kuul was working up an estimate for the water heater. "Looks like seven-fifty for the tank and I'll only charge you another two-fifty for labor. Skip here works for free."

"Good boy, Skip," Al said. "Man needs to help his fellow man, it all comes back around. And Justice for All, man...take Brolin for example; a day after washing Leo's ass in salt water Josey Wales turned his kid down for a role in J. Edgar, played by..."

"Leo," Kuul finished. "Al, harmony and balance can be found even in the face of urinary troubles when we learn to love and trust ourselves. The Great Father teaches us that *Hozho*, our sacred connection to Mother Earth, is renewed by our good deeds." Al was hanging on every word. Skip was surprised he wasn't taking notes. Kuul's mock countenance turned into a playful grin, "Replenishing the Great Water counts. Brolin should have thought of that."

"On the nose, blood brother," Al said, pointing at his famous nasal appendage.

"You want a warm water blessing for the new heater? I'm running a special this month; two for the price of one. I'll throw in an algae *fria* blessing for your pool pump. It looks a touch *verde* out there."

"Add the spa and we've got a deal. I had Donnie Brasco over and the pH crashed," Al winked.

• • •

Skip and Kuul were watching the sunset from atop Kuul's classic 1977 Winnebago Brave, nicknamed *Man Who Runs with Thorn in Foot*. The brilliant overhead streaks of burnt orange, ochre, red, and soft pink reflected against the aged metal.

The Brave rested on a slight rise overlooking a deep arroyo where there had once been a spring, evidenced by a graceful patch of pink flowering desert willow and a lone cottonwood with deep enough roots to find water hidden in the parched earth. Two distant, wavy, purple, lines marked the Black and Bradshaw Mountains, the beginning of Arizona's basin-range country. In between were low hills and gullies packed with scrub bushes, fields of cactus, and the occasional mesquite or juniper tree.

The landscape was exploding in color, painted with yellow blooming prickly pear and brittle bush, scarlet cholla and ocotillo spikes, white flowering stalks of banana yucca, Skip's favorite poppy-sized red blossoms atop the small hedgehog cacti, and wildflowers in every tint of the rainbow. At dusk even the dusty sage showed off their gray-blue foliage.

Thorn in Foot was parked in a gravel pull-off from a Forest Service Road. Kuul's camp seemed remote, seven miles past the end of the paved road at Doe Mesa, but it was still only thirty minutes from town. A generator and full water tank were all he needed. He could see the stars out his bedroom window. A three-by-three bathroom, when he didn't feel like using a bush, was jammed beside a serviceable kitchenette with a propane stove and mini-fridge. A worn couch and swiveling pilot and copilot seats functioned as a living room. A set of bald tires honored the RV's name.

Dusk, last light, was when Kuul could best sense his ancestors and listen to their stories in his head. On special evenings a deer appeared to him as a dancing ghost chanting wishes of happiness. The deer brought the messages from the ancient ones. It never stayed long and melted into the night as it turned black. His vision didn't change if Skip was there, his spirit was silent. The man could sit watching the changing panorama for hours without saying a word. They'd never spoken of the deer, whether or not his friend had seen it was his own secret.

"You're happy here," Skip stated quietly. He wasn't asking a question. The loneliness of the desert was making him philosophical. He was pondering what it meant to be happy. The longer he remained quiet the longer the question nagged him. Maybe being part of someone else's happiness was all he could hope for. Maybe that was enough.

"I see things out here I don't see elsewhere," Kuul said. "Happy? Maybe, but it's deeper than that Kemo. It's about finding your place in life and a time where you belong. Being here, at this moment, is where my ancestors tell me to be. Knowing that, it's not so hard fixing rich white men's toilets. You, me, them, the antelope, the sky, the rivers – we're all one and all in this world together."

For most of the day they'd been together with Al. Ace had a heater in stock, so they had been able to replace it on the spot. The heater, pool, and spa had all been properly sanctified, and Kuul had sold the actor an annual Blessing Plan which included a ten-percent discount if any evil spirits caused a calcium buildup, a recurring problem with Sedona's water but a boon for its plumbers. His customers understood the plumbing blessings were a bunch of bunk, but in wealthy Sedona the pseudo-liberals bent over backward to respect the indigenous culture. And Kuul was happy to take advantage of their shallow sensitivities.

"It could be the Cheers star," Kuul contemplated after his third cold one. Skip took a sip of his Modelo and glanced at him sideways. A coyote yelped not too far away. "After I pumped out his septic, he showed me his collection of antique *Katsinas* above his bar. He's real proud of a Hopi Mudhead doll he got at *Oraibi*, says it reminds him of Woody."

Skip didn't take him seriously. He knew Danson's home was in a subdivision with city sewer. The joke did, however, get him considering the antiquity sales chain Lilac had told them about. "Do you ever get scat from Facebook?"

"What I don't get out there..." Kuul said waving the neck of his bottle out in front of him, "I get from Craigslist. Never use Facebook, it's just people trying to get rid of their junk. I buy scat from there, a minute later my page is full of shitty advertisements and kinky sex links."

The coyote had been joined by a couple of friends once the moon got brighter. They were probably gathering for a late night raid on Kuul's compost pile. "Why don't we pop a second six-pack," Skip suggested, getting up to open the ice chest. "It's a nice night. I'll spread my roll out up here, watch the Milky Way come and go, and we can check out a few vendors from Craigslist in the morning?"

"No can do Kemo. That's the last of the beer. And, besides, I've got company coming," Kuul said.

"Who is she?" He wasn't very surprised. It was still early, and the Native Romeo had a little black Mayan codex full of willing Juliets.

Kuul grinned. "Bong, my crazy Asian livery driver. Ha!"

"Thought you two were divorced?"

"That's your social construct brother, not mine. Masculine and feminine, two halves of the same being you know. A piece of paper doesn't change that transcendent connection once it's been made. Man and woman have to come together now and then to keep the spirit whole."

Skip laughed. "You're both horny. That's your connection."

Kuul smiled, "She's pulled three tours in a row and her boyfriend was transferred to Tucson. All that bumping and grinding, she called and suggested a little Navajo healing was needed. I think it's that new seat cover she has, sitting on those little rolling wooden balls all day gets her medicine wheel revving."

"Brother, time for the ugly American to split," Skip smirked.

30

BARGAIN AUDIO DEVICES

"**W**INK, ANSWER MY PHONE!" WENDY YELLED FROM THE BATH-room. She had told Wink again and again to change the batteries in his hearing aids. If he hadn't bought the cheapest pair, he could find at Costco maybe he'd hear the ringing.

"What?" Wink yelled back.

Wendy Hemplepopper made shoulder bags to sell at the Art Gallery Coop in West Sedona, not to be confused with the venerable Sedona Art Gallery in Uptown. Anybody who rented a rack and kept it stocked could try selling just about anything at the Coop. Hemplepopper cowhide purses were popular with tourists; she used patches shaped like various cacti on the front flap with an arrowhead button, enough Southwest color to charge $39.99 per purse. She usually sold six or seven a week in season. It certainly beat working at the Milwaukee DMV where she'd spent thirty-five years.

"The phone, answer the phone," she screamed louder. She should have known better than to close the bathroom door, but her colitis was acting up, and she was self-conscious about the noise. Why, she didn't know, living alone with deaf Wink.

He must have finally heard her, or maybe her phone had vibrated off the table beside his lazyboy. Wendy heard him say, *Hello*.

"Hello," Wink yelled holding the phone to his ear. "Hello, hello, hello, damnit, hello," he kept yelling louder, getting mad and beginning to swear at whoever was on the other end playing games.

Wendy had managed to stretch far enough to open the bathroom door. "Flip it open, Wink," she screamed. She was afraid to get a new smartphone, he'd never figure it out.

"What...rip the sink? What the hell are you doing in there?" he yelled back. "*Oh*, wait a minute, I forgot to open the damn thing... Hello..."

All Skip heard was an agitated, "Hello. This is Wink. Who the hell's this?"

Skip had found Wendy Hemplepopper on Craigslist after looking under arts and crafts within a twenty-mile radius of Sedona. "I'm calling for Wendy Hemplepopper...about her purses."

He heard a beeping on the other end of the line followed by the man who'd answered, "God damn batteries. You're going to have to speak up whoever you are." In the background Skip heard a woman yelling, "You should have paid extra for the rechargeable set."

"Wendy Hemplepopper...purses," Skip repeated louder.

"The weather's getting worse?" Wink questioned, repeating what he'd heard. This wasn't sounding good.

"Who is it?" Skip heard the women yell in the distance. "Sounds like the weatherman," Wink yelled back at her. "Tell them to wait a minute," the woman shouted. "Ate the peanut? What the hell are you talking about Wendy?"

Skip chuckled listening to the back-and-forth volleys. He heard a different set of beeps and was expecting to be hung up on. On the other end, Wink was trying to adjust the volume on his hearing aids like the audiology specialist at Costco had shown him and Wendy.

"Who is this?" the man asked. "You better not be trying to sell my wife another subscription. Gotta give it to you though, leading with the weather's a nice touch. Still, I'm getting tired of having to cancel all these damn magazines. Why don't you leave us alone and try selling credit cards to college kids."

"No, no-magazines, my-name-is-Skip-Rhodes. I'm-calling-for-your-wife. I'd-like-to-talk-about-her-craft. Can-you-put-her-on-the-phone... *PLEASE*," Skip shouted, slowly enunciating each word.

"What kind of pervert are you mister, that's not what my wife does. I'll punch your lights out if..."

"Give me the phone, Wink," Skip heard the woman say, she was closer this time. Then the man said, "You better let me handle this, Wendy. This joker wants to skip rope and milk your calf..."

"... Hello, this is Wendy Hemplepopper. Sorry about that, my husband doesn't hear too well. What can I help you with?"

In the background Skip heard Wink, "Don't give them the AMEX number, it's some kind of sick agricultural scam." "Wink, shut up and fix your aids," his wife barked.

"Please, don't apologize," Skip said, trusting Wendy was still the one on the phone. "My name's Skip Rhodes. I saw your purses online and have a couple of questions. I make wallets and your buttons caught my eye; thought I might do something similar. Can I ask where you source your arrowheads?"

"Be a little sharp to sit on, don't you think," Wendy said. Maybe Wink was right about this guy.

"I'm thinking about adding keychains," Skip lied.

"*Oh*, well, that makes sense...my buttons...mostly online, Verde Valley Buy and Sell Club on Facebook, sometimes Craigslist or eBay, if they ship for free. Wink doesn't let me go to the seller, too many sex predators out there. There's a good website I use," she rattled on, still yelling at Wink, who had apparently wandered into the kitchen looking for the oatmeal which was on the third shelf of the pantry next to the boxed raisins.

Skip made three more calls after talking with the Hemplepoppers. He talked with Angel Romero, a tile artist, who got most of his embedded materials from his brother Cesar who wholesaled obsidian and onyx chips from Jalisco. But from time to time he also used an online vendor if Cesar was in the hospital; he suffered from miner's lung. Todd Spunkle, a coyote hair potter in Camp Verde had picked up after Skip started leaving a message after the last coyote howl. Todd was pretty much the same story as Wendy and Angel. He found his own hair...Facebook marketplace or an online source if he was in a pinch; he almost slipped and admitted to using his own. The common theme was they all bought online from the same site.

Skip's last call, Carson Littlehawk Butterman from Cornville, sewed drink coasters and placemats from thrown away saddle blankets. He added a few bells and whistles with items purchased from the same website named *Field to Artist*. The site had a single page saying they were located in Arizona and all pieces were authentic. There was a bold-typed banner certifying their inventory was legally obtained from private non-federal lands. *Who did the certifying wasn't cited.* According to Butterman that type of disclaimer was fairly standard. Payment was through PayPal and shipping was via the U.S. Postal Service with a P.O. Box for returns. Of course, a banner line in smaller print below the P.O. number proclaimed a policy of No Returns and All Sales Final. Again, according to Butterman, that was not uncommon.

Butterman was talkative so Skip kept asking questions. "How do you know *Field to Artist* is legit? Any business can say they are."

"It's the internet not a folding table outside Flagstaff Mall." Skip mumbled *uhuh*, not seeing the distinction, but wanting to keep him talking. "They have a website. They've certified their goods. They ship through the U.S. government. There are testimonials at the bottom of the page," pointed out Butterman. "Why wouldn't they be? Everything online is just content written by someone at the company or paid by them. You read what's there and you either trust them or not. You try it and see if they deliver; if they do, you keep using them. Same way with ads in the mail, right?"

"So, you really don't," Skip said. He didn't bother to mention the Post Office was a private business and not a regulatory agency. They'd ship anything that wouldn't blow up in their trucks; it was other federal agencies' responsibility to catch anything moved illegally.

Butterman impatiently sighed but kept talking, "You said you were a tour guide, right? I bet you take online reservations. How do you know your clients aren't terrorists scouting sites to drop a dirty bomb? Bet you didn't know one of the 9/11 hijackers took the hard-hat tour at Hoover Dam a few months before flying into the World Trade Center?"

Skip had wanted to tell him he was well aware of who the hijackers were and who they had worked for, but he didn't. And using him as an example was wrong, he was the one with the website, not the other way around. "Not the same thing, you swapped the parties," he said.

"Okay," Butterman said. "How do your online clients know you are who you say you are? I doubt many of them run background checks on you before walking out into the middle of nowhere, trusting you to get them back."

The man had a point. But *Field to Artist* still seemed sketchier on the face of things than his business. "They get to meet me before closing the deal, and my reviews are at least signed," he challenged.

"So, they see a pretty face and all of a sudden they know you? *AND* you could have written your online reviews under fake names as easy as your supposed clients," Butterman countered. Skip was really getting tired of his objective logic. He wasn't being arrogant or patronizing, just honest. The inability to tell a real person from a fake one was also hitting a bit too close to home.

"Look, it's a crap shoot buying and selling over an impersonal, electronic, fiber-optics system. I don't necessarily like it, but that's the world we live in. You either don't do it or you accept it the way it is and trust until you've got good reason not to. Sure, I don't have a name and number with *Field and Artist*, but, bottom-line, I haven't had any problems."

Butterman had him, Skip thought.

31

BELT BUCKLES AND FADED JEANS

TWIN ARROWS CASINO WAS HUMMING ON A SATURDAY NIGHT. It was just inside Navajo Nation and just outside Flagstaff city limits. The line into the Grand Falls Buffet extended out the front door. Saturday at the Casino meant one thing, the all-you-could eat Steamship buffet; five hour slow-roasted slabs of beef, rump and all, piled high with cooked whole carrots and potato rounds. It came with all the mouth-watering desserts, fry bread, and pizza a pair of comfort-fit jeans could hold. Plan it right and there was time to eat your fill and still make seven o'clock Bingo.

Skip and Kuul skirted the line, walking beneath the twin turquoise arrows pointing skyward. The arrows were parallel, not broken in a sign of peace or crossed symbolizing friendship, either of which would have sent a warm, welcoming message. But twin arrows did symbolize positivity, which was a nice sentiment to have in one's pocket when rolling dice.

Trey Sasse, the Yavapai Apache tribal archeologist, had a gig in the banquet room for the Navajo Nation Rodeo Association's biannual business meeting which explained the sea of stiff white cowboy hats and pearl-button western shirts in line for the Steamship roast – *if you couldn't ride 'em for eight seconds, cook their butts and eat 'em*. Skip and Kuul were meeting Sasse in the Oasis Lounge after his second performance. Skip wanted to ask him about the *Field and Artist* website, and Kuul knew the banquet manager from Tuba City. He had sweet talked her into sneaking him into Sasse's comedy act. He sheepishly grinned as the plump, black-haired manager pulled him through the kitchen door.

Skip ordered a Lucky Shamrock, a margarita with sour apple puree instead of lime juice. It had been a tough choice between the Shamrock and an Irish Rita with Jameson's, but an emerald colored margarita with green curacao didn't seem right outside of St. Patrick's Day.

The Irish connection had struck Skip as odd until he learned that in 1847 the poor and relocated Choctaw people raised $170 to give to the Irish Relief Committee during the potato famine. Over 150 years later a group of Irish men and women walked the 600-mile Trail of Tears, raising $170,000 to relieve suffering in famine-stricken Somalia — $1,000 for every dollar donated by the Choctaw people. And just last year the Irish government announced an academic scholarship program for Choctaw youth. *In each other's shadows the people live* was an old Irish proverb that could as easily have been a Navajo prayer. The Indians' sacrifice for people they didn't know is still remembered and honored.

Skip was standing at the bar between two friendly cowboys with silver belt buckles, the size of Rhode Island, drinking Arnold Palmers. He'd bought the last round.

"Hey brother, you want to hear a joke?" The short, thicker-set cowboy with the rawhide gloves tucked in his belt, asked. They'd just left the archeologist's show. *"If a Chickasaw man married a woman who was half Potawatomi and half Yavapai, what would their kid be – a Chicken Pot Pie."*

Both cowboys roared at their new joke. With a couple of Shamrocks under his own belt, Skip joined in, *"You guys know how you can tell Santa was Navajo – His elves were Hopi"*. The good-natured laughing abruptly stopped. Both Arnold Palmers showered his face like a sand wedge at Bay Hill. The cowboys muttered something in their Native tongue and sauntered off.

Skip looked around like, *what did I do?* The only person in the lounge who had apparently noticed was a familiar, tall, attractive woman seated in a green vinyl booth across from an elderly Navajo in a business suit. Toni Wathatewa was shaking her head having watched the incident. She was mouthing something to him, so he wiped the Palmers off with a bar napkin and walked over.

"They're Hopi," she said, trying not to laugh and pretending to be offended at his ignorance.

"They were at the *Navajo* Rodeo Association meeting," Skip pointed out. "How was I supposed to know?"

Wathatewa testily scolded, "You only allow stupid white men with childish names at your tour guide events?" Her sculpted eyebrows arched, and black eyes opened wide like she was expecting an answer.

Skip stayed quiet, not the place to start a new Indian War. She was right anyway; reservations were as multicultural and multiracial as anyplace else in the state. Arizona had twenty-seven legally recognized tribes, was one-third Hispanic, welcomed busloads of foreign vacationers, and even allowed Californians in on weekends. Casinos weren't for the locals; far from it.

He recognized Wathatewa's companion as the Casino manager he'd seen on TV commercials. "Henry Begay," the man introduced himself. "We Navajo have a saying, *assume every guest is cold, tired, and hungry, and treat them accordingly.* You're as welcome as our Hopi brothers here at Twin Arrows." He left out that both Skip and the cowboys were free to lose their money at his gaming tables.

"The Yavapai People are poorer; we are not so generous," Wathatewa added. Her comment was addressed to Skip, but he sensed it was really meant for Begay.

Skip smiled at the Navajo and said, "Thank you, sorry about what happened at the bar."

"So, you're a guide, chief. Do you bring anyone into the Nation?" Begay asked.

"On occasion," Skip answered. "Mostly through Cameron on the way to the Canyon. I only do day tours, so Monument Valley and Canyon de Chelly are too far, especially for customers coming from Phoenix."

Begay nodded. "Too bad."

"What brings you up here?" Toni asked. "Aside from insulting customers. The last time I saw you it was pretty much the same thing. At least all parties left standing this time." Begay had a quizzical look which for a Navajo meant his head tilted one-thousandth of an inch. Wathatewa's lip minutely curled in uproarious laughter at her cleverness.

"Trey Sasse - Kuul and I are meeting him after his show," Skip said, ignoring the remark about his fight with Landish and without fully answering her question. He didn't see any reason to bring up antiquity trafficking. The last thing he wanted was to get Sasse in hot water with the Yavapai and Navajo tribal governments. They wouldn't be enthused with anyone, for any reason, poking around their historic sites.

Wathatewa looked at him suspiciously. "Too bad Tonto was missing when you needed him," she said, derogatorily referring to his Mayan friend. There was definitely a class hierarchy amongst Natives, a mixed Yaqui from Mexico with German ancestry claiming Mayan quantum was somewhere near the bottom. "You and the snake charmer still looking into Zula Ballsy's nephew?"

"Just here for the show and Shamrocks," Skip said. He tipped his glass to Toni and plastered a fake grin he knew she'd see as such. "Henry, thanks for the hospitality and invitation," he said to Begay. "I'll leave you both to your business."

• • •

Skip found an empty stool at the end of the bar, ordered another Lucky Shamrock, and waited on Kuul and Sasse. After fifteen minutes Wathatewa and Begay left, freeing him from the occasional cold glare. Wathatewa was an enigma wrapped in a conundrum, a mighty attractive one, albeit, but an enigma no less. She was hard to figure. Most Native women kept their feelings buried deep, a sly smile or brief chuckle being a big display of emotion. Their stoicism borne from leading hard lives, their proud husbands and sons forced to look for work hundreds of miles from home, and the diseases of unemployment, alcoholism, and racism destroying their families and communities. The strong ones endured and led their people. Toni was one of those. He would have liked her help, but doubted his good intentions would bridge her hard cultural divide.

Not long after Wathatewa left, Sasse and Kuul came in and the three men sat in the same booth she and Begay had used.

"You should have heard him, Kemo. He had those Navajo wranglers rolling on the floor. Tell my friend the one about the Navajo and Apache war. Man, they were dying," Kuul was still laughing.

"Buy me one of those Shamrocks and you've got it," Sasse said, cashing in on his popularity. Kuul nodded and headed to the bar to order. Trey smiled at Skip, "The Navajo and Apache were having a war and the Apache were losing. So, the Apache decided to steal sticks of dynamite from white miners. They threw them in the Navajo camp but lost the war...when the Navajos lit the fuses and threw them back."

It took Skip a moment then he got it; the Apache hadn't been smart enough to light the fuses, but the Navajo were. He hoped for Sasse's sake there hadn't been any Apache rounders in the crowd alongside the Hopi cowboys. Skip had heard the story before, but not as a joke, rather as a historical metaphor on how the Navajos adapted to new technologies and adopted other people's culture versus the Apache who held onto their traditional customs and spurned outside ideas. Sasse's joke might be a hit on Dinetah, but it'd get him shot at White Mountain or San Carlos.

Kuul came back with another round of Lucky Shamrocks and sat beside Sasse. Skip pushed his drink back, "No thanks, unless you're driving back. I guarantee there's an Arizona trooper at the I40 exit waiting for weaving Broncos and Chevy pickups."

"They comp'd me a night at the hotel," Sasse grinned, sliding the extra drink his way. "So, what are you guys wanting to know this time," the Director of Tribal Archeology asked.

Skip brought him up to speed on what they had learned regarding Zebulon and the possibility of his disappearance being related to area looting. He left out the question of Zeb's role and that they had been shot at in Red Spirit Canyon. "What I'd like to ask is if you're familiar with a website called *Field and Artist*?"

"Zebulon was better than most," the Director reaffirmed. "*Field and Artist* I'm very familiar with though not from using it. It's run by a past Verde Valley Archeology Center employee."

"Legit?" Skip interjected.

"Far as anyone knows. It's not really possible to track the origin of everything that's sold online. Most small stuff, what they sell, doesn't come with certificates of authenticity. It's just too common. Even if you illegally stick an arrowhead in your pocket hiking on public land who's to say that's where it came from. There's no antiquity detector you pass through at the trailheads."

"Who's the employee?"

Sasse hesitated before going on, "Look, I don't like spreading rumors. He's not doing anything wrong that I'm aware of...*but*..."

the Director glanced around to make sure no one was listening and lowered his voice, "Do you recall the Director of the VVAC is new. You met him, right?" Skip nodded. "Well, you also probably remember the previous Director was fired for sexually suggestive tours to schoolchildren. But that was only part of it. He'd also hired some shady characters as part-time field workers. The Center's financial management was a mess from what I've heard, and their inventory controls were lacking, which if you're running a museum is job number one."

"So, what's that got to do with *Field and Artist*?" Skip asked.

"Maybe nothing," Sasse whispered. "The website belongs to one of his previous employees that was let go with him. Most of the items listed for sale *supposedly* come from his ranchette and those are his to do with as he pleases. But the rumor is he was fired when the Board became concerned he might have been selling off some of the uncatalogued items they didn't have room to display. I don't think they had any proof or they would have prosecuted and tried to have the missing items returned."

"Or the Board covered it up. Not wanting any bad publicity. I'd guess that kind of thing would ding donations," Kuul chimed in.

"Again, it's all rumors, and I hate spreading them," Sasse said. He was halfway done with the second Shamrock. The gleam in his eyes wasn't all conspiratorial.

"You think some of what's on the website came from the Museum?" Skip asked.

The Director of Tribal Archeology shook his head. "No, that would be really dumb. There are too many other people that would notice, Board members and other staff and volunteers that have been there a long time. Besides, the stuff he's selling is small-time, nothing major, certainly nothing worth getting fired over or going to jail for," Sasse said, downing the last of the lucky Irish weed.

He leaned in, looking at Skip then Kuul, "I heard you guys went out there?"

"Where?" Skip asked. He was pretty sure he knew where Sasse meant.

"Red Spirit Canyon. I heard someone took pot shots at both of you," Sasse whispered looking to both of them for confirmation and not getting any. "You need to be careful, best to avoid it, that's a long way out there and the cavalry's way back in town."

"We'll keep that in mind," Skip said.

A group of Native and giggling White cowgirls in fringed jackets, tight-fitting jeans, and decorated snakeskin boots entered the lounge and pointed at Sasse. Two of the cuter steer wrestlers came over to their table. They'd all been at his show and wanted autographs. Sasse grinned at Skip and Kuul and asked if they were done. "Watch out for the spurs partner," Kuul joked as Sasse excused himself. The comedian left the table, and as he walked to the bar with his new groupies they heard him say, "Did you hear the one about the horny bull, the distracted cowboy, and the bare bottom barrel rider..."

32

DEACON DELIGHT

ZULA WAS LEANING FORWARD AT A NINETY-DEGREE ANGLE WITH one foot on the ground in her favorite yoga pose - *Live at the Riviera with Dino*. Her left arm outreached and pinched like she was holding a vodka gimlet. It was one way she kept her gluts tight. Lilac was standing behind ready to catch the floating foot if the spry old dancer sprung a hammy. Spike, the javelina, was standing on its back feet stretching for the Kine Bar on the porch railing.

By 9:30 AM, the red bulb on the thermometer was reaching eighty-five. Zula and Lilac had started their session at eight. It was going to be a hot one for sure. The spring rains had stopped and it would be another two months until the monsoons began. Every day between would showcase a brilliant blue sky above the red sandstone formations that stood as sentinels above the Sands. Clouds were typically absent that time of year, unless a lost one floated over the Sierra Nevadas. If they were lucky, a breeze would kick up late afternoons. By 10:30 the blazing sun would rise above the rocks and take charge, dictating what the humans below were allowed to do and when.

Spring was the busiest time in Sedona. High season started in March with spring breakers, mile after mile of cars with California plates winding their way up Highway 179 past the turnoff to Jacks Canyon; five miles from the Sands as the crow flies but at least twenty by paved road. Sedona's spring breakers weren't the college crowd that jammed Lake Havasu hanging off their wealthy parents' houseboats and waterskiing topless; they were families needing a break from their winters. Not counting Christmas thru New Year's, the Sands did half its annual business from Daylight Savings Time through the end of July, the hottest driest time of year.

Landish and his followers were booked for another week, and then they'd be gone. *If it wasn't for the money...*Zula thought, bent over, looking at the upside down rocks through her knees. The tension between Whopper Boy and her favorite boarder was testing the Zen principles of self-restraint Lilac had tried teaching her. Every time Skip and Landish bumped heads she lost track of her breath counts. She pretty clearly saw the nature of their minds, but a bar owner couldn't just sit down and meditate whenever she felt like it.

She and Lilac reassembled in the Warrior-One pose, hips square to the front, backs erect, legs split with the left one stepping forward and the right stretched back bracing the stance, their arms raised and hands clasped with the index fingers pointing to the heavens. They looked like two-thirds of Charlie's Angels. Of course the younger angel's hips were thinner, her back had no scoliosis, the legs were long and toned, no baggies were under her arms, and the free-flowing red hair was a red cape for nearby alpha males who thought they could handle her.

When Skip walked up with a thermos of coffee and two extra cups, Lilac lowered her pointed fingers and cocked an imaginary hammer...without a hello, good morning, or so happy you're alive. She was ready to pull the trigger. *And she's instructing me in Zen, the Buddha-nature, and how to NOT focus on a single object,* Zula thought. *Who was teaching her?*

"*My lower chakras are blocked,*" Lilac warned him. "*Stay back.*" He stopped and stood to the side, sipping away, watching them work through their final *asanas* before cooling off and closing with Lilac's traditional Namaste, hands over their chests, bringing their *yings* and *yangs* in conjunction. Skip hoped balance had been restored.

"Honey, I'll take a cup of that," Zula said to Skip, not giving him a chance to say anything that would get him shot for real.

"Ethiopian," Skip said, pouring a cup. Lilac was still cooling down with a cow pose stretch.

"As long as it's black." Zula took a sip and smacked her lips, praying Lilac held no ill will toward the Horn of Africa. "She put these old bones through the ringer this morning. Girl's in a mood," she said looking over her cup at Skip, mouthing *Be Careful!* "I think it's her sacral chakra, unsuccessful toxic relationships block a healthy sense of sexuality," she whispered.

Lilac was chanting, *I am connected to my community. I am connected to my family. My sensual sexuality serves as a fuel to my creative endeavors.* She was sitting with her legs in front and touching her toes. *I am connected to my community. I am connected to my family. My sensual sexuality serves as a fuel to my creative endeavors...*

"I do my best," Skip whispered back to Zula. He'd read Lilac's cropped T-shirt and come to the same conclusion. "How are your chakras doing?" he joked. "I want to update you on a few things we're finding out that might have involved Zebulon."

"They're wide open. Nothing wrong with my creative endeavors. Haven't had a hot flash in twenty years, and I can still ring the bell if the right man pushes the buzzer."

TMI. Skip was sorry he asked about her chakras and changed the subject. He filled her in on his thinking that Zebulon's accident might not have been accidental and about their finds at Red Spirit Canyon. Lilac had finished refueling her sexuality, undoubtedly with enlightened knowledge that it no longer included him. She joined the conversation, telling Zula about her trip to Phoenix and follow-up with *"John Cooper, a close friend."* Zula shot Skip a look that said, *Better get your act together dumbass*. Neither of them mentioned the two shootings.

"So, you two are suggesting Zebulon ransacked sacred sites and sold illegally obtained artifacts to rich foreigners," Zula challenged, war signals smoking from her ears.

"Not what I'm saying," both Skip and Lilac said in unison. "It's just looking like he might have ridden into the wrong place at the wrong time," Lilac corrected her. "At most, he might have known who he ran into," Skip added.

"Maybe he was out there trying to catch them? Ever think of that?" Zula said, offering a different explanation. "It would have been like him to go it alone and try to get some proof before accusing anyone."

Skip hadn't thought of that possibility. He made a mental note to work it through in his head later. It made sense. The kid didn't have any parents to talk to; he was probably used to solving his own problems. And he had the knowledge and was in a position to get suspicious if he saw or heard anything off kilter. Maybe Zula was onto something.

"He was a good kid!" his great aunt emphatically echoed the oft repeated refrain. She stared at both of them making sure they were paying attention. She wanted to give them a break but was mad at the conclusion they seemed to be working toward. She might believe in Buddha-nature and stuck chakras, but random coincidence? That was just too far out there. "You two work through your confused energies. The negativity around your auras isn't solving anything. I've got to go get the meeting room set up for Landish. He has another *Show* this afternoon. Last one he says."

• • •

Landish started the meeting like it was a 1905 Pentecostal revival meeting in Kansas. Sweat already staining the underarms of his suit, he opened with a solicitous promotional prayer to the *"final frontier"* while the aluminum foil clad deacon and several of his buddies passed around an offering bucket. The *SOB's* boom box had been appropriated and Paul McCartney and Wings were singing the praises of *Magneto and Titanium Man* in the background. All Skip could think of was *Band on the Run*.

"In the name of the maker of all galaxies, his holy offspring Modar, who we know as Jesus Christ, and the Church of Alien Interstellar Connection with myself as its leader, I'm ready to risk my body and soul to represent our shared faith and vision to establish an interplanetary life-force connection with our brothers from *Obikinobedo*." The fat man took several deep breaths, "I've sent an encoded orbital text message to their leader arranging the date and time of our joining in supernatural harmony. Before I tell you their chosen hour of appointment..." Landish dramatically paused, he had the small crowd on the edge of their folding seats.

"What a bunch of bullshit," Lilac whispered to Skip. They were standing in the back of the room. Her outlook had improved after the mantra and two cups of coffee, but she was now a bit twitchy. "Why didn't you hit this joker harder? I thought it was the Church of Astro Departure?"

"He's excited. It's hard to keep your details straight. Probably a sugar high."

Minnie Two Feathers, still hoping for a bunion cure, stood up two rows from the front and shouted, *"Hallelujah, Spirit Man!"* Her husband Clyde slid down in his chair. Minnie had offered to make her huckleberry lemon bars if he drove her to the meeting. She'd also promised to keep her purse closed, but he was getting worried. She hadn't been this worked up since before her last good sweat. He was praying too, praying it wouldn't cost him the new buck knife he had on layaway at Walmart.

"Thank you, sister, for your encouragement! But Modar needs to see more than words before welcoming us on the magical mystery tour," Landish shouted from his makeshift altar - two stacked, orange, drink coolers from the bar's kitchen. He'd balanced them on a wobbly step stool to bring it to the right height. Aluminum Boy had neglected to empty them, and the water kept sloshing back and forth and leaking each time the big man pounded the plastic tray he'd put across the top. His last outburst had spilt another pint.

Landish pointed at Two Feathers and yelled, *"DONATE TO JESUS AND DELIVER OBOKOBEMDO FROM SATAN!"* as a pimple-faced deacon scampered across the room with an offering bucket to cash in on Minnie's excitement. No way, Clyde thought. The deacon hadn't seen the pool of spilled water on the polished floor, but Clyde had.

"Oh, shit," the deacon cried as Clyde squirted a shot of butt cream on the water and laughed. He'd come prepared. The deacon slid into the first row of seats like Lou Brock stealing second. Fortunately, Agnes the librarian and her sister Gladys were already on their feet joining the chorus of *Hallelujahs* when the deacon took out their chair legs. Steel-Calves Kempdinger wasn't so moved. Before she could react, the base-stealing kid skated under her chair, snatching it from beneath her like a tablecloth yanked clean with the place setting still in place. Kempdinger's steel calves held her suspended in a crouch, and disaster would have been averted if not for a spasm in her thigh...*PLOP*...sitting on the deacon's face she began squirming and slapping the top of his head with her fanny pack... screaming for water to stop the cramp. The Baptists turned their backs in shame, praying for her salvation; Doosey Cumbersome and the barista started making out to McCartney crooning, *"Stuck inside these four walls...forever."* Big Bob Baker jumped up, threw a bottle of raspberry seltzer at Kempdinger and started taking fallacious pictures for the Red Rock News.

Public fellatio didn't silence Landish. It egged him on. "The *Obikinobeans* wanted to wait until our summer solstice, but I pointed out Venus was in celestial alignment sooner and we needed to take advantage of the light..." he shouted over the small nervous crowd.

"In alignment with what?" a voice shouted. Skip and Lilac scanned the crowd and couldn't tell who had yelled the question. The whole meeting was devolving into a scene from a western remake of the Rocky Horror Picture Show.

The noise was crescendoing with Kempdinger screaming at her molester, yelling at him to get off her despite her being on top pinching his throat with her knees. Agnes in a #MeToo moment had regained her composure and was smacking him with a Carl Sagan book she'd brought. Doosey had half-swallowed the barista's tongue. Big Bob had switched to a zoom lens for close-ups, "Jesus, Kempdinger, let him breath," he said snapping away, hoping the color setting captured the poor kid's blue face. It was turning purple.

Landish screamed as loud as he could, "The bell rock vortex!"

He was now flustered by the growing distraction of the botched play at second base. "It's where they've told me to lead my congregation and jump...to be transported to the terrestrial realm of harmonic creativity and begin our journey of spiritual enlightenment and cosmic peace. The Church of Astro Coital Imperialism is sacrificing me for the betterment of humankind, *for all of you,*" Landish shouted with his arms spread to the mayhem before him, trying to recapture their attention. *"WE NEED YOUR FINANCIAL CONTRIBUTIONS!"*

"I think he meant *orbital,* not coital" Skip laughed, elbowing Lilac. He hoped Big Bob had taken video. "He gets confused about the alien tribe's name too."

Having lost control, Landish searched his pockets for the bag of tropical flavored Skittles he stashed before the meeting. They weren't his favorite, but the Circle K was out of originals. He nodded hurriedly to a follower off to the side, making circles with his hand telling her to move; she switched cassettes in the boom box and raised her tattooed arm in a salute to the cosmos, crying, "The King Lives". Elvis Presley started singing an A Cappella Amazing Grace in his throaty Biloxi drawl.

"*Damnit!*" Landish exploded. It was supposed to be Josh Groban's, *You Raise Me Up.*

Lilac had no problem projecting over Elvis's moaning, *to save a wretch like me.* She'd heard enough. The sight of an angry six-foot Amazonian woman using two chairs as symbols and wearing a cut-off T-shirt that said, *I am Woman Hear Me Roar,* got everyone's attention, except for Doosey who had wrestled the barista on the floor in a Kempdinger position.

"*NOBODY'S JUMPING OFF BELL ROCK,*" she yelled pointing at the red-faced Doctor as if she was coming for him. The last person to do it didn't get picked up by aliens, they got scraped up by Search and Rescue."

Zula had taken Lilac's cue and walked to the front of the room beside Landish. "This bad joke is *over! Three-dollar house margaritas in the SOB.*"

Kempdinger had finally gotten off the pimple-faced deacon and was helping him to his feet. They exchanged numbers. Big Bob had put his camera away, and Clyde had managed to convince Minnie a little tequila would settle her nerves. Agnes and Gladys had excused themselves and made it to the door, Mustang was picking them both up; Mr. Speer would not have approved. Elvis and the Baptists were finishing with a drawn-out *AMEN.*

Landish angrily watched *His* crowd filtering into the Lazy *S*OB bypassing the collection buckets. He stomped toward Lilac and Skip. Sky had been standing with the other deacons; she caught up to Reggie knowing he was cruising toward another bruising.

"Turn around," she told him, but the big man wasn't listening. She knew Reggie had been lucky to survive his last encounter with Skip with only a swollen eye and broken lip. There was no one around to save him this time, certainly not the red-haired wildcat.

Landish didn't stop charging until he was nose to nose with Lilac. "The Lord and the *Obikinidoans* tell me what to do, not you! Bell Rock's a public trail and I'll lead my flock up there whenever and however I chose."

"I've got the Police and Fire Chiefs on speed dial, they're both friends," Lilac said, not backing down. "How about we call them now and you can explain your plan. You aren't the first charlatan that's flown through our town."

Sky had moved beside Skip, lightly touching his hand which was balled into a fist. The hair on his forearm was raised, like a dog backed into a corner in fight mode. She kept the gentle touch and cupped her hand over his. His muscles relaxed and color returned to his white knuckles. Landish might survive the next few minutes, she thought. *Maybe.* Sky glanced at Skip's stone face and immediately understood the danger hadn't passed, it'd only become more lethal instead of reactionary.

Landish broke off his staring contest with Lilac and stepped back deescalating their encounter. He could feel the energy coming from Rhodes. A face-to-face confrontation wouldn't end well and that's where this was heading. The man was dangerous and he didn't scare easily, that much he'd learned. His brother had tried and been unable to find anything out about the quick-tempered tour guide. The background they'd discovered before his arrival in Sedona was superficial at best. That was troubling. Whoever he was, Rhodes had been in a crazed frenzy and ready to kill him a few nights earlier.

"You need to keep your girlfriend in tow," Landish spat at Skip. "People that jump into the middle of things not their business tend to get hurt."

"I don't jump, I kick, hard. Is that a threat from you or your alien friends?" Lilac said, stabbing her finger at his face. She didn't need Skip's help and she certainly wasn't his girlfriend. "A phony swindler with an eating disorder doesn't scare me, and any little green men with a lick of sense aren't siding with a cheap con artist. How much in donations have you raised here? I'd like to see your non-profit license and state solicitation certificate."

Landish glared at her.

"Arnold Landon," Skip said coldly with zero emotion. "Did time in Illinois for fraud. Selling timeshares in the Everglades I think it was. This is his third or fourth church. Not the first one that's bilked extraterrestrial revenue from susceptible locals and then disappeared." He was ignoring Landish and speaking directly to Sky. There was no empathy in his voice or attempt to sugar-coat the truth to make her feel better; just a matter-of-fact delivery like he was reading from a personnel file.

"Reggie?" Sky said turning to him, her eyes tearing. Landon didn't respond. He just shot daggers at Skip. "Reggie, tell them it isn't true. It can't be," Sky half-begged, her wavering voice betraying her doubts, tears running down her cheeks. A few painful seconds passed before Landish turned to her, his stare changing to a smirk. He opened his mouth to speak. Sky slapped him open-handed across his face.

Landish rubbed his lips and looked at his fingers, making a show of checking if there was any blood. "And you were abducted? Who you kidding, *Clara*, you're no different," he sneered. "It was a made-up story to excuse your running away from Daddy. You're just a stupid little girl who served a purpose."

Sky tried slapping Landish again, but he caught her hand. He let it go when Skip stepped closer. She was crying now. "Oh God," she sobbed, then turned and ran out the door.

Skip faced the fat man who had wisely backed up, "That's just the tip of what I know, *Arnold*. I think it's time you take your traveling circus elsewhere. If you're still here in the morning, the FBI...yeah, you're on their radar again...will get a call from a source much higher placed than me."

"I'm not the only one with secrets. Stay tuned, Rhodes. This isn't over," Landish fumed and stormed out the same door Sky had fled through.

Lilac had stood aside, closely following the interplay between the other three people. She didn't like being a bystander in a fight she started. She liked to finish what she began, she didn't need Skip stepping in and taking control. But *Landish, Landon*, whoever he was, had piqued her curiosity. The Doctor, as much as she despised him, had made the same diagnosis she had about Skip Rhodes – there was a past he didn't share.

"What was that about secrets? What secrets? What higher source?" she asked the only other person left in the room, the only one she knew she'd never get an answer from. "And who's Clara?"

33

URINE FOR A TOUGH TIME

"**K**UUL COULDN'T," SKIP EXPLAINED ONCE AGAIN. "THE WATER line below Nick's bedroom bar sink was leaking. He wasn't going to be *Leaving Las Vegas* to come fix it himself."

Skip and Lilac had reached the ridgetop at the head of Red Spirit Canyon. The sandy ground in front of the granary appeared undisturbed since he'd last been there. Lilac had started in on him the moment they left the trailhead. Avoiding answering her questions had been the bulk of their conversation for the last three hours, *not counting the last two-and-a-half years*, which had led to one argument after another; the last disagreement being over why Skip hadn't brought Kuul instead of her.

"Why did you come?" Skip finally asked in exasperation as they took off their packs. First, she had grilled him on what secrets he was keeping, and then it was the higher source he'd warned *Arnold* with. She hadn't bought the "secrets" were Landish's less-than-imaginative ploy to cause him trouble. Nor did she let his jest slide about the *"source"* being Modar the *Obiwabidinubian* who had probably been in contact with the government for years.

"To watch your lousy six, that's why. Every time someone comes out here, they get snuck up on."

"At least you care."

They were resting in the shadow of the rock wall wherein the granary was located. Skip had started thinking of the open area as a plaza. In another fifteen minutes, thirty tops, the sun would be high enough to replace the cool shade with hot sunlight.

"Exactly what are you looking for?" Lilac asked for the umpteenth time. She knew the answer, *He didn't have a clue*, but all she'd gotten so far was a vague, *we're missing something*. Bugging him was her entertainment for the day; it sure wasn't his scintillating conversation.

Lilac had given up ever finding out exactly what happened to Zeb. It had been three years. Any evidence here had long since been blown or carried away or desiccated like her young friend. Everything they'd been looking into was just theory, a possible way of explaining what had happened. And their hypothesis had been Zeb was innocent, which could be a faulty supposition. They hadn't found one piece of evidence or had a single idea that couldn't be alternatively explained. Discovering what he'd been doing here and why and with or for whom wasn't likely going to happen after all this time. Long lost secrets didn't just come bundled in nicely wrapped packages with pretty bows. The more she learned the more she thought it might be best if the package was never delivered, better for Zula anyway.

While she mused and sulked, Skip had disappeared through the bushes into the granary. Kuul had told her there wasn't much there: the coals of an old fire, piles of spilled seeds, and the petroglyph indicating a people's journey. Nothing she hadn't seen before or cared to share with Mr. Secrets; the southwest was full of similar sites. She screwed the cap back on her water bottle and changed her mind; she might as well take a look.

Skip walked out of the bushes before she had a chance. On seeing her, he stopped. *A woman can tell when a man is checking out her tits, which is what his eyes were locked on. Honestly?*

"Not happening," she said, warmly enough to keep the possibility open if he played his cards right. She hated the thought of walking all this way for nothing.

"Huh?"

"Nothing," Lilac said, frowning. Casanova looked as confused as ever. He pointed at her chest, and began walking toward her, waving both hands like a blind man feeling for a pole. *Lost as ever.*

As he got closer, she saw an orange speckle of light dancing on the back of his waving hands. He twisted to look back toward the rock wall. As he turned, Lilac noticed the same speck of light reflecting off the metal button on her flannel top. That was what Skip had seen. She followed his gaze up the rocks to a crack in the sandstone. Just below the top of the wall was a hollowed crack the diameter of a baseball. The sunlight was shining thru the hole causing the small circle of light on her shirt.

Lilac moved and looked for the light behind her. She picked it up bouncing across the shiny leaves of a manzanita bush. The bush was part of a cluster of scrub and twisted junipers growing by the edge of the cliff overlooking the south side of the canyon. Skip had followed it too and caught up with her. The light suddenly disappeared. They both looked back above the granary and the hole was hidden again in shadows.

"From my vantage leaving the granary it looked like a lighted arrow," Skip said. "I first thought someone was pointing a laser at you. I was about to yell before realizing what it was."

"Just the sun shining through that crack," Lilac said. "Same thing happens everywhere rocks split or there's an eroded hole that aligns with the arc of the sun. Since the aspect of the earth to the sun changes it's not that uncommon. Weird when it happens though, if you're not expecting it."

"Maybe," Skip inattentively said.

He was poking around in the thick acacias and manzanitas where the light had disappeared. There was just enough room to slide sideways between the bushes to avoid their thorns. The acacia was a wicked plant; landscapers used it below windows to discourage burglars. The plants here were old and wild. He reached a twisted juniper growing out of rock, its gnarly limbs drooping all the way to the ground. There were a couple of smaller sucker trees growing up through it, creating a dense cover and screening the edge of the ridge.

"What are you looking for?" Lilac yelled.

"Probably crazy, but the light arrow made me think of the petroglyph in the granary; a circle with a long line leading to a square. Kuul believed it meant there was once a village or settlement near here. Maybe the light pointed to their home?"

"Not likely. The angle's a little different every day. There are places where that kind of event happens at solstices or times of the year that coincide with planting cycles. But there's nothing special about today."

Skip had pushed his way through the juniper limbs. There had been an opening just wide and high enough to duck through near the main trunk. He could see where limbs had been cut off from the ground to shoulder height.

"There's an opening under here..." he called back. An alleyway had been cleared thru the branches on the backside. The cut, dried limbs were piled up behind where the drooping branches on the back of the tree reached the ground, right near the edge of the drop off into the canyon below. He started pulling dead branches off the pile."

"There's an orange fiberglass extension ladder!" he yelled excitedly.

Lilac had followed him but he hadn't noticed, "So I see." She walked past the pile of brush hiding the ladder and looked over the edge. "Thirty, thirty-five feet down there's a six or seven foot ledge," she estimated. "How tall is the ladder?"

"Werner 32 feet, 375-pound capacity," Skip read out loud.

• • •

Set back from the ledge that Lilac had seen from above were two small cliff dwellings. They had been built into a shallow cave that had once been a pocket of mudstone encapsulated by a layer of harder limestone. As the layer of limestone wore down, the softer mudstone was exposed and eroded away leaving the opening. *Sinagua* farmers had taken advantage of the cool temperature inside and built their homes overlooking their fields in the bottom of the canyon. Both homes had a single doorway set in mortared walls made from the same limestone as the cliff face. The dark shadows, angle, and vegetation on the narrow ledge had kept them hidden from below.

The ladder was just long enough to reach the ledge, with the top rung a foot below the edge of the cliff. Skip and Lilac had scouted the ridge but hadn't found another obvious way down. The first of the two dwellings was three rooms deep; Skip and Lilac were in the last room, shining a flashlight on the back wall, gawking at the elaborate scene depicting hunters with drawn bows chasing and killing what they guessed were deer or elk and bighorn sheep. The larger animals had antler racks; the smaller ones curved horns. A shaman figure was standing in the middle with a humped back and three legs, one arm raised and holding a stick. A section of the wall had been chiseled off.

In the second room they had found intact painted pots neatly lined against one wall. On another wall were rustic stands made from juniper limbs with stacks of textiles, worn but still in one piece. There were also baskets filled with sea shells, large and small. Empty alcoves had been carved into the limestone sidewalls, like shrines for a family saint in an old Italian villa. *Something valuable had been displayed there.* Stone and yucca woven fetishes in the shapes of bears, coyotes, owls, and eagles were scattered in a corner. Decaying poles were lying on the floor. Skip could see the holes in the short ceiling and floor where he guessed they had originally stood. Why, he couldn't figure. Maybe it was to keep food off the floor away from rodents or maybe they had supported animal skin walls separating the rooms.

"How long since you think someone was in here?" Lilac asked, she was carefully dusting the side of a brown clay pot painted with a striped-red design. She also saw black-and-white Anasazi pots with their intricate geometric designs. One piece had a speckle-painted mountain lion as a handle. There were also bowls that she recognized as being from the Hohokam culture further south, with crudely painted cranes, turtles, and snakes decorating the bottoms.

"Not long, the ladder looks newer, and it was too clean to have been laying there for years in the weather. Nothing growing through it either."

"This pottery is amazing and it's from all over, not just the *Sinagua*. I think this might have been a trader's home. There's *Anasazi, Hohokam, Mogollan*, and these shells are from the Pacific," Lilac said, amazed at the breadth of what they were seeing. "This is a *MAJOR* find. God knows what's already been looted; whoever found it did a hack job on the glyphs. If it weren't for the ladder and the damage, I would have guessed we were the first people in here since the *Sinagua* left. I can almost hear them even though it's been hundreds of years."

"They'll be back," Skip said.

"I hope so."

"The looters, I mean. There's a lot of money left in here."

"Transporting items from here undetected has to be a nightmare," Lilac mused. "It's not like you can back a panel truck up to the door. You'd have to take piece-by-piece up top, careful not to break anything. These pots are extremely fragile. They'd have to be wrapped, crated, and then hauled seven miles to the trailhead. This work would take a crew, at least two or three. You'd have to do it at night, you wouldn't want to risk running into hikers on Jacks Canyon."

"Probably take years," Skip said, giving Lilac a meaningful look.

"Zeb?"

"Circumstantial maybe, but with his background in archeology and the crowd we know he was hanging with, I don't know if I can buy his being out here as a coincidence. There must be dozens of mapped bike trails in Sedona, Lilac. We're two miles from any of them."

"Let's go investigate the other dwelling," she said, not yet ready to judge the dead. "There are lots of... "

Before she finished her sentence, Skip swore and darted toward the opening to the dwelling. Lilac ran after him. Bursting into the sunlight on the ledge she watched Skip leap in the air trying to grab the bottom of the ladder that was being pulled up the side of the cliff. His fingers slipped off the bottom rung, and he fell hard back to the ledge, one foot landing awkwardly on a rock. Lilac screamed as his leg buckled and he bounced over the edge.

"Did he go over?" she heard a voice up top ask another person who said, "I couldn't tell for sure, I think so." Both voices laughed.

Lilac ignored them and ran to where Skip had vanished. She hadn't heard him scream, not that he would. Stopping just before the edge she glanced up to where she'd heard the voices. Getting shot or having a boulder thrown on her would only make the situation worse. The ladder was gone, and she didn't see anyone, but she did hear scuffling. She grabbed for her Glock and remembered it was in her holster inside the dwelling. She'd taken it off to lean into one of the bigger pots. *Damn! Running back without checking on Skip wasn't an option.* She looked up one more time, *SCREW IT!* She got down on all fours and then laid flat to look over the edge like her Search and Rescue training had taught her. She'd seen the end result of too many falls to hold out much hope. It was at least a seventy foot straight drop and the chances of surviving that high of a fall onto the rocks below wasn't good. Lilac took a deep breath and peaked over the rim.

"Hi," Skip said grimacing, gritting his teeth. He was looking up in pain at Lilac, hanging onto a dead branch just below the ledge with his right hand. He had managed to find a foothold with the tip of one boot. "It's my knee, you'll have to help me up."

Lilac sneaked another glance to the top over her shoulder, *So far so good.* She found a depression in the rock ledge behind her feet and dug the toes of her hiking boots in, lowering her arm down to Skip's free hand. He tightly grasped the underside of her wrist and she did the same, creating a firm arm lock.

"I'll try to find another foothold, but I'm not much good with a busted leg," he said, glad it was a six-foot yoga instructor with tight abs who had hold of him.

"No excuses. On three," Lilac said. "One-two-three..."

Skip felt the weight come off his foot that had found the toehold. Lilac was groaning and he could see the muscles in her neck bulging. Lying down, her core was supported by solid rock, but she'd only be able to raise him a foot at most before she'd need to regrip or else lower him back down. He raised his good knee, and his foot found the stub of a higher root. It gave a little but held enough that he took a gamble. He let go of the branch with his right hand. The root he'd found with his foot broke with his shift in weight. Lilac was holding all his 185 pounds with one arm. He reached up and grabbed the edge of the ledge with his fingers, clawing until he found a tiny crack.

"Can you grab my right wrist?" Lilac grunted. She turned it upside down and laid it beside his hand.

Skip looked up at her, "Drop me, Lilac! I'll pull you over." As strong as she was, she couldn't have much left. He could feel the shaking in her arm.

"Shut up and grab my wrist! I'll swing you until you can get a leg on the ledge."

"Lilac," Skip calmly said. "Drop me, swinging won't work with my knee. You'd have to pull me up deadweight. Honey, it's over, I... I..." he stuttered.

"Just hold on," she said. She squeezed the wrist she had hold of tighter, signaling letting him fall wasn't an option.

They shared a last look and Lilac closed her eyes, steeling herself. She knew she was about to get all his weight again. He let go of his hold and they quickly locked their second wrists. He was dangling in the air with both arms fully extended above his head. It was all up to Lilac now. She tensed her muscles again and groaned against the weight. She pulled until she couldn't pull her arms back farther without letting go. *Eight inches.* Not much, but enough for Skip to get his elbows up over the edge, taking some of the weight off her. She slid one hand and then the other farther down his arms and regripped. With his wiggling she pulled him until his waist was over the rock ledge. His first scream had been as his damaged knee came over the edge.

They were both exhausted lying on the ledge when they heard clapping up above. "Pay up, I told you she'd save him," a voice said, familiar to both Skip and Lilac. "Shut up!" another voice barked.

"Landish," Skip whispered to Lilac. His mind flashed a mental picture of the Whopper- laden big man hiking Jacks Canyon. *No time to solve that inconsistency now*, he thought.

Lilac was breathing heavily and her arms felt like jello, but she sprang up and ran to get her gun. *Maybe they'd be stupid enough to lean over and give her a shot.* At thirty feet all she needed was a two-inch window.

"Landon! You Skittles-sucking-pig!" Skip yelled, hoping he'd lean over, giving Lilac a window of opportunity.

"What's so hard about keeping your mouth shut?" the other voice chastised Landish.

"They're not getting out of there, what's it matter?" Landish argued back. He leaned over and yelled down to Skip, "You got what you deserve. I'm finished here and Sky's leaving with..."

The fat man's gibe was cut off by a thud into the tree he was standing beside. He'd moved at the last moment, and Lilac's shot had missed by less than an inch. "*BITCH!*" he screamed as a second shot tore a chunk off his left shoe, grazing his big toe. If not for his brother pulling him back the third shot would have ripped into his testicles, torn through his suspensory ligament, and ended somewhere in his gut. Angrily, Lilac shouted a stream of less-than-complimentary adjectives and emptied ten more rounds into blue sky.

After her last shot, a power bar landed on the ledge in a final taunt. "See how long this lasts," Landish laughed. "Hey sweet cheeks. Watch your back. Your boyfriend isn't who you think he is. You better save those last bullets to shoot the asshole and cut off his beefsteak when you get hungry. Just do it while you're still wet enough to enjoy it."

"You're sick," Lilac screamed up.

"Water?" Skip mouthed to Lilac, realizing that was their real problem. He'd stupidly left his up top.

"No," she mouthed pointing up.

They'd both left their backpacks up top like a couple of greenhorns; the excitement of their discovery having replaced their good sense.

"How about some water, too?" Skip called up, thinking it didn't hurt to ask.

An empty Gatorade bottle bounced on the ledge. "Urine in for a tough time," the other voice called down. Both men started laughing.

34

POLE VAULTING

LILAC HELPED A GIMPY SKIP HOBBLE OVER TO THE LITTLE BIT of shade between the doors to the ruins. They hadn't heard anything more from Landish or his companion since the empty bottle landed. That was three hours ago. With only a few hours of sunlight left it seemed certain they would be spending the night with their *Sinagua* hosts.

"How's the knee feeling?" Lilac had fished a two-pill package of aspirin from her jean pocket. Their emergency first aid kit was up top with their water bottles and phones. Skip had refused the aspirin to save for later.

"Fine."

Lilac could see it was swollen. They had zipped the leg off his khakis to assess the damage. The skin was abraded, though not as bad as the nylon pants. The swelling around his kneecap was complimented by a darkening bruise. The good news was he could still bend it and stand. It hurt but held. Lilac had him get up and move every fifteen minutes and then elevate it.

"I don't think you tore any ligaments or busted the cap. It seems it's just a deep sprain. When we get out of here, you'll need medevacked as soon as we get in service.

"I'll be okay," Skip answered.

"You try hiking out of here and you will mess something up. You're going to wait up top while I hike out to where I can make a call. That's if you can get that far."

Skip nodded. He knew better than to argue with Florence Nightingale. There wasn't a doubt in his mind their bags and phones would be gone when they found a way up top. When the time came, he would find a suitable stick to use as a crutch and walk out. In the meantime, job number one was finding a way either back up to the ridge or down to the canyon floor. Lilac had already scouted along the edge of the ledge and nixed down as impossible.

Skip was thinking the *Sinagua* people had to have a way to and from their home; up seemed far easier, safer, and less than half the distance. He knew they would have placed a kiva pole or two at different levels to climb on, but they also would have had a trail of some sort. If they managed to walk up and down the Grand Canyon, they certainly did the same here. It was less than forty feet.

He hobbled along the front of the first dwelling examining the mortar work. Lilac watched him and shrugged, "Your leg, do what you want." Halfway between the door opening and left edge of the cliff he noticed that stones were missing in the wall. He could tell they hadn't just fallen out; the stonework had been intention-ally recessed and mortared two inches into the face of the wall. He stepped into the first hole with his good leg; the second higher hole he couldn't bend his bad knee enough to reach.

"Come here, I might have found something."

Lilac came and saw what he'd found. She quickly scampered up the mortared wall using the toeholds like steps. By their spacing it was obvious that's what they were. "They stop here." She was standing on the top row of stacked stones, leaning against the limestone cliff with her feet level to his eyes, still more than twenty feet below the ridgetop.

"Go along the row you're standing on. Do you see any indents or holes in the rock or stone?" Skip asked. He was thinking he might know how his Sinagua friends came and went – maybe.

"There's a hole down this way," Lilac started edging her way against the cliff along the top of the mortared wall. "It's in the top of the wall, about four inches square and just as deep," she said inspecting it.

"Stay there," Skip said and disappeared into the first dwelling. Lilac saw the end of one of the poles they'd seen inside slide out the door. She watched Skip scoot the rest of it out onto the ledge. The pole was about eight feet tall and there were a series of knots where limbs had once been cut off. She knew at once what Skip had found – Native ladders.

She started to climb back down, but Skip repeated, "Stay there, I can stand it up and push it to you. Put it in…"

"I'm with you," Lilac said. *Mansplaining*, she thought.

Without too much trouble Skip got the pole in position. With his pushing and Lilac's pulling she got it on the row of stones and placed in the hole in no time. She leaned the pole straight up the cliff where it rolled into a chiseled notch securing its top. Lilac climbed up the knots and found the pole rested beside another horizontal ledge on the cliff. It couldn't have been more than ten feet wide and a step deep. She was still a good fifteen feet below the top. Looking at the narrow ledge she spied another hole cut into the rock.

"Is there another pole?" she called down to Skip. He limped back inside, and a second shorter pole appeared. "Hold on, I'm coming back down."

Their problem was getting the second pole up to the horizontal ledge fifteen feet above the landing outside the dwellings.

Lilac lifted the second pole to check its weight. She could carry it on level ground, but no way could she climb the first pole carrying the second one. And even if she could, she'd then have to cling against the cliff face, moving herself and the second pole along a narrow ten foot ledge over to where it fit. It was a job requiring two healthy people.

"There's no way I can get that second pole up there without falling." They both glanced at the edge Skip had gone over. "There'd be no stopping me if I fell."

"I've got to somehow make it up the steps in the mortared wall. It's only six feet," Skip said determinedly. "You can go up first and I'll lift both poles to you. Then you help me up. If I can make it there, I'll be able to inch along the top of the wall and lift the second pole to you right by where it goes."

"It'll still be short of the top. Is there a third pole?" Lilac pointed out.

"No, but one step at a time. Maybe when you get up the second pole, you'll be able to free climb the rest of the way, or you'll find more chiseled steps."

Lilac went back up the steps in the wall. Skip raised the first pole which she notched in place. He lifted the second smaller pole to her and she rested it on the top of the wall below where he'd need to lift it to her. Now it was all up to Skip to climb the ancient stairs. His knee had loosened a bit from all the activity and he managed to get his second foot into the second step. But raising his weight on the bad leg was a no-go. It took Lilac pulling him from up above to straighten his bad knee and reach the third step with his good leg. It hurt like hell, but working together he got to the top of the wall, winded, his strength running low, and the bad knee nearly nonfunctional.

Lilac climbed the first pole, inched across the cliff face to the second ladder base and waited on Skip to catch his breath. After a couple of minutes he carefully stepped along the top of the mortared wall to below where Lilac was standing. Bending, he balanced himself against the cliff wall to grab the second pole and lift it to Lilac. He had the pole standing up and started lifting it when his knee buckled. *Shit*. There were two bad choices, let go of the pole to keep from falling or fall with it. The pole fell to the landing outside the dwelling, flipped once...and was teetering on end at the edge of the ledge...*please please fall backwards*. Skip moaned as a gust from the Gods decided the matter against them.

"Why don't I try free climbing the last fifteen feet?" Lilac suggested. She had climbed back down to the ledge. Skip had refused her help with the steps; going down, gravity was on his side – if not the wind. She did get him to pop the two aspirin, which dulled his throbbing knee but hadn't improved his mood.

"Too dangerous, and it's getting dark. It's my fault, I shouldn't have dropped the friggin' pole."

"Let's check out the second dwelling while we can still see," Lilac said, heading to the opening. "It looks the same. Maybe we'll find more poles and can try again in the morning." They both accepted they were spending the night in the ruins.

Skip, groaning and swearing, managed to stand and joined her in the first room. It was almost identical to the other dwelling with the exception of being completely emptied of any artifacts. All they found were newer pine slats, a couple of broken crates, and a few scattered nails. "Looks like this was Bad Santa's workshop. Wonder how they got out of here, a sleigh and mule deer?" he asked sarcastically thinking of the missing ladder.

The second and third rooms were also empty. The gouged back wall in the last room meant there had been another set of petroglyphs. More work scraps and a half-empty plastic bottle of water laid on the floor. "That should buy us an extra couple of days in the Presidential Suite," Skip quipped. "My knee's really tightening up. That aspirin is not lasting long."

"It's the swelling, stay off it. At least we can use the slats for a fire," Lilac said. "If this house was as full as the first one, they've been working here a long time."

Skip was investigating the corner of the back wall. The light was almost gone, and shadows were filling the room. He felt air moving on his leg and ran his hands down the wall. Above the floor his fingers found a crack.

"Let me see your flashlight." Lilac kept it clipped onto her holster.

"Why?"

"There's a crack over here, lower to the floor."

Lilac shone the flashlight toward where he was standing. Like in Dwelling One the back wall was where the cave dead-ended into rock, but the texture where Skip was now digging was slightly different. The color of the rock was the same, but it looked smoother.

"I felt air," Skip said. He had managed to kneel on his good knee with his bad leg stretched out behind him. "There's a crack here. It's loose." He was chipping the crack with his pocketknife, and it was getting bigger. "This isn't rock...it's stucco...dried mud. It sounds hollow," he said pounding the surface with his fist.

Lilac was shining her light on the wall around the crack. She traced a faint outline of where the wall had been patched. "I think its mortar," she said. "There was an opening here." She started scratching along the outline with the end of her flashlight.

After a half hour of scraping and finding more cracks, they uncovered a stacked stone section roughly the size needed for a person to crawl through. "This stonework looks newer than what was done in the outside wall, still old, but it's not the same workmanship," Skip said. "Let's see if we can knock it in." Sitting down in front of the stacked stone, it only took four good kicks with their three feet before the opening collapsed inward.

Lilac crawled in first. Skip followed. They crept through a tight tunnel several yards long, Skip dragging his bum knee and banging his head more than once, but not about to miss out on the adventure. Finally, the passageway opened into a large chamber that went farther back into the cliff. The mudstone deposit had been much deeper and bigger in this section, and they had just enough height to stand. The ceiling was dome-shaped and covered with pictograph paintings of stars, planets, streaking comets, and sun symbols. The paintings were divided into four quadrants with different placements of stars and planets. Stone benches lined the perimeter. *Kuul's astrologically attuned ancestors would be jealous.*

"Different seasons," Lilac said, pointing out the different positions of the Big Dipper. "It's a celestial chart."

Skip had wandered deeper into the chamber. "This room was walled-in in 1873, maybe 74."

"It's gotta be older than that, look at the ceiling. This is definitely *Sinagua*. The later tribes didn't like to go near these places – bad spirits," Lilac said. "How can you be so exact?"

She walked to where Skip was standing. He grasped her hand holding the flashlight and pointed it to the ground. "That's why." Lying on the floor were two piles of blue and gray rags covering two skeletons.

"Those are U.S. infantry uniforms! How in the world did they manage to get themselves walled in the back of a *Sinagua* ruin?"

Skip remembered Sasse's story about the Yavapai massacre, "There was a massacre in this canyon in 1873. Trey Sasse is recording an oral history at the Tribal Center offices and one of the elders told it to him. The cavalry cornered a band of Yavapai and killed every man, woman, and child. How these two ended up in here, I don't have a clue."

Skip pulled the clothing off the skeletons, "Their legs are disarticulated and look at the skulls, they're bashed." He noticed small holes in the bones like they'd been hammered with an ice pick, "I think those are from Beetles."

"And those are arrows," Lilac said pointing at sticks stuck in the two torsos.

"They didn't go quietly into the night, that's for sure. Looks like they were tortured." They looked for any identification or equipment that might help identify the remains. There was nothing left but the uniforms, which were rags. Even the metal buttons had been removed.

Lilac was deep in thought. The soldiers had surely been killed and left here by Natives. The 1873 date fit. But if they had been part of the massacre their bodies would have been recovered back then by their own troops. Meaning there would be a record of these ruins. "Did Sasse say if the Yavapai were trapped in here?" she asked. "There has to be some connection."

"Not that I remember. He knew about the granary on the ridge, but he didn't say anything about these ruins. He did give Kuul a case of woolies with a story about the Yavapai still believing there were bad spirits out here."

"Hmmm," Lilac murmured. "I bet the Yavapai retreated up here and these soldiers took part in the massacre. Maybe they came back later to loot the site. The army at Camp Verde and a few early ranchers were the first Europeans in the valley since the Spanish, if you don't count the mountain men. They were the first to discover the ruins and pueblos. Soldiering back then was a pretty boring career choice except when they were campaigning against the tribes. Most of the year they just drilled, drank, and tried to stay busy, restless boys with time on their hands. That's how the antiquity trade in the Southwest got started."

Skip was working their story out in his head, "And these two got caught by Natives and payback's a bitch," Skip said. "If they were out here on their own it'd explain why there's no record of these ruins. Whoever caught them probably hid the bodies to avoid the cavalry's reprisal."

"Maybe. We'll never know for sure, but I bet we'll find a record of two AWOL soldiers that year."

"That second voice," Skip said, thinking out loud. Something about the massacre story was nagging him. "Did you recognize it?"

• • •

Lilac had gathered the discarded packing materials in the front room of Dwelling Two. It had taken her less than a minute to shave off a handful of splinters from the pine slats, rub two of the larger pieces together, and get a fire started. Even though the temperature had reached the mid-90s earlier, once the sun set the desert got cold. Neither of them had brought jackets or sweaters, they'd planned on being back in their warm beds by this time.

Another pair of aspirin buried in the small coin pocket of her jeans had helped Skip's swelling go down. He wasn't complaining, but she knew he was in pain. She had found a pot just the right size to put under his knee to ease the strain. He was lying propped up by the fire staring at the flames. It had been quite a day and tomorrow... well, tomorrow was anyone's guess. Neither one of them would be falling asleep anytime soon.

"What did Landish mean?" Lilac asked with as little accusation in her tone as possible. She didn't want to be mad at him given their circumstances and his injury. And she knew he had been refusing the water to save it for her. She put a few more slats on the fire, they wouldn't last long. The light illuminating his face revealed no reaction to her question, not a flicker of concern she had circled back to Landish's warning.

"What?"

"The secrets and his telling me you aren't who I think you are." Skip's playing dumb was irritating. He knew what she was referencing. Sure, Landish was a liar but even liars told the truth occasionally.

"Deflection from a con artist caught red-handed," Skip said. "He was just driving a wedge."

"It didn't seem like that." She wasn't ready to let it go. If she was going to be stuck with him in an Indian graveyard and possibly die of exposure and thirst, he owed her an honest answer. "Every time I've asked you about before you came to Sedona, you've gone all zero dark thirty. I think I deserve to know who I'm on this ledge with...don't you?"

"I am who you think I am," Skip said cryptically.

"Thanks for being so open!"

The fire had burned down and only a few bluish flames were lighting the room. It was a moonless night and all they could see was the silhouette of the door, beyond which were a few early stars that seemed close enough to touch. The walls had disappeared in inky darkness. Lilac wondered if a *Sinagua* couple had huddled around a fire here a thousand years ago arguing about their lives and future. There were ghosts here, she could feel them.

Skip laid the rest of the way down and rolled over away from the fire, away from her questions. She was surprised when he spoke.

"There are things I can't tell you...I don't want to tell you. You're better off trusting who I am now."

"But..."

"Lilac, leave it be," he said icily.

35

COFFEE, INTRAVENOUS DRIPS, OR ME

"SWEETIE, YOU DID THE RIGHT THING STAYING HERE," ZULA Ballsy told Sky. "I can use some help tending the *SOB* and with the cabins." Zula had offered her a job, at least temporarily until the poor thing figured out what she wanted to do. At the girl's request, and against her better judgement, she'd made her a cup of rosemary-spiked yucca flower tea to toast her employment. To Zula, it tasted like she'd dug up a weed and brewed it in soapy water. She'd have a hot cup of black coffee when they finished their talk. But right now, empathy was the order of the day.

"I know aliens are real. They took my appendix," Sky said. "This is good tea," Sky exclaimed, changing direction quicker than a hummingbird on crack. "Did you make a pot? I guess I need to learn where the supplies are stocked."

"We're out of rosemary," Zula hastily said. "Honey, most aliens are good people, the green mob Landish attracts would have taken more than your appendix. That Whopper bastard could talk the life out of a Shriner convention, and they'd pay him to do it. Believe me - you're better off without him. How about some coffee?"

Sky was fishing rosemary sprigs from the bottom of her cup and feeding them to Spike. The javelina had taken a liking to her ever since the night of the party when she'd snuck him a Corona. "It's not just that he doesn't believe my story. There's a part of him that scares me."

"Landish shouldn't scare you, Honey. He's all bluster."

"No, not him. Skip. One minute his aura's all muddy red and there's a memory and anger he can't let go of. The next minute it's a white honesty and he seems so pure. That night at the fire it was black and ruthless. He's like the phantom from the musical, you know."

"Oh . . . now he's harder. I don't know jack about auras, but he's the kind of man who only sees straight ahead. It's that directness that's scary. You're right about them other colors, but I think you can boil it all down to some unresolved grief. The anger and darkness come from there. He's as honest as the day is long about everything other than that."

"I - don't - know," Sky said, stretching her words as she did her thoughts. She had come to Zula in tears, having split with her Reggie, and totally confused about her future and her feelings for Skip. Reggie had been in a hurry to leave after Skip's ultimatum. He'd asked her to go with him but wasn't willing to give her time to think it over.

"Sky, his word is as good as gold at my bank. I'm not too worried about who he was. A little mystery is a good thing. He reminds me of Sinatra, always knows what he's doing and confident enough he doesn't give a hoot who follows. Frank held the Rat Pack together the same way Skip does here in his own solid quiet way."

Sky laughed a little, "Sounds like the song – *And let the record show I did it my way*," she said, singing the last line.

"Pretty voice," Zula clapped. "I've been thinking about adding live entertainment at the *SOB*." She gave the younger girl a friendly questioning look.

"Maybe, I'll think about it. I do play the guitar and know a lot of Joni Mitchell songs. But it'd be for free, you've already offered me more than enough."

"We'll work on your repertoire," Zula smiled. She was warming to the idea of having an assistant she could rely on to help manage the retreat. If things worked out, maybe she'd be able to take a vacation. Ballsey was a name still good for a comp'd room off the strip.

Spike had finished the rosemary sprigs and was nosing around Zula's legs. If she was sitting on the porch, he was expecting bacon. *You like her too, don't you boy*, she thought, patting the stiff ring of fur behind his head. She had sent Sky to get a carafe of coffee and leftover ham in the *SOB* fridge. Cubes of ham with *queso* and salsa on a Ritz had been last night's half-priced bar apps. Zula heard a honk and the AAA Plumbers to the Stars van pulled into the retreat. Kuul parked next to Lilac's jeep, the only other auto in the lot.

"Where is everyone?" he yelled out, seeing Zula was alone.

"Landish and his crew, except the girl, checked out early," Zula answered as the big Mayan walked up the porch steps. "I don't have another booking until next week. Thank your Great Spirit," she said looking up, opening her arms. "How about some coffee, the girl's bringing a pot."

"That girl, Sky?" Kuul asked. Zula nodded. "Trouble amongst the rocks for our friend," Kuul cheekily commented.

"A little competition is always a good thing," the old dancer winked.

"You seen Skip? I tried calling but nada, nothing, just his smart-alecky message to *Not* leave a message unless you are booking a tour. I don't think he really cares." Zula shrugged. "I wanted to tell him about the suspicious *National Treasure* collection I saw at Cage's. You know he gets moonstruck by any bit of bling that catches his eye."

Sky backed out the screen door carrying a tray. "Oh, Hi," she said on seeing Kuul.

"*Yatahey*," the Navajo said in movie Injun.

Zula rolled her eyes, "He's looking for Skip. I was just about to tell him he hadn't made his normal early morning appearance." Sky poured two cups of the thickest coffee she'd ever seen, handing one to Zula and offering the second mug to Kuul who shook his head *no*.

"You only have two cups, go ahead," he said to Sky.

Sky looked at the honey floating on the gooey black surface that Zula told her to add and thought of the poor bees who had worked so hard only to have their fruits confiscated. "I don't mind," she said, handing the cup to Kuul.

"The Bronco's been out of the corral since yesterday morning, now that I think about it," Zula said. "He didn't come over last night either. I chocked it up to Landish still being here. Sorry Honey." Actually, she thought his seclusion had more to do with the girl than the fat man.

"That jeep?" Kuul said, nodding toward the parking lot, meaning *Where's Lilac*?

With Sky hanging around, Zula had hoped to avoid explaining why Lilac's jeep had been there since yesterday...overnight. She didn't know for sure but could make a good guess. The poor girl was scrambled enough already. Lilac and Skip were probably shacked up and the Bronco in the shop again.

"They left yesterday morning. I watched them put their backpacks in his Bronco. They'd argued over which car to take," Sky reported, surprising both Zula and Kuul.

And she still stuck around this morning, mooning over Skip, Zula thought. There was more to this free spirited pig-tailed painted-toed girl than met the eye. Zula had to admire her commitment and confidence. Despite the zany appearance and alien stories, she was obviously a straight-ahead *Knows-what-to-do* type of girl, just like someone else they knew.

Backpacks, Kuul thought. Skip had tried to get him back out to Red Spirit Canyon, but he'd scheduled the installation of the water filtering system at Nick's. *He had probably talked Lilac into going instead.*

"And you're sure they haven't come back?"

"Pretty sure," Sky said sheepishly glancing sideways at Zula, "I've been watching."

• • •

Kuul found the Bronco at Jacks Canyon trailhead. His only predicament was whether or not to take his IV nurse from Phoenix. He'd invited her to his Hogan, and they were hooking up in Sedona before heading north. Brandy worked at a private clinic in Scottsdale that offered subscription detox and nutrient IVs and therapeutic massages. Al had introduced them and Kuul had signed up for a Chelator Hydro drip and scalp rub, good for pulling heavy metals out and hangovers. Sitting in her chair with a needle in his arm, Kuul had fascinated her with indigenous plant remedies. They'd struck a deal; Kuul would brew Bushy Birds Beak tea to shorten her menstrual cycles and Brandy knew a special massage that doubled the output of sperm.

When Kuul suggested a hike before the medical exchange, Brandy said, *"I'm loaded with liquid electrolytes and aminos, exercise is nature's aphrodisiac you know,"* and slipped into the soled moccasins she'd brought for the Hogan. With any luck they wouldn't find Skip and her Vitamin E and B12 energy shots would kick in somewhere along the trail.

It wasn't hard to find the path Skip and Lilac had taken. He tracked them across the same off-trail approach to Red Spirit Canyon they'd taken on their last hike. But to impress Brandy, he made a point of stopping to inspect broken twigs and knelt to study the deer and bobcat tracks they'd passed. Most impressive to the nurse was the Mayan healer preparing a natural supplement of juniper berry puree from a pile of dried coyote scat. They were high in antioxidants and mixed well with the potassium drip in her hydro pack.

Brandy had no problem keeping up with the wily Native tracker; they reached the switchbacks by mid-day with having only stopped twice, once for the scat snack and again for an open-air massage and shared bottle of Yippyjiz Energy Juice. By the time they climbed to the ridge top, Kuul could smell her sweat, citrusy and stringent like lemon-lime Gatorade with a dash of fecal matter.

Kuul led Brandy toward the granary. She was excited about using ancient corn pollen as an additive to her massage oils. Kneeling in the sand, he pointed to two sets of footprints, one heading toward the granary and another going in the other direction. Fancying the edible oil idea, he followed the former. After several steps, he stopped, holding his hand up scout style. "Voices!"

. . .

"I was behind the juniper tree uncovering the ladder!" Skip argued. Lilac's patience had evaporated when they couldn't find the power bar for breakfast. She'd been quick to accuse him of eating it while she was sleeping. Neither of them had had anything for over thirty hours except sips of stale water. They'd spent a lot of calories since leaving the Bronco.

"So, it's my fault our bottles and packs are up top?" Lilac barked back. "It's a good thing there are two ruins down here. Tonight, you're barracking with the soldier boys."

"You were the last one with our gear," Skip shot back.

"Forget sleeping with soldier blue, this place isn't big enough for both of us," Lilac shouted the traditional western movie challenge. "I've got the gun. Take your pick, jump or shut up!"

"You're out of shells," Skip chided, not backing down. "Besides, my knee..." he groaned, rubbing the scratches and trying out his best Basset hound look. When Lilac was hungry all bets were off. He felt like the punk at the end of Dirty Harry only he didn't want to rely on an empty clip.

"Busted knee or not, shooting you would make my day. Not to mention conserving water. Just try me and..."

Lilac stopped her threat as the knotted end of a rope hit him on his head, knocking him down. *Good.* She looked up to the edge of the cliff and saw Kuul with a girl in blue scrubs sucking from a plastic bag. *Thank God.*

The Mayan yelled down, "He hurt?"

Lilac nodded yes.

"Well, if you don't shoot him, make a harness and we'll pull him up first."

"Good to see you Kuul. Give me a minute to think it over."

36

PROTECTIVE PIGEON
AND HERO PIG

SKIP'S KNEE WAS PROPPED ON A CIRCUS CIRCUS SOUVENIR pillow. He was lying in the glider on his porch having a lengthy conversation with his buddy Don Julio. Don had doused himself with prickly pear syrup, opened up, and was pouring out his soul. Zula had insisted on adding liniment to his aspirin regimen and rubbed his knee with a smelly goop, claiming it worked miracles for her bursitis. Alone, back at his cabin, he'd given Don a couple of extra-strength ibuprofen. Not only was he pain free but feeling sweet, sour, and well-lubed.

On the way back from Red Spirit Canyon, while Brandy had administered a field Hydration and Healthy Relation drip to Skip, they had agreed to turn the whole mess over to Chief Hooton in the morning. Lilac had said she was done and argued it was time to get the officials involved; they'd been shot at twice and left for dead at the ruins. They knew at least one of their assailants: Landish. Kuul had agreed once they'd told him what they'd found in the ruins; the ladder, nails, and lumber were physical proof of a serious crime. Skip had pointed out they still didn't know whether or not Zebulon had been involved, although he admitted they probably never would.

Around midnight he'd left his drinking buddy sitting on the porch and stumbled to bed. It hadn't taken long for Escobar to find him. They were running through the same Halloween house of horrors with the addition of two cavalry dragoons on horseback joining the chase. This time Escobar had closed in and started poking his machete on Skip's back shoulder...

"Wake up," he heard Escobar say, the poking getting harder but somehow not breaking the skin.

"Let's do it here and get it over with," one of the dragoons said.

He heard Escobar yell at the younger voice. His thick accent was gone. The haze clouding Skip's mind began to lift, and he opened his eyes. He'd been hard asleep and being awakened so suddenly was disorienting. He looked around his room for Escobar and his bloody machete. The fog lifted, his eyes and mind clearing. It wasn't the cartel henchman. Trey Sasse, the tribal archeologist/Jack Benny of the reservation world, was standing beside his bed. A younger man he didn't recognize wearing a ski cap advertising Red Bull was at the foot. He focused on Red Bull who was holding a Walther .22 with silencer.

"You boys want a night cap," Skip smirked. "Thanks for the Gatorade by the way," he said to Sasse.

Sasse smiled, "I wondered if you recognized my voice. When my young colleague went back out there today and found you were gone...well, I had to assume you did."

"So, what know?" Skip said sitting up. His brain spun inside his head, and his mouth was dry. *Don wasn't helping.* Red Bull took a step back, keeping the Walther pointed at his chest.

"Now we take a long walk in the woods. Skip Rhodes is going to disappear into the night the same way he arrived – no one knowing anything about you." Sasse had been holding his right hand behind his back and brought out a matching Walther as Skip swung his legs to the floor and stood. "Just in case you're thinking about jumping my friend."

Skip didn't have any choice but to play along. It was a mistake on their part to not do him here. He might have a chance outside in the dark. He'd have to act fast, and it wouldn't be easy with the throbbing in his head and being a tad dizzy. At least he still had his shoes on. He tried buying some time.

"I should have suspected after you tried scaring us away from the canyon with the graveyard warning. Very slick how you got Kuul to be the one to actually remark about *not disrupting the spirits.*

Sasse grinned smartly, "You both should have listened better. Even our shooting at you and your fake Navajo didn't work."

A bad feeling, a panicked sense of alarm, passed through Skip's mind. *Kuul and Lilac knew as much as he did.* "Kuul, Lilac," he stammered.

"I told you there was nothing out there, but you and your girl-friend had to see for yourselves. You should have left it alone," Sasse said, realizing what Skip was thinking and intentionally torturing him. "They're fine. *FOR NOW,*" he grinned. "We decided to cut off the headfirst. Let's go." Sasse motioned his Walther at the door.

Red Bull prodded him with his gun to move. That was opportunity number one; Skip decided to let it pass. He could take out Red Bull, but that would be it. Sasse was locked and loaded and too far away to reach. The odds of disabling him before he fired weren't in his favor; he could get off one maybe even two shots. Then again, the man wasn't trained, he might hesitate just enough… *no, he needed to be patient. It wouldn't be just his life he gambled, but also Lilac's and Kuul's.* Skip walked into the cabin's living area and stopped by the open screen door.

"So, what was Landish's connection?" Skip asked, stalling for time.

"You're stalling," Sasse warned and then seemed to reconsider. "I guess it doesn't hurt to bring you up to speed. A man ought to know what he's dying for." Sasse was standing just out of reach to his right and Red Bull had taken up position to Skip's rear.

"Landish is my long lost little brother," Sasse said. "He found me when he was up in Utah. Unfortunately, it was after he had started his alien scam. I couldn't convince him to drop it, but I did talk him into coming to Sedona."

"The cousin?" Skip said, putting the pieces together and wanting to keep him talking. He slowly turned to face Sasse, not wanting to put him on the defensive. Red Bull was now in his peripheral vision.

"I almost cut him loose when I found out he was running his mouth about *his cousin*. But once you started sticking your face into my business I needed another hand. Plus business, as I explained to you, is picking up. He didn't have any scruples; it was just a matter of giving him directions. He didn't get any growing up."

"Was it you or Landish I chased?"

Sasse laughed devilishly, "You almost killed him making him run that way. He wanted to quit after that. I had to threaten to expose his scam. Of course, he could have done the same with me. You might say it was a Mexican standoff. We both had to do what the other wanted. I promised him he could finish his meetings and then we'd go our own ways. Stay in touch maybe, but no more working together. I could have used him in New Mexico, but in the end he just wasn't reliable."

"Why not have Red Bull back there play the prowler?"

"I was making a delivery," Red Bull answered. "Let's cut the talking and get this over with," he said to Sasse.

"You heard him, youth are always in such a hurry," Sasse said. "In this case, he's probably right. We're going to the creek and take the trail away from the lodge. No sense bothering Zula Ballsy and her guests. Get moving."

Skip stopped on the last porch step. "One last question. Humor me." As long as Sasse was in a talkative mood he might as well ask, "Zebulon Ballsy, was he collaborating with you?"

"He was a friend," Red Bull answered, his tone betraying he was upset by what had happened to him.

Sasse stared at Skip. "If it hadn't been for him, we wouldn't be here now, would we? Zebulon Ballsy..." Sasse said the name slowly, making up his mind what to say. *Because of the kid he now would have to empty out the ruins quicker than he had planned. He'd hoped to keep filling orders for a few more years, keeping the ruins as his own personal warehouse.*

"He was too smart for his own good," Sasse started. "He was working with us...sure. He was the one who found the ruins. He was a volunteer at the tribal center and helped me transcribe the story about the massacre. Native elders like retelling their history to younger people. Kid went out there, put two and two together, found the dwellings and came to me with a plan. He had even made contacts online with brokers in Asia."

Skip noticed Red Bull was getting fidgety. He was rocking back and forth and had touched his free hand to his forehead during Sasse's monologue. Clearly, he was still affected by his friend's death. Lilac's cop friend had reported Zebulon had been hanging around with a bad crowd. Maybe Red Bull was part of that crowd.

"So, you killed him?"

"No other choice. He mistakenly started thinking it was his business and that he deserved an equal share," Sasse said.

Red Bull was rubbing his head again, "It was an accident...at least in the beginning. He wasn't supposed to have been there..."

"Time's up. Time to take a walk," Sasse said, holding his gun on Skip and gesturing toward the creek.

They walked across the clearing in silence. A hundred different scenarios were running through Skip's mind, none of which included his passively being led along a trail and marched into the woods to be shot in the back of the head. If he was going out it wasn't going to be like that. Which is exactly why he had taken preemptive measures, of course he hadn't thought it would be a tribal archeologist that would come for him. He also hadn't planned on anyone so easily getting the drop on him. He'd grown soft and complacent, and it might cost him.

His last defense, his best shot, was hidden in the sycamore at the bottom of the stone stairway leading to the creek. He would have to make his move there and hope for the best. Skip gave himself a 50-50 chance. He hadn't counted on being unarmed. On the plus side, he was facing an inexperienced operator in Sasse and an obviously conflicted kid. He'd faced far more dangerous adversaries.

On the backside of the sycamore, he'd hidden a backup trigger to a booby trap in the clearing - his kill zone. It was rigged to use on approaching trouble coming *from* the creek. Hopefully it would cause enough of a distraction for him to make a move. It was all he had. *Two more steps*. Sasse and Red Bull were both behind him thinking they were safe and in charge. He knew once he tripped the trigger, the clearing would be flooded with blinding spotlights he'd camouflaged in the trees surrounding its perimeter. C4 charges would rock the night and be heard all the way in town.

He also knew that would be the end of his time in Sedona and with the people who'd adopted him. There would be no explaining the trap. It was too professionally staged.

One more step...Skip was beside the tree and casually reached his hand around the trunk as if he were using it as a handrail. *Now! He didn't have a choice...*

"Hold it right there!" Zula Ballsy yelled. Skip kept his hand on the trigger but held off tripping it. Zula had stepped out of the dark

holding her 12-gauge Beretta Silver Pigeon. *"THE FIRST MOTHER OF A RUSSIAN WHORE THAT MOVES GETS A BUCKSHOT ENEMA!"*

Skip dropped his hand and relaxed, "What took you so long?"

"Drop the guns, boys! Spike, keep an eye on Zorro," Zula said, pointing at the masked Red Bull. Spike was beside the shotgun-toting showgirl snorting and scratching the ground. "Drop them," she repeated. "One word from me and that pig will rip your throat out and eat your balls for a late snack." Spike pawed the red earth and acting without orders charged Red Bull.

The kid panicked and raised his Walther at the javelina. *BOOM!* A cloud of lead spherical projectiles hit Red Bull in his shooting shoulder knocking him backwards. "Get the bacon," Zula yelled as Spike launched his hairy body on top of the screaming intruder.

Sasse raised his Walther and zinged a silenced shot at Zula. Skip heard the whoosh as the bullet left the barrel and expected to hear the soft thump as it hit flesh. Instead, he heard it hit metal. "God Dammit," Zula yelled, the shotgun flying from her hands. Sasse's shot had hit the Silver Pigeon. The archeologist was taking dead aim at the unarmed dancer.

Skip grabbed his gun hand, pushing the silencer up. Sasse's second shot splintered a limb on the sycamore sending a shower of leaves and branches downward. A dead limb fell knocking Skip on the arm, causing him to let go of the Walther. With his gun suddenly free, Sasse fired prematurely; Skip jerked his body violently backwards just enough to avoid the .22 caliber bullet. The hiss from the close silencer sounded like a rattler as the shot just missed his head.

His violent jerk had cost him his balance. Losing his footing on the uneven stone steps he crashed to the ground. Sasse was standing over him, grinning, breathing hard. He leveled the gun deliberately, taking his time. Skip rolled to his left as Sasse fired, the bullet grazed his jeans and splattered the ground beside his hip. He froze as Sasse took two steps back, out of his reach. His eyes were protruding with excitement and rippled veins bulged on his forehead.

"You should have left things alone," Sasse shrieked.

Zula was creeping toward him. He waved the gun at her, "Don't move!"

He turned the gun back to Skip and aimed between his eyes, "You first. Goodbye ... "

From the corner of his vision Skip saw a black blur arc through the air above him with bared fangs. The gun flew out of Sasse's hand as the flying javelina crashed into him. The archeologist fell screaming. Spike's front feet were pinning his chest, bloody teeth chomping the air in front of his face. Sasse was holding the animal's cheeks trying to keep the teeth off him.

Zula grabbed her Beretta, covering the struggling archeologist. "Spike, let him breath boy!" The proud peccary jumped off and pissed on the man's face in a sign of disdain. Skip found the Walther and checked on Red Bull who was alive but looked like two-day-old road kill lying in a demolition derby arena.

"Damn pig," Sasse whimpered.

"Don't call him a pig, he doesn't like it," Zula Ballsy said. Spike stuck his snout in the air and woofed.

37

CAMPFIRE STORIES

I T HAD BEEN A MONTH SINCE ZULA, WITH SKIP LIMPING ALONG, marched Trey Sasse and Red Bull into Hoot Hooton's office at the end of her Beretta twelve gauge demanding justice.

"The breeze has died down," Kuul observed, twisting a cap off another bottle of Modelo *Negra*. "I can smell rain, but it's going to miss us. Camp Verde will get nailed, the big storms always move in line with the mountains - south of here."

Monsoon season had started, and most evenings ushered in a brief but violent storm to water the desert and cool off its residents. Sedona got its share, but not nearly as much as the Asian- Indian name suggested.

"I think we're safe," Skip said, throwing another mesquite log on the fire. The tangy scent made him hungry for barbecued chips and sloppy joes.

The two friends were sitting around the stone fire pit behind the O'Bryan cabin. It was in the heat of the summer and neither of them was very busy. The tour business was in a seasonal lull except for families on summer vacations and they were more interested in bumpy jeep rides to keep the kids happy and spending their money on T-shirts with a picture of Geronimo. It would be after Labor Day before Sedona Chi's calendar started filling up. Kuul was in the same boat, with the part-time celebrities having closed their second or third homes in Sedona and gone back to L.A. or New York; once they returned he'd be swamped with calls to fix minor leaks, replace washers, and perform autumn blessings, but for now he was lucky to get three calls a week. It was a quiet, slow time.

"What's the latest with the case?" Kuul asked, rearranging the log Skip had placed on the fire. He propped it up with two half-burnt logs to create a tepee. "A tepee keeps the smoke going straight up instead of blowing on us."

"A tepee?" Skip shook his head. The rearrangement had sent a shower of golden sparks above the blue flames, the glow from the brighter fire unveiling more of the dark night.

"Only one in Arizona," Kuul joked.

"The case is quiet. Chief Hooton couldn't wait to dump it all on the FBI and wash his hands. Zula and I were in last week and made statements," Skip laughed at the memory. Kuul's expression asked what was so funny. "Every time the FBI agents asked Hooton to confirm something, that lazy eye took off like a dog chasing a squirrel. It bounced all around and back again and ended up pointing straight to the ceiling. Freaked the FBI guys out."

"I still can't believe Sasse turned against the People. Their sacred sites and culture were what they were paying him to protect. They trusted him with their stories. One of us should have picked it up at the Casino when he asked about our being shot at. There was only one way he could have known that; he was fishing to see if we suspected him. Too bad we can't stake him out over an ant hill."

"He'll do some time. How long is going to depend on how much he rolls up. The FBI said he is talking. They are bringing colleagues in from Interior and the BIA. They said it could end up in fifty or more indictments. Unfortunately, murder looks like it's off the menu; they've charged him with accidental homicide. Despite what he told me, there's no evidence, and he and the kid are sticking to Zeb's death being unintentional. They're also pretty solid on his having been involved, which didn't make the authorities too sympathetic. I had to physically wrap my arms around Zula and carry her out the station."

"The truth may never come out Kemo; time and wind erode everything. All I know is the best way to judge a man's character is by what those who knew him thought of him. Zebulon Ballsy was a standup *bilaga'ana* - white man."

"Here's to Zeb," Skip said, tilting his beer and clinking it with Kuul's.

He placed two more logs on the tepee to keep it from falling in. It was good to be outdoors; the smells of a campfire, the sounds of cicadas and crickets, the mesmerizing solitude of a crackling fire, the taste of the ice cold beers. He felt at peace - cocooned in a warm bubble in the wilderness, past troubles and sad memories lost in the dark night. Skip was home and he didn't want to ever leave. He'd fight hard to stay.

"The Dine' have Landish," Kuul said. Skip looked at him, about to ask how, and then realized he didn't really care. The authorities were looking for him and so far, he hadn't turned up. "They have him in the Window Rock jail. Caught him in Tuba City selling fake turquoise. Stupid, thinking he could get away with that there."

"He'll be extradited...should be scalped," Skip said.

Kuul winked, "We never did that Kemo, that was the Spanish and *Mexicanos*." *Mexicanos* was the name for North Americans living in what was then old Mexico. "We had other ways."

Skip smiled at the thought of the fat man locked up in Window Rock without Whoppers or Skittles. "About the only good that came from this is the Verde Valley Archeology Museum has a real find on their hands. The ruins were on Forest Service property, off the res-ervation. Their new director is smart; with the Yavapai archeolo-gist job empty, he reached out to Toni Wathatewa and the Yavapai/Apache council to preserve and catalog the finds. They plan to rotate displays between the Museum and Tribal Center. One of the soldiers had kept a journal; it was found with some other items in a satchel buried in the corner. They're both going to use it in an anti-looting campaign."

"Karma," Kuul laughed. He grabbed two more Mexican beers from the cooler and tossed one to Skip. "So, Kemo," he said study-ing his friend's half-lit profile, "How about we go up to Cameron for Navajo stew sometime soon? Things are getting heavy with the IV nurse, we finally made it to the Hogan and she's dying to try a cou-ple's energy drip on her next visit. She keeps asking about you and Lilac. She has a new Siberian Ginseng therapy for reducing erotic tension and synchronizing your moods."

Skip chuckled at another of his friend's offbeat girlfriends, the idea of synchronizing anything with the volatile gun-toting yoga instructor, and his own romantic predicaments.

"Probably not Lilac," he grinned. Kuul gave him a *You've got to be kidding me look* and laughed.

Skip shrugged, "Sky's sticking around helping Zula and work-ing at the Alien Encounters Meditation and Flexibility Center. I promised to take her to Bell Rock vortex at sunrise on the winter solstice, so long as she doesn't jump."

38

SIX MONTHS LATER

Shanghai Night

HENRY HARPER PASSED HIS AUSTRALIAN PASSPORT, VISA PAPERS, and Entry Registration Card to the uniformed customs officer at Shanghai's Pudong International Airport. She was young, pretty, professionally pleasant, and had a red bow tied around her hair like Minnie Mouse. Harper asked in perfect Mandarin if she had been to Shanghai Disneyland. His guess paid off with a polite smile and automatic stamp in his book, and directions to baggage in perfect English. With no luggage, he went straight to the exit and looked for a driver holding a name card that said Benjamin Smith.

It had been near midnight when Harper's, now Smith's, flight arrived. He'd come to fulfill a favor. At exactly 1:30 AM the driver had dropped him off at the busy east end of Nanjing Road. It was as crowded then as it had been at 1:00 PM. Nanjing Road was China's premier shopping street, it starts at the historic Bund in the east, once home to Western imperialists until the Japanese occupation, and ends in the west at the junction of *Jing'an* Temple and West *Yan'an* Street.

Smith's contact was waiting for him in an alley beside the Seventh Heaven Hotel across from Century Square and a dark block off the main Road. He was handed a neatly wrapped package in brown paper and given a tourist map of Nanjing Road with the shop's location indicated by a small sticky dot to be removed after the job was finished.

Smith sat in the square until 2:15 AM and then walked three blocks west on Nanjing Road before turning onto a side street by Jack Jones Oriental Shopping. He walked past several university buildings, crossed *Fengyang* Road, and stopped across the street from a nondescript, brightly-painted Indian building with a single sign that read...*Gallery and Fine Collectibles*.

The shop was closed but his packet had included a five digit code for the alarm and another access code for the door. His instructions were to take the service elevator in the back up to the owner's ornate residential quarters. He'd also been given codes for the elevator and the steel door beyond it that led to the penthouse's kitchen entrance. The owner was a wealthy trader in his 70s who lived alone and traded in international antiquities. Smith's orders were to assassinate the man as he slept and confirm death with a video delivered to the contact waiting at the Seventh Heaven Hotel.

At 2:45 Smith woke the elderly half Chinese/half Japanese man sleeping in his antique elaborately carved Chinese opium bed. Instead of killing him immediately, he ordered the man to take him to his subterranean rooms. The man had stood quietly by as Smith photographed the androgynous figure with the protruding penis. The pictures would be anonymously delivered to an old colleague in the Department of Interior. It might take years, but once it went public the Chinese government would, in the end, have no choice but to repatriate the artifact to the Yavapai Apache Tribe.

The Chinese man was then returned to his bedroom. The man had pleaded for his life and offered a bribe that would have given Smith enough to disappear and live anywhere he chose in luxury. He refused. Smith allowed him to smoke a large dose of opium before lying back down in bed. He executed his orders, took the video, and was back on Nanjing Road by 3:15. He passed off the video and the contact gave him keys to a Seventh Heaven hotel room. Smith slept for four hours and at 8:00 AM took an unregistered taxi back to Pudong where Henry Harper checked in for a Chinese Eastern Airline flight to Bangkok.

Twenty-eight hours and two stops later Harper was relaxing in the VIP lounge at Bangkok's Suvarnabhumi International Airport waiting for his long haul flight to San Francisco. The lounge was an old haunt, he had decompressed there many times before. He asked a beautiful Balinese bartender in a flowered sarong for a prickly pear margarita. Harper had to settle for dragon fruit.

AUTHOR'S NOTE

Paul Johnson

I HOPE YOU ENJOYED THE NOVEL, AND IT LEADS YOU TO VISIT this remarkable part of our country. Please leave a review if you did...enjoy the book that is. It's how authors sell their stories.

If you do visit Sedona, you will find most of the places contained in these pages exist in some shape or form. The interior arrangements of particular restaurants, bars, casinos, and museums may be different due to my fitting them to the character and plot needs. Three places you won't find are the Sands Retreat, Red Spirit Canyon, and the ruins in the climatic scenes. All three are entirely fictional, though any hike out of town will quickly get you into canyons with towering red cliffs.

Different stories contained herein about Native history are factual. Though I may make light of certain fictional characters at time, I hope by reading the book you begin to understand the eradicating impact European conquest and settlement had on Native People's lives, ancestors, and culture – past, present, and into the future.

If you want to read more of Skip and Kuul's adventures, check-out the second book in the series:

WHITEWATER HONEYMOON

A horrifying scream...wild splashing... and frantic yells for help from the raging, frothing Colorado River...

So begins Skip's and Kuul's next adventure. A scandalous movie star and her mother book a tour with Skip to follow in the footsteps of a honeymoon couple who disappeared rafting the Colorado in 1928. The action takes them from the sandstone cliffs of Sedona, into the depths of the Grand Canyon, and finally to the remote Hualapai Reservation, where shocking answers are discovered. Expect your favorite characters from *Tale of the Broken Spoke* to return and to learn more about Skip's troubled backstory.

ABOUT THE AUTHOR

PAUL JOHNSON IS A TOUR GUIDE AND AUTHOR WORKING IN Sedona, Arizona. Sedona is a small artsy town that gets upwards of five million visitors each year, all aspiring to balance their chakras, get lost in beautiful red rock canyons, and levitate over sacred vortexes. He has toured thousands of visitors to natural and cultural sites in Sedona, Grand Canyon, and various Native Nations. Paul shares stories, geologies, and histories to educate his guests about the Southwest's multicultural past and present, which often find their way into his books.

Tale of the Broken Spoke is the first book in the *Sedona Chi Mystery* series. Skip Rhodes second adventure is *Whitewater Honeymoon*, available as an eBook or paperback at most online retailers. Paul is currently working on the third book in the series, scheduled for release in early 2024, which delves deeper into the character Kukulkan Balthazar and his Mayan heritage.